Tainted Essence

Re Della Strada

Book Three

Samantha Barrett

Azlan and Bruce,

Watching the two of you grow up has been one of the greatest experiences of my life.
I couldn't be prouder of the young men you two have become.
Keep being the dippy Faleti's that you are and never change.
Aunty loves you so freaking much!

TRIGGERS

Note to reader, this book is a cross over from the Murdoch Mafia, Memento Mori and Godfathers Of The Night. You DO NOT need to have read those series before starting this one. This book is set on the same timeline as London has fallen from the Godfathers Of The Night.

Kidnapping
PTSD
Dub con
Degrading
Rape
Torture
Forced Proximity
Domestic violence (not by MMC)
Cum swapping
Child abuse (not by FMC or MMC)
Child rape (not by MMC or FMC)
Murder
Cyber Stalking

If you find something triggering that has not been listed please email authorsamanthabarrett@gmail.com. I do endeavor to include all triggers but what I may not find triggering others may so please be kind and reach out to me so I may include those triggers here rather than reporting to Amazon.

Chapter One

Destiny

"Six months. That is all the time you have to get in the mindset and shape for this fight, this is your last chance to take her down, Dest." I crack my neck from side to side and allow the fire inside me to burn hot. This is my shot, Dad's right. Six months isn't long, but it's what we have, and I'm going to win this.

I have to!

If I lose this fight she won't let me continue to chase my dream, fighting is in my DNA. The very freaking gym I train in, my father used to run until he handed it over to my uncle. I shake out my arms and bounce on the balls of my feet as I crack my neck side to side. My skin is slick with sweat from sparring for hours but I still have pent up energy I need to release. I normally hang out with my friends and go dancing or have a few drinks but thanks to some fuckers making threats against my family once again, I'm on house arrest.

Growing up with the last name Murdoch a lot of people think everything is easy for me. The outside world thinks my family is rich because they own hotels, casinos and a bunch of other businesses but they're wrong. My family is *the* mafia. My dad has tried his best to shield me from that but it's pretty hard when your mother is the drug lord for the Bratva and is the only person alive with the formula that can liquidize cocaine and then reform it. For years people have tried coming after my mom, but my uncles and dad have always protected her, not that she needs it because my mom is a fucking badass.

"Hit the showers, take tomorrow off to rest." I spit my mouth guard into my gloved hand and glare at my dad.

"I'm not taking a day off, I need to train—"

He pins me with a look that has me clamping my mouth closed. "Destiny, you are going to burn out before you even get the title fight, you have another two to win before the main event. Rest." He turns his back on me and climbs out of the ring. I stare after him wanting to say more, but don't. He's taken the time to step in and train me while I look for another trainer thanks to my last one quitting because he couldn't handle my attitude.

"You look like a sack of shit." I spin around and glare at the little shit.

"Aren't you supposed to be back in Greece?" London smirks and shoots me one of her *no one tells me what the fuck to do* looks. London is my cousin Royal's daughter and she may only be nineteen, six years younger than me, but she is fucking ruthless and has faced the trials of the Greeks and lived to tell the story. No one, and I mean no one, fucks with her. Everyone except for Uncle Bishop and Aunt Kiara are weary of her because she has a tendency to stab first and ask questions later.

"I want to be back there getting railed seven ways to hell by Artemis but my bitch ass dad sent me here to *learn*." I fight my smirk from breaking free, she is the heiress to the *Memento Mori* and will be the one to take over the Murdoch family, but she is also engaged to the Don of the Godfathers Of The Night, thus making her the most powerful woman in the world. But she doesn't allow that power to go to her head, she's still just London.

"Sucks having a dad that doesn't give a shit about what you want, doesn't it?"

"My dad can eat rotten assholes for all I care. I'm only here willingly because Grandpa promised to help me fuck with my dad and we all know that fucking with him is my favorite pastime." I smile and shake my head. The shit she does to my poor cousin would have me committed. If he didn't love her as much as he does, I know he would have dropped her in a hole years ago. I jump out of the ring and begin to unglove my hands, London surprisingly helps, which is odd because this girl never helps anyone. "Stop looking at me like that, it's fucking creepy."

"You helping me is *creepy*." I still and eye her cautiously for a long minute, she doesn't cower or even twitch under the pressure of my gaze. "Why are you really here, London, and don't spit some bullshit about your dad because you and I both know he doesn't have any pull over you."

She presses her tongue into her cheek to keep from smiling. "Your mom called me after Nytress and Unique said no."

I grind my teeth and try to tamper the anger rising inside me. "*No* to what?"

"Convincing you to give up fighting and go to law school." I narrow my eyes at the little shit.

"You think *you* are the one to convince me to do that?"

She shakes her head and smirks. "Fuck no! I'm here to help you loosen the fuck up and get your head in the game. Cronos is back from being away with Amelia. He is here with me and is also willing to help you. You know I never do as I'm told, the fact Aunt Anya thinks I would fly here to convince you to give up and take the pussy route is fucking nuts. She should know me better than that."

"You're a devious little shit, aren't you?" This bitch beams and nods like a crazy person. We fall into easy conversation as I pack my bag and get ready to head out, my muscles tense and burn but it's a delicious feeling. I long to feel this burn daily. London and I exit the gym side by side, and neither of us feel the need to fill the silence with mundane chit-chat. Much like me, she isn't a talker. Nytress and Unique are the opposite, they never shut up. London's father, Royal, is a few years older than me. He, Chanel, Chaos and Havoc were always together. They formed their own crew, *Memento Mori.*

We were never really close or talked much until Havoc was murdered. Amelia, our oldest cousin, never kept in contact either until Havoc died. His death seemed to spark something in all of us cousins and the need to check in with each other weekly became a thing. We all realized we had lost so much time never getting to know our own family because of our age gap. Royal and Chanel are thirty. Chaos is thirty-one and Amelia is turning thirty-six this year. Nytress, Unique and me are the youngest at twenty-five, twenty-four and twenty-three.

We all may talk once a week through text message but that's it as Chaos, Chanel and Royal still stick to themselves, Amelia lives in Chicago still pretending that she isn't a Murdoch while me, Unique and Nytress are the ones left here in New York with our families. Actually, soon it will be just me since the two girls are planning a round-the-world trip and Uncle Rook isn't happy about his babies flying the coop.

Once we reach my car I feel a little lighter and not so wound up, so I turn to London and smirk. "So, how about a night out?"

Her eyes darken and I fight not to groan, this girl is Lucifer's greatest creation.

"What did you have in mind? I'm down to cause mayhem and make my fiancé squirm a bit."

Shaking my head I chuckle at her antics. "What did Artemis do this time?"

She shrugs. "Nothing, I'm just keeping him on his toes and reminding him that being with me is a gift he should cherish because I'm a fucking prize."

Artemis has to be one of the most courageous men I

know in order to put up with London and all the shit she puts him through.

"Get in, I have to go back to my apartment and shower, then we'll head out."

"I'll call Nos and tell him where to meet us," she answers.

Much like me, London isn't a girly girl type. She and I are similar in that aspect but I don't harbor a sour attitude like she does. The Lift drops us off out front of the new club that opened a few weeks back. I found out from Nytress that this is the *it* place in the city to be, she and Unique have been here almost every weekend since it opened. Unique's boyfriend and his cousin own it so I know London will have no issue getting in, plus her last name alone will grant her entry into any place she likes.

We walk by patrons who are lined up waiting to be granted access to the inside. Some of the girls send us snotty looks, clearly not impressed by our appearance. London is wearing a simple tube top paired with skin tight skinny jeans while I'm wearing jeans, Converse and a white crop tee that falls off one shoulder. I don't spend a lot of time worrying over how I look, I don't even wear makeup. The most effort I put into myself tonight was washing my hair and wearing it down. London has her brown hair tied in a high ponytail, it's getting longer now since those fuckers cut it when they kidnapped her.

I shudder at the thought of what she went through. I may be training to fight in the octagon and be able to beat the shit out of men twice my size, but that is my choice. Being taken and forced to submit to the will of someone else is my worst nightmare. My phone vibrating in my pocket pulls me from those dark thoughts. I tap London on the shoulder, halting her. She rolls her eyes and waits as I retrieve my phone and groan at the sight of my father's name on the screen. I show London who it is before I answer.

"You said to take the night off and now you're bugging me, why?" I say with an irritated edge to my voice.

"Where are you?" I note the hint of worry in his tone but choose to ignore it.

"Out." I dart my gaze to the line of people when some guys start catcalling us. I shake my head at London, hoping she heeds my warning and doesn't kill them.

"It's not safe—" Before he can finish, London snatches the phone out of my grasp and ends the call, pocketing my phone while I glare at her.

"I did you a favor, now let's go before I break their noses." I don't argue as I follow after her, knowing that threat wasn't idle and she really would break those assholes noses. Unlike her, I can't be caught fighting out of the ring or else I will be barred from entering the octagon and that is not something I will ever risk. The bouncer takes one look at us before nodding his head and waving us through. I shudder in disgust at the hungry looks he shoots our way.

Men are pigs!

The bass from the music reverberates through my body.

London grabs my hand and shoulders her way through the crowd of people. I have no idea how the hell she knows where to go but I don't protest. A guy tries to reach for me but I shove him back with my free hand. I had assumed she would lead us to a VIP area or something, where I know Unique and Nytress hangout when they come here, but nope, she shocks the shit out of me when we stop in the middle of the packed dance floor.

Frowning I lean forward and shout. "What are we doing?"

I pull and see the devilish glint in her eyes and fight not to groan, she's up to something. "My man is up there watching." She flicks her gaze behind me discreetly. I play along and pretend to feel the beat as I dance around her with my arms above my head and swaying my hips as I look up and see Artemis, Cronos, Unique's boyfriend Kelly and the two girls themselves who wiggle their fingers in a wave. "Is Artemis about to lose his shit?" London shouts. I turn my gaze back to her and smile.

"He's shouldering people out of his way to get to you." She throws her head back and laughs. I marvel at her for a moment loving the way she is so confident within herself. Artemis is head over heels in love with her and anyone with eyes can see that man would die for her without thought. I think that's the only reason Royal hasn't killed him. It takes him two minutes tops before he is barging his way through partygoers and wrapping his arms around London from behind, then burying his face in the crook of her neck.

I turn away from them the moment her eyes turn hazy,

that shit is gross and I don't need to hear what he is saying in order to know it's going to end with them fucking in a public restroom. I come to a halt at the sight of the guy standing in front of me. I cock my head to the side at the familiarity of him, then it dawns on me.

He's the guy from Wave's party that hit on me. I narrow my eyes at the cocky bastard as he runs his gaze down the length of my body like he has a right. The moment he sinks his teeth into his bottom lip, I give up on fighting the eye roll and allow it to break free.

"You don't seem happy to see me, *Slayer*." I inhale a sharp intake of air at the sound of him calling me by my fighting name. Every fighter has a nickname or a name they go by in the ring. Mine is Havoc Slayer. I chose to incorporate Havoc's name as a tribute to my cousin. The fact he tried to turn my fighting name into a pet name is cheesy as fuck. I attempt to brush past him and head upstairs, but the bastard wraps an arm around my waist and spins me so my back is flush against his chest. I draw my arm forward, ready to elbow him in the ribs but the moment his lips graze the shell of my ear I hesitate. It's his words that have me turning to stone.

"Russian hitmen are in this club right now and they are coming for you."

Chapter Two

Taylan

I feel her stiffen in my hold. I sway my hips, trying to act casual as I let the beat lead me in my moves. To everyone else we look like two people sharing an intimate moment but the truth is, we are strangers. Knox sent me here to deal with the Murdochs, *Memento Mori* and Godfather's. Wave, Xan and Trey are here too. Knox won't leave Lake while she is pregnant and I can't blame him, but the fact we have a huge Russian problem right now makes it inconvenient for him to not be traveling and Bishop Murdoch isn't the type of man you ask to come to you because your wife is carrying your sister's kid. Bishop's a good guy and we've been working with him for years now, but we aren't friendly enough to ask him for shit like that.

"What the fuck is that supposed to mean?" she grits out as she sways her hips going along with my charade. I fight back a groan when she grinds her ass into my dick. I flick my gaze to Artemis and give him a nod. At my confirmation, he begins to pull London away and signals to his brother upstairs to follow him.

"We need to move, Destiny, I'm not fucking with you right now." She lifts her head to watch Cronos and her two cousins descend the stairs.

"Not until you tell me what the fuck is going on! I don't even know you." She tries to free herself of my hold but I refuse to allow her to move an inch.

"Andreas has lost control of Russia. The Crows are trying to get it under control but it's proving difficult because the Russians want the formula your mother uses for themselves. Since they can't get to her, they are coming for you, hoping your mom will hand it over in exchange for you." I feel her breathing accelerate. I tighten my hold, trying to reassure her without words that I won't let them touch her.

"I need to get to my dad," she says as she pushes away from me. This time I let her but before she can get too far I snag her hand in mine and drag her behind me as I try to catch up with Artemis and Cronos. I was heading back to my hotel when Xan called and told me that Andreas had given them all a heads up that hitmen were coming for Destiny. Gage had a lock on her location and said they would handle it but they are over twenty minutes away, so I made a call to Artemis who said he was waiting for the girls to show up and decided to lend a hand.

As we near the exit, I spot Art and Nos but they freeze in the doorway at the sound of screeching tires. Nos turns to me and shakes his head.

Fuck!

I dart my gaze around the club and spot a neon *exit* sign. "This way!" I order as I drag Destiny after me, rushing toward the exit. If it was just me and the two guys I would have stayed and fought but with four women, three of which I have no idea if they can shoot a gun—London I know for a fact can throw knives and shoot. I shove the door open and we all stumble into an alley out the back.

"My car's around the other side," Artemis says drawing my attention to him. He pulls two guns from his waistband and hands one to London just as Nos grabs his own guns.

"Give me one of those," Destiny demands. Nos doesn't hesitate as he hands one over to her. She yanks her hand free and pops the clip checking how many rounds she has, then draws the barrel and checks the safety before turning to me with a pointed look.

"What?" I ask.

"If you have a spare gun give it to Nytress or Unique," she snaps.

"They can shoot?" I ask in disbelief as I look at the two girls in question. They both wear skin tight dresses, six-inch heels and look like Italian Barbies.

"We're fucking Murdochs, of course we can all shoot and fight, you idiot," Destiny snarls as she brushes past me. I pull my spare out of my waistband and hand it to Unique, who takes it without argument and goes through the same checks her cousin just did, then the both of them run after Destiny. I marvel at the sight of them running in fucking skyscraper heels.

"Don't ever underestimate my family again because it will cost you your fucking life," London seethes as she shoulders past me. Nos, Artemis and I follow after them.

"She's a peach, isn't she?" Artemis says about his girl. I shoot the idiot a glare as we push ourselves ahead of the girls and lead the pack around the corner. I raise my hand halting them all in their tracks as I press against the brick wall of the club and poke my head out to check if the coast is clear. When I don't see anyone with guns raised, I wave them forward. Nos leads the girls across the road where mine and Artemis's cars are parked as we take up the rear.

"There!" I hear someone shout, fuck. I raise my gun and aim at one of the fuckers shouldering people who are standing in line to enter the club. I can't risk taking the shot and hitting an innocent person.

"Get in the fucking car!" Artemis roars, but a gun firing from behind us has me dropping into a crouch. I turn back and glare at London, unlike me she clearly doesn't have an issue with hitting a civilian. People scream and begin to run in every direction. We use that chaotic diversion to our advantage. London, Art, Nos and the two girls jump in his car. Destiny looks pissed that she can't fit and right now with those fuckers returning fire I don't have time to argue, I snag her arm and fire off two shoots before dragging her to my car. She jumps in without complaint. I'm a second behind Artemis as he pulls away. I reach across and grip the back of Destiny's neck, pushing her head down as I duck low when we pass a fucker who shoots at our cars.

"Let me go!" she screams. I do so only when we are far

enough from those cunts. I can feel her glaring at the side of my face but I don't dare look at her as I maneuver my way through the city. I know she wants to say more but when my phone begins to ring through the sound system in the car she remains silent. I answer the call using the button on the steering wheel.

"Yeah?" I say in lieu of a greeting.

"Taylan, what the fuck happened?" I relax the slightest bit at the sound of Chaos's voice.

"I got to the club just in time, Artemis has Rook's girls—"

"Where the fuck is my daughter?" *Royal hollers.* No matter how well London can defend herself, her father will never not see her as his little girl.

"She's with Artemis and Cronos, he's bringing them back to you."

"What about Destiny? Where is she?"

Before I can answer the strange voice she beats me to it. "I'm right here, Dad." I hear him sigh on the other end of the phone.

"I want you to bring my daughter to Bishop's." My eyes widen in surprise. In all the years we have been dealing with the Murdochs, none of us have ever been to their *compound* as Chaos calls it. We always meet them at the hotel we are staying at or one of their clubs. Unlike their parents, Royal and Chaos host us at their houses. Kacey and Sin have had us at their house a few times, but we mostly hang out at Royal's when we're in Miami.

"Why?" Destiny barks. "I want to go home back to *my*

place!" Their argument becomes background noise as I spot four cars gaining on us at top speed.

"Fuck!" I growl. Destiny darts her gaze to the side mirror then spins in her seat to look out the back window of my Camaro.

"They're chasing us," she mutters more to herself.

"Add Artemis to the call," I say through gritted teeth as I cut into the next lane, ignoring the sound of the blaring horn coming from the car behind me as I cut it off to keep up with Artemis. She does as I say. He picks up before the first ring can finish.

"We have a tail," he says.

"I know," I answer.

"How many?" comes from Bishop, I can tell the bass of his voice anywhere.

"Bishop?" Artemis questions.

"They're all on the line, I added you so we could come up with a plan," I say, cutting the chitchat short as I weave in and out of traffic trying to dodge these Russian fuckers chasing us.

"I have Luka, Rook, Knight, Vin, Kacey and Chanel with three carloads of our men coming for you. I have your location locked now and I'm tracking you through the CCTV footage in the city."

"Uncle King, we can lose them if we split up. That will buy us time—"

Gage cuts Destiny off before she can continue. "No. You keep heading back and the others will—"

She returns the favor and cuts her father off this time.

"No. I've been trained to deal with this shit since I was kid, I know what to do. Send Chanel and Kacey to my location and send the others after London and Artemis." Before anyone can utter another word she ends the call, this time I do chance a look at her in surprise. "What?" she snaps as she rolls her window down and flicks the safety on her gun off.

"What the fuck are you doing?" I snap.

"Take the next left, there's five cars chasing us, not four. Two will go after them and three will come after us," she says in a matter of fact tone.

"How do you know that?" I ask as she unfastens her seatbelt.

"I'm the one they need to leverage my mother for the formula, not them. They know who London is and if they are dumb enough to try to take out Bishop Murdoch's granddaughter, they know it means death. They would know this is a suicide mission anyway, because there is no way Royal won't skin them alive for endangering his baby girl."

Fuck it!

I bank left and sure enough, three cars follow us. I plant my foot down on the gas as I dodge in and out of cars, trying to get away. When I spy her out of the corner of my eye pushing out the window and resting her ass on the edge, I dart my arm out to try pull her back inside the fucking car. When she fires the first shot, I leave her be and grind my teeth in rage—if she falls to her fucking death, I know without a doubt that I will be executed by her family.

The cunts return fire. Instead of ducking back inside the safety of the car like I thought she would, she surprises me when she stays put and fires off round after round, finally landing a shot on one of the cars, sending it careening into one of the parked vehicles at the curb. The two behind it don't slow down. She ducks back inside the car and secures her seatbelt like she didn't just act like she was fucking Rambo.

"What the fuck was that?" I seethe.

"Me helping you, dipshit. Take the next right and then head back toward the club. We'll lose them in the frenzy of people." I tighten my grip on the steering wheel, not liking her ordering me around, I'm not used to that shit. Knox may be the Don and my formal title may be underboss, but we don't operate like that. We're partners. With Xander not being with us, we had to learn to cope as a duo instead of a trio. Xan pledged his loyalty to Wave and that shit earned both mine and Knox's respect. He's a brother and best friend, the fact he was willing to go to war with us in order to stand by her side showed us how much he loves Wave.

"Here, take this," I say as I hand her my gun.

"Why?" she queries.

"Three more cars just joined the chase, the fact they aren't trying to take out the two chasing us means they are with them." She turns in her seat and curses just as my phone rings. I answer the call knowing who it is.

"I already know, Artemis," I say.

"We're doubling back—"

I cut him off before he can continue. "No. It's too late, there's a road block ahead." Destiny follows my line of sight to see three SUVs parked across the road, blocking it with men standing with machine guns, I slow down buying us some time as I try to think of a plan.

"Hang on, I'm adding Royal to the call." Within a second Royal's voice filters through the speakers.

"Ram those fuckers and don't stop," he snarls.

"I'm in a rental car, no bulletproof glass and I'm not risking her," I sneer.

"Destiny, you fucking run. Do you hear me?" The sheer panic in Gage's tone has me feeling like a complete waste of space that I am the reason his daughter is in this position.

Destiny looks to me as she answers, "I won't let them get the formula." My brows raise at her insinuation. I snatch the gun from her grasp and glare at her.

"Listen to me, we have three seconds tops before I hit the brakes. You don't fight, you do as they say," I say hoping she obeys me.

"Taylan, they will kill you," comes from Chaos.

"No, they won't." Destiny frowns at my answer. I shoot her wink. "No one knows who Royal Murdoch is..." I let my sentence trail off as I toss my gun in the back.

"You sneaky son of a bitch," Royal says, I can hear the humor in his tone as I bring the car to a stop and I turn to Destiny.

"When we get out, you shout out anything you see about these guys, we don't know who they are, anything you say they will be able to hear and track." I tear my gaze from her to see the fuckers in front of us approaching. "Royal, mute the call, Gage won't like what he hears and I can't risk him fucking this one chance we have until you all find us."

"Protect her with your life. Destiny, I'm coming for you, kill as many as you can, champ." At the sound of her father's voice, she turns rigid.

"Bye, Daddy," she whispers as she shoves her door open and climbs out with her hands up.

"I'll lay my life down for hers, I'll keep her safe," I vow before I rush to follow after her.

Chapter Three

Destiny

It takes them four seconds from the moment Taylan climbs out to come at me. "Ski masks, AK-47's, MG 42 and 43's, M60 rifle, License plate G49-2368," is all I manage to say before I take a left jab to the mouth. The metallic tangy flavor of my blood fills my mouth as I stumble backward. "Come on, motherfucker!" I scream in false bravado.

"Don't fucking touch her, you cocksucker!" Taylan roars as he tries to fight off the fuckers holding him back. For a split second my gaze collides with his and that's when I see fear, not for himself but for me. The trance is broken when another hit lands to my stomach. I gasp and drop to my knees as two cunts grab my arms and yank them behind me. I feel a cable tie slip around my wrists a second before a black bag is placed over my head and I'm dragged toward a car. "Slayer?" I hear Taylan call out, I open my mouth to answer but my head is shoved from the back and I smack into something hard and solid. I grind my teeth fighting to keep from crying out at the pain radiating through my skull.

I'm dizzy and have black spots dancing at the edge of my vision as I'm thrown inside, what I can only assume, the trunk of a car. Before I can get my bearings or get my head to stop spinning something—no, someone is thrown on top of me. I gasp and groan from the impact as I try to roll out from under them but it's a fucking hard when your hands are tied.

"Your cousin's coming along, get comfortable, it's a long ride," a man with a thick Russian accent says, then the hood is yanked off my head. I slam my eyes closed against the light. The trunk is slammed, then I'm bathed in darkness. I try to regulate my breathing and remain calm as the car takes off. I sigh in relief when the body rolls off me except I remember what Taylan said and put two and two together, the body is Taylan.

"Taylan?" I whisper shout, trying to gain his attention. When the driver hits the brakes, it shines enough light inside for me to see his eyes are closed. He's knocked out. I feel around with my fingers hoping to find something to cut these restraints off, but after a couple minutes I growl in frustration.

"Argh," Taylan groans out. I have no idea why the fuck this idiot would risk his life for me. The last time I saw him I told him to die and I would fake cry at his funeral. "Slayer?" he moans and shifts.

"I'm here," I answer.

He rolls onto his back, hissing in pain. They clearly

worked him over pretty well if he's in this amount of pain. "You okay?"

"I got a fat lump on the back of my head and a pounding headache from getting my face smacked into something but I'll live," I deadpan.

"There's a guy who wasn't wearing a mask and barking orders in Russian, he's the one we need to talk to."

"Why?"

"Because he's the boss or at least he's the one running this thing," he says in a clipped tone.

"Why are you pretending to be Royal?" I whisper, trying to keep my voice low in case they can hear us talking inside the car.

"Same reason I'm calling you Slayer instead of your name."

"What?" I'm confused as hell now.

"You will deny being Anya Murdoch's daughter, you will claim to be Rook's kid. If they think you aren't Destiny, that will buy us some time for our people to find us."

That actually makes sense but he still hasn't answered my other question. "Why are you pretending to be Royal?"

"You don't think I can pull it off?" The fact he is trying to joke at a time like this grates on my freaking nerves.

"Royal has a New York accent and you sound Canadi-an!" I hiss.

He's silent for a moment and I begin to fidget as the events of the night catch up with me. "If they knew I wasn't important they would have put a bullet in my head and you would be left alone with them. Saying I'm him means I'm valuable and them thinking you are Rook's kid means you are worth nothing but them thinking I am Bishop's…" He lets his sentence trail off.

I nod my head even though he can't see me. "Which means you will take the brunt of their anger while I don't. They will torture you so Uncle Bishop forces my mom to give up her formula," I mutter dejectedly.

"I won't let them hurt you, Slayer," he says quietly.

A whoosh of air escapes me. "Why? I'm not your problem, you don't even know me."

"I may not know you personally but I do know your family, they came to our aid—"

"Stop bullshitting and tell me the truth!" I snap—there is no fucking way he would risk his life because he feels like he owes my family.

"I like you."

I snort. "Nice try, no one likes me. Now, tell me why you are really here."

"That is the reason, I obeyed Knox's orders to come here in the hopes I would see you again." I lull my head to the side and squint against the darkness, trying to see him in the dark but can only make out the outline of his face.

"Nice try, Romeo."

"Believe what you want but it's the truth. I'm a man, Slayer, and there is no fucking way I would have let them take me out like a bitch while they ran away with you, that shit isn't in my DNA."

"So you have a hero complex?"

He scoffs. "Fuck, you're no good for my ego."

"Never will be, either. I don't have time to fluff men's egos so they can feel better about themselves. I'm a fighter, not some piece of meat for them to stick their cock into."

He whistles between his teeth. "I said I liked you, I never said I wanted to fuck you."

I grind my teeth and remind myself he is my only ally here. "I will never let you fuck me. I refuse to be like my cousins and London who got sidetracked by cocks. I have a dream and I will fucking achieve it."

"Who are you trying to convince, me or yourself?" he counters. I refuse to answer him because his question hit too close to home. My arms feel numb and my body is aching from being cramped inside this trunk with Taylan plastered against me. We haven't spoken a word since I refused to answer him but I feel the car slowing down and tense in anticipation. "When they pop the trunk, don't fight, play the damsel—"

"I'm no fucking damsel!" I seethe.

"Play the fucking part of one, you fight against these guys and they will make it their mission to break you."

"They can try," I retort.

"They won't beat you, Slayer, they'll rape you and that is something that *will* break you." For the first time since this whole fucking thing started I feel fear. It travels through my body at a rapid pace. I realize for the first time in my life that my last name won't save me, it will be the cause of my demise. "I won't let them touch you, *Destiny*." The conviction in which he says that has me wanting to believe him.

"You can't make a promise like that," I whisper as the car

comes to a stop and shuts off. I close my eyes and will myself to remain calm. Kidnapping is becoming a rite of passage in my family at this rate, why couldn't we be normal?

"Normal is overrated." I balk, I said that shit out loud. "It's not a promise, it's a vow. I will take whatever they dish out and redirect their anger to me, you remain silent and you will stay alive." Before more can be said the trunk is opened. I close my eyes against the harsh light. "Fuck you!" Taylan snarls as he is yanked out of the trunk. I snap my eyes open. Hands grab me, and I force myself not to fight against them and heed his advice. I look around, taking stock of my surroundings. We're in a large warehouse that is vacant except for seven cars. The fucker shifts his hold from my arm to gripping a handful of my hair. I hiss earning a chuckle from the bastard.

"The budes krichat saa menia?" (Will you scream for me?) I grind my teeth as he drags me by my hair through a door into what looks like a storage room. He yanks me to a halt by my hair as three guys wrestle Taylan into a chair. They cut the tie binding his wrists before securing his wrists and ankles by cuffs to the metal chair. Once they are finished with him they come to me. I don't fight as they chain me the same way they did him except when they finish, they don't step back. The bastard who brought me in here leans in so his lips brush mine, his rancid breath has me fighting to not gag. He darts his tongue out and licks a trail from the corner of my mouth along my jaw. I turn my head, locking eyes with Taylan who is vibrating with anger at the sight of the fucker slobbering on me.

"Rook is going to kill you," he forces out through clenched teeth. The fucker doesn't stop licking. He places his hands on the tops of my thighs and sucks the shell of my ear into his mouth, my face contorting as I stare at Taylan. His gaze bores into mine, he can see the unfiltered horror in my gaze when the bastard forces his hands between my legs and cups my pussy through my jeans. I whimper. "Nytress, keep looking at me." The guy freezes at the sound of my cousin's name and pulls back. I see confusion in his eyes as he looks between us. He grips the back of his ski mask and yanks it off. I note he has a jagged scar down his left cheek and I see burns around his neck.

"*Kogo the nachren vzyal?*" (Who the fuck did you take?) He asks the three guys.

"*My poshli za ney, boris skazal, chto eto ona,*" (We followed her, Boris said she was the one.) one of the guys answers.

Licker glares down at me and I can see the rage filtering beneath the surface of his eyes. "*Pozvoni bossu, pryamo seichas!*" (Call the boss, now!) Taylan and I remain silent as the four of them storm out of the room, slamming the door closed and locking it behind themselves. I sag with relief into my chair, then clench my fists to try to stop myself from trembling, the last thing I want them to see is me quaking in fear just from being licked and... I slam my eyes closed and fight off the intrusive thoughts.

He didn't touch me!

I keep saying that over and over again in my head forcing myself to believe it. If these disgusting fuckers think I will allow them to grope me and touch me however they please, then they have another fucking thing coming. I am a Murdoch and we are fighters!

"I may have bought us some time but they won't be gone for long," Taylan says barely above a whisper. I don't respond, I'm too lost in my thoughts trying to devise a plan on getting the fuck out of here. My hands being cable tied was something I could have worked with and broken them or something like that but handcuffs? That is a hard fucking no. "Slayer?"

"What?" I snap as I turn to look at him. The intensity in which he looks at me would have women dropping their panties and begging him to slide his cock inside their desperate pussies but not me.

"You're gonna be okay."

I scoff. "Making another promise you can't keep?"

His brows furrow causing a deep V in the middle of his forehead. "*When* we get out of here, you are going to be thanking me for everything I am about to go through in order to keep you safe until the cavalry arrives." I tear my gaze from him and tilt my head back, staring up at the ceiling. If I had just stayed home tonight instead of going out I wouldn't be here, I'd be in bed with my laptop watching YouTube videos of my next opponent and studying everything about them. I should be trying to find a new trainer instead of being chained to a fucking chair!

This is the price you pay for your mother being born a Volkov.

Chapter Four

Taylan

The silence between us stretches, I feel no need to fill the void and reassure her. She's a feisty one and will handle this situation well. Most girls would be a sobbing mess right now but not Destiny, she's stoic and trying to process everything that led her to being chained beside me. I can't help but admire how fucking gorgeous she is. Since the first moment I saw her at Wave's party, I was struck stupid by how beautiful she is.

I made that stupid bet with Kimber and I know that greedy bitch will come to collect, unlike Knox and Xan I don't do feelings. Having a woman drag me around by the balls doesn't appeal to me. My famous motto has always been *find em, feel em, fuck em, forget em.* Feelings are for the weak and it is for that reason alone why I know we will get out of this. Knox and Xan would be going crazy right now if they were locked up with their girls but unlike me, Destiny isn't my girl so I don't have the compulsion to act like a dick and draw the Russian's attention.

Don't get me wrong, I won't stand by while they hurt her. No man worth his fucking weight in salt would ever stand by and be okay with cunts pawing at a woman or hitting them.

"When they come back, they aren't going to beat you," she says, shocking me out of my thoughts and drawing my attention back to her. Those gray eyes stare at me with resignation.

"Why do you say that?"

Her face is blank of all emotion as she speaks. "Because you gave them a reason to use me against you."

I reel back. "No the fuck I didn't," I defend.

"You screamed at them to leave me alone when they grabbed us, just before you spoke in my defense instead of remaining silent. They are going to use me to get you to talk."

"I have nothing to say," I grit out through clenched teeth.

"You don't but I do. You will break and offer up the truth willingly about who we both are because you won't be able to stomach the sight of them beating me or... raping me." Realization dawns on me as I process her words. I feel my face slacken as dread washes over me. "Don't feel bad, even the best of us break but unlike you, I was trained from birth how to endure this type of shit by my mother. She went through a similar situation, so she wanted me to be ready in case I should ever find myself in a position like this."

I shake my head trying to deny what she is saying. "It won't come to that," I argue.

"It will. You know it will. You need to close your eyes and not watch because I will never give them the information they need."

"Why not?" I can hear the anger in my tone.

"The moment they have what they need we will both be dead, it is the only leverage I have until my family finds us. If I give them what they want, they will kill me to get back at my mother for abandoning Russia for my dad and leaving it to be run by a gay man." Shock spurs to life inside me. I had no idea Andreas was gay, not that it matters, but I know Russian men wouldn't exactly relish the idea of being led by a man who shares a bed with another man.

As I stare at her I begin to feel guilty. I made a stupid bet with Kimber to fuck her and then leave for 100k and yet, here she is willing to be tortured just so we can *both* make it out of here alive.

I'm a real piece of shit!

Both of us dart our gazes to the door when the lock clicks. I fight to keep my breathing even as the door is opened and four men wearing masks enter. I brace myself for the beating that is to come but they step aside to allow the fucker with the burned neck through. When he looks at me and smiles I begin to panic —that isn't the look of someone that is coming for you, that is the look of someone that is going to do exactly what Destiny just said. They are going to destroy her in order to get me to talk.

"The boss is on his way and says we can play with you both until he gets here." I fight not to look at Destiny and keep my gaze on this fat fuck in front of me. He licks his lips and grabs his cock in his hand, sneering at Destiny like she's a snack. "You a virgin?" His accent is so thick. The guys behind him begin to chuckle and speak amongst themselves in Russian. It fucking annoys the shit out of me that I can't understand them.

"I was a virgin until I rode your daddy and became your stepmom." My eyes nearly pop out of my head as I choke on my spit at her reply. His face turns beet red as the guys behind him laugh loudly. Destiny smiles up at him, daring him to do his worst. I see him shift his weight onto his back leg, I open my mouth to scream at him not to do it but it's too late, he punches her so hard in the face that her head snaps back.

"You motherfucker!" I roar. "Uncuff me and see what I do to your fat ass, you useless Russian cunt!" His nostrils flare in anger but his attention is drawn back to Destiny when she groans in pain, her chin is on her chest and I see blood staining her shirt. Panic flares to life inside me, I promised her they wouldn't touch her and told her I wouldn't allow them to rape her but I think she's right—I don't know if I can keep that promise.

She lifts her head, I see the strain it takes for her to do that simple movement. Her nose and mouth are bleeding, making her look manic as she smiles up at him.

"Your daddy fucked me harder than that hit." This time, she sees him shift his weight. When he strikes out she ducks and he hits air. He tries to punch her again but she dodges left, he roars out his anger before closing the space between them, grips the back of her head and yanks her back by her hair forcing her to look at him.

"*The budes krichat, suka,*" (You're going to scream, bitch.) he snarls in her face before delivering blow after blow. I fight to get free and scream at the cunt to stop but it falls on deaf ears. I manage to snap the bolts anchoring the chair to the ground and topple sideways. Before the four fuckers can get to me, I kick out and sweep the fat fuck off his feet. When he hits the ground I slam the heel of my boot into his face repeatedly until the other four right my chair and hold me in place. They don't check on their buddy, who is bleeding thanks to his broken nose. Two of them stand in front of me, taking turns hitting me in the face, chest and stomach while their friends hold me still.

It takes one solid right hook to have me seeing spots in the corner of my eyes and another uppercut for me to pass out. I tried to fight it, not wanting to leave Destiny for a second but I'm powerless to stop myself from blacking out.

It's the drumbeat in my head that finally wakes me. I scrunch my face and immediately regret it. I feel the dried blood caked to my face and wince when I try to open my eyes. My face feels like it's swollen, my ribs are burning with every breath I take, my shoulders are screaming in pain. I push all of the pain out of my mind as I slowly lift my head and turn to check on Destiny. The blood in my veins turns to ice when I see her chair empty, the pain forgotten as I dart my gaze around the room. When I spot her in the far corner with her legs to her chest and her arms wrapped around her legs something inside me dies.

Her jeans are gone.

Her face is bloodied.

Bruises mar her forearms.

No! Fuck, they… they fucking…

I can't even think about what she went through. She's shaking, her eyes are open and staring directly at me but they're hollow, she's looking right through me.

"Slayer?" I rasp out, trying to bring her out of her spiral but my voice is weak. I clear my throat and fight not to wince from the pain. "Look at me," I demand.

"They uncuffed you," she says. I frown as I look down and move my arms and legs. I'm shocked. I use every ounce of strength I have to push to my feet, making a groan slip free. I press my hand against my ribs and grit my teeth as I stumble toward her. I press my back against the concrete wall and take a deep breath, knowing this is going to hurt like a bitch. I slide down the wall, biting the inside of my cheek. I taste copper. The air whooshes out of me when my ass hits the ground. I shift and grind my teeth through the pain as I yank my shirt over my head and pull it over her hers. She jerks away from me and I immediately release it and raise my hands as if surrendering.

"It's just a shirt, Slayer." She stares at me for a long moment before swallowing audibly and shrugging it the rest of the way on. She draws the hem over her knees, then rests back against the wall, neither of us saying a word. Honestly, what the fuck can I say, the two things I promised her wouldn't happen did fucking happen. Time seems to stand still as we both sit here getting lost in our thoughts. I don't know how much time has passed since we arrived here but I fucking hope the others are close to barging in here and saving our asses.

I run my gaze over her and watch in amazement as she calms herself and gathers every ounce of courage she possesses. Her gaze darts around the room and finally settles on the cuffs laying on the concrete floor. I drink in the sight of her in my shirt and love the way it looks on her. Without a word she leaps to her feet and grabs the abandoned cuffs off the floor then returns to her place beside me. I watch as she wraps one set of cuffs around her knuckles then uses the other set to do the same before looking at me.

The raw determination in her gaze is astounding, this girl is a fucking oddity. "You're injured." It's not a question, just a fact. "When they come back in, I'm fighting my way out of here. You can either stay or come with me but those are your only two options." I press my fingers into my ribs and wince, they're tender but not broken. I roll my shoulders then crack my neck side to side.

"Nice try, Slayer, but I'm not letting you out of my sight." She brushes off my retort.

"Can you fight?"

I quirk a brow at her. "Against guns? No. Hand to hand?

Fuck yeah." She eyes me warily for a moment before nodding. "What's that look for?"

She purses her lips. "Can you fight *fight* or just brawl?"

I scoff at her insinuation. "I was fighting in the streets while you were still swimming in your daddy's sack, babe."

She scrunches her face in disgust. "You're a pig."

"Hey, we were all conceived the same way. Everyone got shot out of daddy's sack and pushed out of mommy's snatch."

"Not me, dumbass."

"What?"

She huffs clearly annoyed by this line of conversation. "My mom can't carry children, it was a long ass process. They managed to extract some eggs from her, plant my dad's shit in it and then implant it in my aunt. I didn't pop out of *mommy's snatch, I popped* out of my aunt's, dipshit." I stare at her in utter disbelief—I never knew that. At the sound of footfalls outside the door she tenses and jumps to her feet, keeping her hands concealed behind her back. I grunt as I follow her lead but I take a half step in front of her, slightly shielding her from view.

The door opens and we both stiffen in anticipation as we wait for whoever it is to enter. The moment a woman is shoved inside, I gape at the sight in front of me. The door slamming closed shakes me from my stunned state, when the girl climbs to her feet tand turns to me with a smile.

"You owe me for this, asshole," she grits out, motioning to the skintight black leather dress she wears that barely covers her pussy. Her tits are pushed up so high they practically rest on her fucking chin.

"You two know each other?" Destiny asks, drawing our attention to her. She darts her gaze between the both of us, clearly feeling uneasy about something. "Who the fuck are you?"

"Slayer, meet Kimber, the bane of my existence," I mutter. The two girls stand there eyeing each other with untrust and scrutiny.

"Why are you here?" Destiny clips out.

Kimber being the bitch she is rolls her eyes. "I'm here as the entertainment to distract those fuckers while your family breaches the perimeter."

The blood drains from my face as I stare at Kimber. "You didn't?" I breathe out.

"They didn't touch me..." I know what she isn't saying *yet*. When the sound of more footfalls pound outside the door, Destiny rushes forward and grabs the other sets of cuffs and tosses them to Kimber before raising her own hands to show her what to do with them. I dart forward and push both girls behind me as the door opens to reveal that burned fucker. He steps inside, followed by six masked cunts—the fact that fucker isn't wearing a mask tells me he is the under-boss or someone higher than a simple soldier.

The fucker shoots Destiny a sly smirk before stepping aside to reveal a guy in a tailored suit. He looks around my age. His blond hair is slicked back flat against his head, his green eyes flick between the three of us before landing on Destiny who gasps at the sight of the man. I look over my shoulder to see her pale slightly.

"Do you know *him*?" I grit out. She snaps out of it, the shock is quickly replaced by hate but it isn't her that answers it's *him*.

"We know each other really well, don't we, sweetheart?" he says in a tone that holds an edge.

Chapter Five

Destiny

Koda.

My blood begins to boil inside me at the sight of him.

This motherfucker is going to die.

Taylan was wrong, they never thought I was my cousin, they were playing us from the second we got here. Koda would have told them who I was.

"We know each other really well, don't we, sweetheart?" I sneer at the fuckers answer. I can feel Taylan and Kimber staring at me but I refuse to take my eyes off the snake in front of me for a second.

"Who the fuck is he?" Taylan grits out.

"Oh, do tell them who I am to *you*," Koda taunts. "We have plenty of time to catch up on the flight, darling, I just wanted you to see who is behind all of this. Your family sent the whore in to entertain my men thinking it would distract us so they could breach the perimeter but I'm not foolish as you know. I know everything there is to know about your family's tricks, thanks to *you*." Shame washes over me, Koda knows he's hit me where it hurts. "Bring her to me." Taylan and Kimber begin fighting but I just stand here staring at my nightmare.

When the guards finally manage to subdue Taylan and Kimber, one of them grabs my hands and yanks the cuffs free, tossing them to the side before dragging me out of the room by my arm. Taylan and Kimber shout for me to fight but I ignore them, fighting him got me nowhere last time.

He's my cross to bear.

I look around me and take in every detail, I memorize the amount of turns we take and count out the guards as we pass. The moment we enter a little kitchenette, Koda motions toward a seat by a tiny table, then the fucker shoves me into it. I shoot the cunt a glare but say nothing. Koda takes a seat opposite me and waves his men away so we are alone. He places a bottle of water in front of me, I swipe it off the table. The bastard is quick, he strikes out slapping me across my face, splitting my lip open again. I spit the blood on the table between us.

"Still a dog I see," he sneers.

"Still a cocksucker I see," I taunt. His eyes darken as he grinds his teeth, trying to reign in his temper—he was never good at controlling himself.

"Why do you insist on constantly pushing me?"

I scoff. "Because fucking with you has always been my favorite game."

His nostrils flare. "I'll break you again, you know that, don't you?"

I cross my arms over my chest and smile wide as I recline back in my chair. "You may have broke my hymen, *baby*, but you sure as fuck didn't break me."

"Suka!" (Bitch) he snarls, his upper lip twitching as I watch him war within himself. "You know why you are here. Give me what I want and I won't kill you."

I laugh, this motherfucker must be smoking some good fucking herbs if he thinks I will give him what he wants. My laughter is cut off when a hand grips the back of my head and slams my face into the table top. I groan, but bite the inside of my cheek when the cunt behind me yanks me back by my hair only to slam my face again.

"*Dostatochno.*" (Enough.) The bastard releases me. I peer over my shoulder to see it's the cunt with the burnt neck. He leers at me with a hungry look in his eyes. I shoot him a vicious look before turning back to Koda. "You forget who I am and what I am capable of."

"I forget nothing. I remember exactly how your fists feel. I know exactly what you are capable of doing. I'm not that same stupid kid anymore," I grit out through clenched teeth.

"You always did have a way of bringing out the worst in me, didn't you?" The hint of humor in his tone has me grinding my teeth to the point of pain. "Your father will give me what I want."

"No the fuck he won't. You forget, you stupid prick, who trained me to endure everything that you are about to put me through. I may be a Murdoch but I am also a *Volkov*." At the mention of my mother's maiden name his face turns an angry shade of red. He snaps his arm out, tangling his fingers in my hair and yanks me forward. We're nose to nose. I smile, knowing I've hit a nerve. "Do your worst, baby, it won't change the fact that I will always be a Volkov and you will always be nothing but the shit beneath my shoe." To drive my point home and to fuck with him I seal my lips to his relishing in the angry roar that tears from him when he shoves me back. Manic laughter comes from me as I stare at the fucker.

"*Vodi yeye seychas!*" (Waterboard her now!) I brace myself when the fucker obeys his boss and yanks me to my feet by my hair. This time I don't take it like a bitch. I spin around ignoring the burning sensation in my scalp as I jab him right in the throat. Before he can stumble away from me, I rip his gun from his side and unload two bullets in his chest before turning to Koda. The fucker darts out a side door I didn't see earlier.

I race out of the door and shoot one of the guards running at me in the head. I keep my gun raised as I bend down and disarm him. I shove two clips in my bra and take his walkie talkie. I listen to what the men are saying in Russian, dumb fucks have no idea I'm fluent. I take off down the corridor when I hear one of them say that I must have bolted out the back door. I peer around each corner before darting back toward the room Taylan and Kimber are being held in. I sigh in relief when I spot the door open, the moment I enter my eyes widen. Two fuckers hold Taylan down on his knees while another guy is pawing at Kimber, without hesitation I raise my gun and bury a bullet in the back of the bastards head. The two holding Taylan release him and reach for their guns but they're too slow, I lodge a bullet in each of their skulls.

"Russia, if you are going to freak out, now is not the time," Kimber snaps as she begins to grab the fuckers gun that was pawing at her. Taylan rushes to me after getting a gun from the other dead fuckers and comes straight to me. He cups my face between his hands.

"Hang on for a little bit longer, Slayer, can you do that?" Unable to form words, I just nod my head. He pushes his lips to the side and looks like he wants to say more, but I jerk out of his hold when someone orders over the walkie talkie to check on the prisoners.

"We need to move, they're coming back," I say. Taylan orders us to stay behind him as he leads us out of the room. I latch onto my adrenaline, knowing that it is the only thing holding me together right now. Kimber grabs my arm and pushes me in the middle. I shake my head but she shoves me forward again.

"You're worth more alive," she whispers.

"My life is not worth more than yours," I say. Shock colors her features before I tear my gaze away and follow after Taylan. I'm alerted when he begins firing the second he opens a door. I lean against the wall opposite him, then dart my head forward to peer into the warehouse where the cars are parked. Shouts are heard throughout the warehouse and my stomach sinks at the sheer number of men, we can't take them all. "Where is my family?" I ask Kimber.

"They were trying to find a way to breach the fence line, it's rigged with explosives." Something isn't adding up, there is no way my dad wouldn't say fuck it and barrel through the fence at the sound of gunshots. I have this gut feeling that something is wrong. I eye Kimber warily suddenly seeing her in a different light. Her eyes narrow the longer we stand here staring at each other.

Motherfucker!

I grab Taylan's arm and yank him back to me, he whirls around about to snap but I beat him to it. "She's working with them, my family isn't here."

"Slayer, now isn't the time to fuck with me when twenty or so men are out there trying to kill us!" he shouts before snatching the gun off Kimber and then going back to shooting. I raise my gun and point it at her. She stiffens as she looks down the barrel of my gun.

"Come tomorrow I am going to be a mess and probably break down as tonight is the first time I have ever killed someone, but adding you to the list of dead people isn't something I will grapple with." Taylan pushes the door closed and looks between us with worry.

"Put the fucking gun down, she is on our side—"

I cut him off before he can continue. "My family would have blown that fucking fence down, they aren't here are they?" I push. She looks from me to Taylan and the moment he sees the look in her eyes he gasps.

"What have you done?" he mutters.

"He has my daughter, I didn't have a choice, Tay." More

shots can be heard outside the door. I push the gun against her forehead.

"Show us the fucking way out or I will kill you," I seethe. She shoots Taylan a look imploring him to understand. I don't have time for this shit. "Move your ass now!" I shout. She jerks in fright.

"I don't know a way out, I was brought in here the same way you were," she argues. I growl in frustration before demanding Taylan to follow me as I sprint back toward the room Koda had taken me.

"I guess we know what happened to him then," Taylan mumbles at the sight of the burned fuckers body as we race past him. I lean against the wall and crack the side door opening a tiny bit and check to see if the coast is clear before looking back to Kimber.

"Is the fence really wired?" I grit out.

She shakes her head. "Not that I know of." Her bad bitch attitude is now gone. I have half a mind to shoot the bitch in the foot and leave her here but I can tell from the torment in Taylan's eyes that he won't leave her behind.

"If we make a run for it we can reach the fence and jump it before they catch us, can you make it?" I ask him.

He shakes his head as if to clear his thoughts before nodding somberly. "Let me go first," he says in a tone filled with hurt. Who the fuck is she to him? I push that thought out of my mind as he shoves the door open and darts out. I follow behind not caring if Kimber comes with us or not. That bitch played us! Taylan's back glistens when the moonlight hits it. He scales the fence in a matter of seconds. I toss my gun over the fence when I reach it. Just as I ready myself to climb I hear Kimber cry out behind us. She's hunched over grabbing at her ankle, I dart my gaze around and see three guards rushing toward us.

I should leave that two faced bitch!

"Kimber!" Taylan shouts. Fuck! He won't leave her. I rush forward and yank the bitch up by her hair ignoring her protests as I duck low when gunshots ring out. I shove her into the fence.

"Climb!" I scream at her and she cries out in pain when she tries to push off her ankle which is twisted at an odd angle, I grab her waist and use all my strength to push her up. Taylan grabs her wrists and pulls her over the fence. I jump up and scale the fence, just as I'm about to leap over the other side something hits me in the back of the head and sends me tumbling forward, I land on the hard ground with a thud.

"Fuck, get up, Slayer!" Taylan snaps. I reach back up and touch the back of my head wincing in pain, my vision is blurry but the sound of the Russian fucks getting closer has me fighting through the dizziness and pushing to my feet. Taylan has Kimber in his arms as we run as fast as we can ducking and making a zig zag pattern when more shots ring out. My lungs are burning with the effort of pushing myself as much as I can. I'm exhausted and barefoot but I refuse to allow Koda to get what he wants. "This way," Taylan shouts, we round a corner and I sigh at the sight of buildings with lights on, Taylan stops next to a parked car and places

Kimber on her feet beside it as he goes to the driver side and kicks the window in. "Get in!"

I don't argue when he unlocks the doors, slipping into the front seat beside him while the rat climbs into the back. He leans down and rips a few wires out, then rubs two of them together to start the car. He doesn't fuck around as he plants his foot and burns rubber, putting as much distance between us and them.

Chapter Six

Taylan

My heart is racing, my mind is reeling over Kimber's declaration. I have no idea how she knew they had her daughter or what she had planned to do in order to help them but she betrayed me! She wormed her fucking way into my trust circle and then broke it like it meant nothing to her. I hit the interstate and finally chance a look at Destiny. She sits there staring down at her hands as she wrings the hem of my shirt in her grasp. Without thinking too much into it, I reach over and pry one of her hands free before interlocking my fingers with hers. She snaps her wide eyed stare to me.

"You're gonna be okay," I say quietly before turning back to the road. She doesn't pull her hand free or even fight me, she relaxes slightly and sinks back into her chair.

"Where are we going?" I inhale a deep breath at the sound of Kimber's voice. I count to three in my head to try and control the anger simmering beneath the surface at her betrayal. She became someone I could count on and trust in, now she ruined all of that. "Taylan, I had to do it—"

"You didn't have to do shit!" I roar. "You betrayed me. I fucking trusted you, I brought you into my circle and I never fucking let anyone in, Kimber!"

"She's my daughter! I love you, Tay, and I'm sorry for hurting you but they have my kid and I will do anything I have to in order to get her back." I take a calming breath. I understand her reasoning but it doesn't stop it from stinging like a bitch.

"What was the plan?" I ask her as I turn to meet her gaze in the rearview mirror for a second.

"I got a message three days before Wave's party. They knew my name and everything and sent me a picture of my daughter."

She egged me on to chase Destiny, that's why she made the bet!

At the risk of sounding like an asshole I ask, "How do you know that girl is even your daughter?"

"She has a birthmark in the shape of a star behind her ear, that's how I know she is my daughter." I hang my head trying to fight a war within myself. "They said they would return her safely to me if I could get the information they needed."

"I would never fucking tell you!" Destiny sneers.

"She wasn't talking about you," I mutter. "She thought you would tell me and she would use my friendship with her to her advantage to get the information out of me knowing I trust—trusted her." Destiny stares at me for a second before tearing her hand out of my grasp.

"Were you in on this as well?" I snap my head toward her and glare at the minx.

"Oh yes, of course, dear, I enjoy my face being used as a punching bag and love getting my ass beat. Feel sorry enough for me to offer up that formula yet?" I snark. She narrows her eyes, then crosses her arms over her chest and slumps back into her chair with a huff.

"I'm sorry Tay—"

"I don't want to hear it, Kimber. Just... shut up and sit here while I process," I snarl. I have no idea where the fuck to go. I don't have a phone or money to stop and buy a phone or even use a fucking pay phone.

"Get off at the next exit," Destiny says.

"Why?" I question.

"My family has a safe house there, we can clean up and use the phone." She rattles off the address.

"Slayer, I'm not from here so I'm gonna need you to be my GPS for a hot minute." I don't have to be looking at her to know she is rolling her eyes. I fight the smirk from breaking free as she directs me where to go. I can tell she's pissed off but I can't do much about that right now, I need to get to this house and call Knox. I also need to figure out who the fuck that guy was and how she knows him. Kimber's treachery was just the tip of the iceberg. We drive for another twenty or so minutes, I'm so fucking lost and have no idea where the fuck I am. When she points to the small home on the left-hand side of the quiet street, I pull into the driveway and disconnect the wires to shut the car off. Destiny leads us around the back of the modest home, and I fight not to snort when she snags the key from beneath a potted plant.

What an original hiding place.

She lets us in and then rushes around the corner to shut the alarm system off. Kimber and I stand in the entryway as she turns the lights on. I spot a landline on the countertop in the kitchen and make a move for it but Destiny snatches it before I can.

"Give me that!"

She stares me down like she wants to gut me where I stand. "Your boss is a country away and can't wait to hear from his favorite dog. My family is an hour away and will be here before Knox can scratch his ass." I cage her in with my arms gripping the counter on either side of her and getting right in her face. She doesn't cower away, if anything she hardens her gaze.

"I'm not one of your father's men that you can bark orders at, Slayer. I work *with* your family, *not* for them. Don't push me too hard, baby, because you won't like the feeling of my bite."

She presses in closer until her chest is flush against mine and her full lips ghost over my own. "Keep telling yourself that you're an alpha a few hundred times more and you may just believe it. In my world, I outrank you." In a move so bold that it renders me speechless, she pecks me on the lips, then pain radiates through my entire body when she knees me right in the balls and I crumple to my knees before her shouting in pain. "You ever back me into a corner like that again and I'll rip your fucking cock off." She marches her psycho ass out of the kitchen *with* the phone as I kneel here gasping for air.

"She seems... nice." I ignore Kimber as I grip the edge of the counter and haul myself to my feet. I make it to the next room ready to go another round with her when she waves the phone in front of me. Not one to be deterred, I close the space between us and wrap my hand around her throat.

"Who the fuck is this?" I freeze and dart my gaze from the phone to her, she smirks and mouths *speaker phone*. I keep my hand on her throat refusing to lose another round.

"Uncle Bishop, it's me," she answers.

"Destiny, thank fucking God." The relief in his tone is clear. "King, call Gage and tell him she's at *Haven Home*." I inch her backward step by step, she doesn't fight me but she does shoot me a warning look that I choose to ignore. "What happened?" She grunts when I slam her against the wall.

"I'll explain everything when I get home." She tries to sound unaffected by my hold on her but fails.

"Are you okay?" Bishop asks just as she tries to knee me again, but this time I'm prepared and smack her leg away.

"Yeah, just tired. How far away is Dad?"

"King, give me an ETA on Gage?" he calls out to his brother as I lean forward and bury my face in the crook of her neck nipping at the soft skin. She gasps, causing me to smile against her skin. "He's forty minutes away. Hang tight kid. Is Taylan with you?"

"Y-yeah, he's here?" A soft whimper escapes her when my lips brush against the shell of her ear.

"You like me don't you," I taunt quietly so only she can hear. I feel her stiffen but before she can say anything Bishop speaks.

"Can you put him on?"

I pull back and rest my forehead against hers loving that she can't do a fucking thing right now with her uncle listening to every word.

"I'm here," I say.

"What was the damage?"

I stare into her gray eyes as I answer. "Russians. They're after the formula her mother uses to transport the drugs. They took Destiny as leverage and were going to use whatever means they could to get her to talk."

"Fuck, I want you back here with her and ready to give me a full debrief," he demands.

I dart my tongue to moisten my lips and in turn, lick hers too. "I don't work for you, Bishop."

"No you don't but you do work for Knox, who is on his way here now. You get the fuck back here with my niece or your boss will be the least of your worries," he orders before the call drops out. A whoosh of air escapes Destiny when I snatch the phone from her grasp and step back.

"Find some clothes, your father won't like the sight of you in my shirt," I throw out as I head back into the kitchen where Kimber stands leaning against the counter with a raised brow. I shoot her a look that I hope conveys *fuck off* before I step out the back door and call Knox. It rings three times before he answers.

"Taylan?"

I smile. "How'd you know?"

"Thank fuck, are you good?"

Warmth spreads through my chest at my brother's concern. "Yeah, I'm good. Why the fuck are you coming to New York?"

"Because you got kidnapped you stupid fuck!" he shouts.

"Calm the fuck down, dick head, I was just asking."

I can just picture him working his jaw side to side as he tugs on the strands of his hair. "You're a real asshole, you know that, right?"

I chuckle. "Yeah I do. Can you do me a favor and add Wave to this call?"

He hesitates for a second before asking, "Why?"

"Kimber's here and it's not good," I answer truthfully.

"How bad is it?"

I release a long exhale as I scrub a hand down my face and wince in pain. "The Russians that took us have her daughter."

"Fuck! Hang on, I'll add her now." I remain silent and wait for her to answer. Wave still doesn't sleep much so I know she will be awake at this early hour of the morning.

"What?" she says in lieu of a hello.

"Wave, I have Taylan on the line as well, he has something to tell you."

"Tay? You're alive."

"Yeah, Wave, I'm good but Kimber's here."

She's silent for a second before she asks, "Why the fuck is she with you?"

"The Russians that took us blackmailed her, they have her daughter."

"Mother-fucking-cunts!" she snarls. "I'll handle it."

"You need to get to my location now. Gage is nearly here and taking us back to Bishop. If they get their hands on her..." I let my sentence trail off, we all know the Murdochs won't show her any mercy for her betrayal.

"I'm heading there now. I'll send you the address. Meet us there, Wave, but you get Kimber and get the fuck out. We cannot go to war with this family, they are too fucking powerful." I know that hurt Knox's pride to say but he's right, with his wife pregnant with Wave's baby none of us are willing to put her in harm's way. Wave is a blood-thirsty bitch but even she won't go to war and risk the safety of her best friend and child with her guys.

"Text it to me now," she says before she drops out of the call.

"Taylan, make sure Kimber keeps her mouth shut and doesn't utter a word until Wave gets her out."

"Got it," I say then end the call and head back inside to break the news to Kimber. She stands there with a guilty look on her face. I hate that she broke my trust but I hate myself more for understanding why she did it. "We're being taken to the Murdochs, you keep your mouth shut and don't utter a fucking word. Knox and Wave are meeting us there, the moment she gets there you leave with her without an argument, am I clear?" My tone leaves no room for argument.

"You're not going to kill me?" I hear the surprise in her voice.

"No." Her shoulders sag in relief but I'm not done. "We are no longer friends, Kimber." Her mouth opens to argue but I push on. "You broke my trust, you want to earn it back then prove to me you can be loyal. The only reason I didn't kill you is because I know what finding your daughter means to you."

Her eyes turn misty and I begin to think she may cry but to her credit, she doesn't let her tears fall. "I understand."

"Good, now go find some clothes while I try and convince the demon upstairs not to rat you out to her fami-ly." She shoots me a look that says, good fucking luck. I have a feeling I'm going to need all the luck I can get to convince this hard-headed minx to keep her trap shut.

Chapter Seven

Destiny

I found some clothes in the dresser in the master bedroom, they are men's clothes but I'm not complaining. I drop them on the bed and head straight for the adjoining bathroom, I need to wash the fucking night away. I pull off Taylan's shirt and toss my bra and panties to the side as I step under the spray of hot water. I let it cascade over me as I stand beneath it with my eyes closed.

The night's events flash like a movie on the backs of my closed lids, I see the faces of the men whose lives I took and cover my mouth with my hand to muffle the sob that tears out of me. Yes, I have been trained from a young age to fight and endure the worst forms of torture by my mother. I know how to stay alive but training and actually doing it are two totally different things. I took the lives of five men tonight and in the moment I didn't hesitate, it was them or me and I chose *me*.

I'm a killer!

I love MMA and the thrill it gives me to fight, it's mine. Not my family's or anyone else's, this is just mine. I don't have to share it or worry about the FBI, CIA, or DEA coming after me. I know what my family does and I respect that they choose to live their lives the way they do, but I don't want to make my living that way. More sobs claw their way out of me as I think about what I did tonight. My head is still throbbing from where one of those fuckers threw a rock at it when I fell over the fence. I should be grateful it wasn't a bullet.

Then there is Koda—seeing him tonight was a shock I never saw coming. I thought he was a part of my past, I really thought I had left that nightmare behind me but it turns out, yet again my last name fucked me over royally. He knew who I was the first moment we met. I was young and dumb and thought he hung the fucking moon. He was my teacher. I cover my face with both hands as emotion overcomes me, I can't stop the sounds from forcing their way past my lips, my whole body shaking from the force of it.

When I feel arms wrap around me I gasp and try to get free, but the instant he buries his face in the crook of my neck and speaks, I stop fighting.

"It was you or them, Slayer. You did what any person in your situation would have done." I hang my head in shame, yes they hurt me but I played God tonight.

"I killed them," I choke out. He spins me in his arms and cups my face between his hands, forcing me to look up at him.

"They would have killed you or done worse if you didn't do what you did. You saved Kimber from being raped, you saved my life and that has to count for something." The fact his gaze never waivers to catch a look at my naked body has me respecting him a little.

"I don't cry."

He smiles. "I never thought you were the crying type. We can act like this never happened if that helps?" He will never know how much him keeping this moment to ourselves means to me. Before I can stop them, more tears leak from my eyes. I close my eyes not wanting him to see me in my most vulnerable state but to my surprise he doesn't call me out on acting like a girl, instead he wraps his arms around me and buries my face in his chest. I wrap my arms around his waist and smile to myself when the tips of my fingers brush the top of his jeans. He had enough respect for me to keep his clothes on instead of using my weakened state to his advantage.

At this rate, I might actually be sad at his funeral if he did die.

His hold on me tightens as he places a kiss on the top of my head. Something passes between us at this moment, I don't know what it is but I can feel a shift between us. He slowly pulls back and reaches up to grasp my face between his hands and swipes away my tears with his thumbs. His blue eyes burn with such an intensity that it has my breath hitching. I feel my heart rate begin to pick up as he slowly leans down, giving me every opportunity to back out but I don't move an inch.

He stops for a second the moment his lips are a breath from mine, offering me one last out but I don't take it. When his lips touch mine, a chorus of butterflies take flight inside my belly. His hold shifts as one hand grips my waist to pull me closer to deepen the kiss. His tongue swipes mine and I moan at the taste of him. Taylan doesn't ask permission to lead, he just does it like it's in his make up to be the one calling the shots. I wrap my arms around his neck, needing more of him. When he shifts his hand to grip the back of my head, I hiss in pain and he immediately draws back and stares down at me with concern.

"Did I hurt you?" The worry in his tone is clear as he runs his gaze over me checking for injury. I feel heat creeping up the back of my neck when he gulps audibly at my nakedness as if he is only realizing for the first time now that I'm in my birthday suit. His eyes darken and stay rooted on my body. "Fuck, you are gorgeous," he rasps out.

At the risk of sounding like a *girl*, I feel warm at his compliment. I'm used to being told I'm a great fighter, I have a good stance or throw an amazing hook but I never get complimented on my looks. It feels strange to be compli-mented on something so trivial and yet my mind seems to be lapping up the praise like a dog wanting to be pet by its owner. My throat feels dry and without thought I lick my lips to moisten them. Taylan's eyes follow the move.

When he leans forward and captures my lips, his move-ments are strong and sure. He doesn't ask for permission, but grips the back of my neck and tightens his hold on my waist. The rough material of his jeans chaffs against my heated skin. My head is all messed up, my body aches and hurts but the longer he kisses me everything seems to fade away, until he is the only thing I can focus on. I melt into him, drawing him closer by the belt loops of his jeans and moan into his mouth.

He grips the backs of my thighs and lifts me. I lock my arms and legs as he walks us forward until my bare back meets the cold tiled wall of the shower. An ache begins to build inside me so I grind against him needing friction but he breaks the kiss and looks at me intently.

"Destin.," It's so strange hearing my name from his lips, the way he says it has me wanting to moan. "If this isn't what you want... tell me now and I'll leave. You've been through a lot in the past twenty-four hours and I don't want to take advantage of you—"

"Taylan, don't try to be a good guy right now, I just need you to make me feel something that isn't despair and a broken feeling that is trying to consume me."

His eyes turn dark as his features harden. "I don't do feelings, Slayer. This is a one-time deal, you good with that?"

I fight the urge to roll my eyes. "Yes, now hurry the hell up before my dad gets here and kills both of us." My words seem to be his undoing. He reaches between us to open his jeans, but his knuckles brush against my bare pussy drawing a gasp from me. The bastard shoots me a cocky smirk and winks as he pops the button and pushes his zipper down. I can see the strain on his face and know the pain from his ribs is giving him grief but his need to fuck me drives him to ignore it.

Once his cock is free he doesn't fuck around with teasing me or even checking to see if I'm wet, he positions himself at my entrance then meets my stare. "Last chance to tell me to stop."

"Do it," I push. A glint I can't decipher enters his gaze as he pushes inside me. I want to say it's easy and he slips inside me with ease but the truth is, he barely gets the head of his cock inside me before I'm panting and digging my nails into his shoulders trying to keep from crying out. There's a strain on his face, his jaw is locked as he fights to go slow and not slam inside me.

"Breathe," he grits out, without realizing it I've been holding my breath and suck in a large intake of air as he pushes in further drawing a strangled sound from me. The self-satisfied smirk on his face annoys me but the fucker has every right to feel proud of himself, because his cock is fucking huge and my poor pussy is stretching to its limits. God it burns but in a delicious way that has me unable to remain silent and throwing my head back. Taylan leans forward and captures my nipple in his hot mouth, drawing a sharp cry from deep within my throat.

My body reacts and pushes forward, forcing his cock further inside me. Taylan releases my nipple with a pained groan as he buries his face in the crook of my neck.

"Jesus Christ, you're killing me, Slayer," he growls.

"Fuck me, I need you to do it now," I demand. I expect him to reject me or refuse to move fast but instead, he slams the remainder of the way inside forcing a scream to tear out of me that has my own ears ringing. Our breathing is labored as we both try to calm ourselves. I feel so full, my pussy pulses around his large girth trying to accommodate his size. I'm not a virgin but the amount of pain I am in right now from his monster cock you would think I am.

"You're so fucking tight!" he grits out through clenched teeth. All I can do is stare at him as I try to breathe through the pain, whatever he sees in my eyes has his features pulling taut. "You okay?" I nod. "I need the words or I pull out and we stop, consent needs to be verbal, Slayer." My brows raise in surprise, I didn't expect him to be so worried about needing me to voice my consent.

"Yes," I rasp out.

"Yes what?"

"Yes. I want you to fuck me, is that what you wanted to hear, you—" Before I can finish telling him how much of a controlling asshole he is, he pulls almost all the way out before thrusting back inside me. A loud moan escapes my lips as he repeats the same movement. I lull my head, allowing him free access to nip and suck at my neck. He doesn't bite hard enough to leave a bruise but the slight pinch of pain mixed with the pleasure he is inflicting on my body has my mind blanking. All I can focus on is how good he feels inside me, the way his cock strokes that sweet spot inside me has me making sounds unfamiliar to my own ears. As the pressure inside me begins to build, my hold on him tightens. "Taylan," I moan his name like he's the answer to a prayer.

"That's right, baby, scream my name." The dark look in his eyes would frighten most women but not me, I relish in the darkness I see buried in the depths of those blue eyes. I grip the strands of his brown hair and tug, loving the growl that escapes him. I silence his next groan when I seal my lips to his and begin pushing down on his cock, meeting him thrust for thrust. The undeniable feeling of my orgasm cresting has me in a frenzy. The need to come outweighs all rational thought. I feel like a crazed woman as I begin to scrape my nails along his back, swallowing his hiss of pain. When the tension inside me becomes too much, I break the kiss and throw my head back.

"Fuck, Taylan! I'm coming," I cry out as he slams inside me one more time before I'm screaming his name as I come harder than I ever have before. He doesn't slow his pace or allow me to ease down from the high, instead he increases the speed in which he fucks me. I've barely come down before I feel another orgasm building. My shocked gaze meets his and I feel a hint of fear when I see determination in his gaze. I shake my head. "I can't," I whimper.

"You can and you fucking will. I want to feel that cunt strangling my cock as I come deep inside this perfect fucking pussy." His dirty words have me groaning, I want to fight him and plead that he stops but my body has other ideas. This is new for me, I've never come twice during sex or even had a lover that cared enough to make sure I was satisfied.

"Taylan, I can't." I try to plead again even as I feel the need to come building inside me rapidly. I loathe to admit it, but I fear that this second orgasm will have me passing out.

"Yeah, you can. You're gonna take this cock and come all over it so you know who this pussy belongs to." The pure dominance in his tone is what seals the deal. I hate when men try to assert their dominance and act like women are their property to be owned, but hearing him stake his claim over my pussy, sends me tumbling over the edge.

"Fuck!" I scream so loud my throat turns hoarse, this orgasm feels like it's splitting me in half. If it wasn't for his hold on me, I would swear that I was a puddle on the ground.

"Good girl," he praises me a second before he roars out his own release. A pang of annoyance hits me in the chest, I hate that I wanted to hear him come with my name on his lips! The both of us are breathless and panting, like we went seven rounds in the ring. Aftershocks continue to wrack my body as I try to regulate my breathing. You would think being an athlete that I would be used to hard workouts, but sex with Taylan... that is a whole new level of cardio! He doesn't meet my stare as he slowly eases out of me. I wince in pain and notice the slight look of guilt in his eyes before he masks it. He keeps a hold on my hips when he places me on my feet, and the moment he is sure that I am steady, he releases me and steps back.

Not two seconds ago we couldn't get close enough to each other but now, we both want to be as far away from each other as we can. I know that was just sex and nothing more, we both needed to decompress and take our minds off what happened, but I can't stop my mind from wondering why it felt so right to be in his arms.

"I didn't come up here for that... just so you know." I quirk a brow at him but don't call him on his bullshit.

"Why did you come up here then?" I try to keep my face

blank of emotions but the moment I feel his cum leaking out of me and trailing down the inside of my thighs I cringe. His gaze drops and when he sees what has me cringing, a possessive look enters those blue eyes that has my breath hitching. He darts his tongue out to moisten his lips. I attempt to close my legs but he shoots me a glare that has me stilling.

"Fuck I like the sight of my cum trailing down those delicious thighs." Without uttering another word he drops to his knees, shocking the fuck out of me. Utterly stunned and at a loss at to what he is doing, I just stand here and watch as he swipes the cum on my thigh with his pointer finger, looks up at me and slowly pushes that cum covered finger inside my sensitive pussy drawing a whimper from me. "Throw your leg over my shoulder," he demands. I narrow my eyes down at him.

"Why?" I gasp and my eyes shoot wide when he hooks that finger inside me.

"You may think you are the boss and you are... in the ring, but when it comes to me getting what I want, I'm in charge and right now, what I want is to taste my cum inside this pussy so throw your fucking leg over my shoulder so I can eat your cunt." My jaw unhinges. As if my body and mind are no longer in sync, my leg lifts and hangs over his shoulder without consent. The fucker shoots me a cocky smirk and winks. I try to formulate a response but it dies on my tongue the moment his own swipes through my slick folds, drawing a sharp cry from me.

I'm stunned again for the second time, most men would never want to taste their own releases but not Taylan. He suctions his lips over my entrance and sucks. I whimper when his groans send vibrations through me. My hand tangles in his hair holding him in place when he pushes his tongue inside me. My other leg begins to tremble and almost gives out but he grips the globes of my ass, pulling my pussy in closer as he laps at it, drawing mewls of pleasure from me.

"Fuck, my cum tastes so good inside you, baby. I need you to come on my face and then push the rest out. I need to taste your come mixed with mine."

Sweet baby fucking Jesus!

I'm already so sensitive and know I won't last long, I can't draw this orgasm out, I need it now!

"Suck my clit and finger fuck that pussy and you will have me seeing stars in seconds." His eyes darken.

"When you come, you will be seeing me, not fucking stars. Those fucking things don't get the reward I worked for. I want your eyes on me, Slayer. I want you to see what *I* am doing to you." His challenge sparks something inside me. My gaze remains locked in his as he buries two fingers inside me, crooking them at the perfect angle to hit my G-spot. Shudders rock through me. The second he sucks my clit into his mouth and pumps those fingers inside me I detonate, screaming his name so loud there is no doubt that Kimber heard me. My leg wants to give out as he yanks his fingers free and suctions his lips to my entrance. Without thought, I push and watch as his eyes roll back and he swallows the remainder of his cum from inside me.

A warm sensation washes over me as I stare down at him,

I have never seen a sexier sight than the one I am looking at right now.

"Fuck, we taste so good together, baby," he moans. I hold his gaze as I reach down and press a single finger inside myself. He watches my every movement. When I bring that finger to my lips, his mouth parts and a hungry look enters his gaze as I wrap my lips around the digit and suck it clean. I moan at the salty taste of his cum mixed with the tangy taste of my release.

Our release tastes like they were made for each other.

"Fuck, Slayer, I never hit the same pussy twice but I think I can make an exception for you, baby." Before I can answer him, the pounding on the bedroom door has him jumping to his feet.

"Get the fuck out here now, Gage just arrived," Kimber shouts. Taylan and I lock gazes for a second before we both scramble to get the fuck out of the shower and make ourselves presentable so my dad doesn't kill him and start a war with the Re Della Strada.

Chapter Eight

Taylan

I know without even making it down the stairs that Gage will know I've fucked his daughter. That isn't even the part that has me worrying, it's the fact I got so wrapped up in her pussy that I forgot to tell her to keep her mouth shut about Kimber. Before we can round the corner into the kitchen I grab her arm and pull her back. She spins around and glares at me ready to tell me to fuck off, but I press on before she can, making sure to keep my voice low enough for only her to hear.

"I'll keep my mouth shut about Koda if you don't say anything about Kimber." Her nostrils flare in indignation, her eyes even darken as her anger begins to rise.

"Why the fuck would I care if you told them about Koda?" I release my hold on her and cross my arms over my chest pinning her with a smug look.

"Does daddy dearest know you fucked him?" Her jaw

locks, if looks could kill there is no doubt in my mind that I would be burning alive right now.

"You just made an enemy out of the wrong Murdoch, you bastard. Your bitch is safe for now," she grits out, but I can tell she isn't done. She presses in closer so we are flush against each other. "You've just become my main focus after I take the head off that snake. Run while you can, Taylan, because unlike my family, I don't sneak or hide my tracks. You'll know it's me coming for you when the time is right." She pulls back, shooting me one last scathing look before she marches off. I stare at the back of her head in surprise. I didn't expect her to be so... intriguing but fuck, she is holding my attention without even trying and given what her last name is, that is fucking dangerous.

To not make it so obvious we were just together, I wait a minute before following in after Destiny. The moment I enter the room, I spot her wrapped up in her father's embrace. A hand lands on my shoulder pulling my attention from Gage and Destiny to see Royal and Sin standing beside me.

"Glad to see you in one piece." I turn and shake Royal's hand and nod to Sin.

"Yeah well, that's all thanks to your cousin over there." Royal's face pinches.

"Destiny?" he questions, clearly shocked by my admission. Sin's face mimics his shock.

I shrug my shoulders. "I guess she isn't just a badass in the ring." I spy her looking at me from the corner of my eye. I give her my attention and smirk when she sneers. "Clearly the constant resting bitch face runs in your family." Royal snorts a laugh while Sin promises to gut me if I ever say that shit again. Worst part, I actually believe that Chanel would do it, she isn't exactly known for making idle threats. Kimber moves to stand next to me. Rather than letting everyone know there is a divide between me and her, I shift so she is included in the conversation. Once Gage's men finish their sweep of the house, we are all ushered outside. I climb into the car we stole so we can dump it on the way. Kimber joins me, but as I start the car and put it in reverse I have to slam on the brakes when I see Destiny standing behind the car in the rearview mirror. She stands there for a second longer before she climbs into the backseat.

Before I can ask her what the fuck she is doing she speaks. "Drive now before my dad realizes I'm not with Royal."

"Why?" I ask.

"Because you owe me an explanation about why I'm not ratting the bitch out that got me kidnapped." I grit my teeth, doing as she says knowing if I don't, it's Kimber's life on the line. The three of us remain silent for a couple of miles until Kimber finally breaks it.

"Why would you help me?" she asks Destiny.

She keeps her gaze focused out the window as she answers. "I never said it was you I was helping," she claps back.

Kimber growls. "Why the fuck are you helping at all then?"

Destiny pulls her gaze from the window to glare at

Kimber. "Because your bodyguard is blackmailing me and if I am to go with this, I want to know why you are being protected." I roll my lips over my teeth, she's a lot smarter than I gave her credit for.

I answer instead of Kimber. "Where we come from we don't turn our backs on people we care about because they made a mistake."

Destiny scoffs. "I'd like to go to that place." Her answer brings a frown to my face. "If I agree to help you *lie* to my family and hide her treachery, what assurances do I have that the bitch won't sell me out again?"

Kimber slouches in her seat, making the smart choice to keep her mouth shut and leaving me to deal with this errant demon. I mull over her question for a while trying to come up with a good answer but the one conclusion I keep coming back to doesn't exactly work in my favor, but when I see Gage flashing his headlights behind me, indicating to pull over and dump the car, I know I'm out of time.

"I'll train you for your title fight. I know you need a trainer and believe it or not, I'm fucking good at what I do." Her face scrunches at my reply.

"I'd rather forfeit than have the likes of you training me," she snarls.

"I'm your best option. I give you my word that you will win that title with me as your trainer as long as you keep your end of the deal." I pull over and put the car in park but don't move to get out, waiting for Destiny to answer me.

"Prove to me you're worthy of the chance to train me and I'll consider it but make no mistake, Tay Tay, I won't be fucking you again." I smirk as I meet her gaze in the rearview mirror.

"Find em, feel em, fuck em and forget em is my motto, Slayer." Her cheeks redden at my reply, clearly pissed off that I brushed her off without a second of hesitation.

"I guess you won the bet," Kimber breathes out before she exits the car. I keep the anger from splaying across my face. Destiny looks confused for a second before I tear my gaze from hers and climb out of the car, shooting Kimber a scathing look over the roof.

"You'll pay for that," I vow. The little bitch just shrugs.

"She's outta your league and you and I both know it. Best to set the boundaries now." If we didn't have an audience, I would have my hand wrapped around Kimber's throat right now. The bet was made as a joke... kind of but I know Destiny won't see it that way.

That bet is going to bite me in the ass, I can just feel it.

The ride to the Murdoch compound is filled with tension, my mind is reeling over what is going to happen. I need to speak to Knox first before talking to Bishop, he needs to know about what happened and the deal I made with Destiny to keep Kimber breathing. If the Murdochs found out she ratted out one of their own they would kill her on the spot. It's going to be hard enough explaining to them why she was there to begin with.

As we make our way through the gates that are manned

with armed guards, I spot the six houses that line either side of the road. It's true, they all really do live in their own community. Gage drives past the houses and comes to a stop in front of the largest house at the end that is separate from the six. I can see a small guest house just off to the side of it. What draws my attention is the sight of Knox leaning against his car in front of us with Wave, Xander and Trey beside him.

Thank fuck!

As soon as I climb out, I reach back inside the car and grab Kimber's arm, dragging her after me. Wave shoots me a look of warning not to hurt her friend but I choose to ignore it. We are in this shit because of Kimber not trusting us enough to come clean and ask for our help. If she had done that we would have helped her and got her daughter back but instead, we're all here trying to keep the peace and work out a way to keep the Murdochs in the dark.

"You good?" Knox asks when I come to stop in front of them.

"Yeah. She needs to get out of here now," I say. Wave nods and motions for Kimber to get in her car. Kimber shifts to face me but I refuse to look at her, keeping my gaze on Knox.

"For what it's worth, I am sorry, Taylan, but my daughter means more to me than anything in this world." I slowly turn to face her, the look on my face has her backing up a step and Wave creeping in closer ready to put me down if I make the wrong move.

"You meant something to *me*!" I grit out in an even tone,

her eyes turn misty. "I would have helped you. I would have gone to fucking war for you, Kimber. That's what you meant to me but you broke that when you lied to me." Her bottom lip trembles but she doesn't allow her tears to fall. She shoots me one last pleading look before nodding and making her way to the car with her head down. I can hear Gage and the others behind us making their way into the house but I don't make a move to follow after them.

"If they try to come for her, you let them know that they will be at war with the Da Luca Crime Family. I don't give a fuck what their last name is or what she did, she is my family and I will protect my own, Taylan, regardless of what you think." Wave's tone leaves no room for argument. She doesn't stick around for my answer as she goes after Kimber, leaving the four of us here with mere minutes to spare before we are summoned to meet with the Don of the biggest crime family in the US.

"They try to come for her, we won't stand down. I won't let my girl go to war without me by her side," Xander decrees.

"No one is going to war, if they try to go after my sister then they will be at war with the Re Della Strada as well," Knox snaps. "My wife is pregnant with your kid. Remind my sister of that fact would ya before she starts something she can't finish on her own." Xan and Trey both shoot my best friend an angry look.

"You don't think we fucking know that? Wave has moved our entire operations to Canada so she can be closer to Lake through the pregnancy. Nano is running things in Ireland until after the baby is born. Don't ever use our kid against us again because it won't be a war that ends you, Knoxville, it will be me!" Trey snarls before storming off after Wave.

"He's right. Wrap this shit up here and do whatever you have to so that a war doesn't break out because I'm not losing my girl or putting Lake and the baby in harm's way because Kimber fucked up." Xander storms off leaving me and Knox to deal with this shitstorm.

"I'm getting real fucking sick and tired of everyone thinking they can get away with demanding shit from me and talking to me like I won't put a fucking bullet in their heads." I shoot him a deadpan look.

"You gonna kill Xan and your sister?"

He narrows his eyes at me. "No, but I would kill Trey and deal with my sister's tantrum."

I smile and shake my head. "You hurt Wave and your wife would murder you." He throws his head back and groans.

"I had to go and fall in love with a ball-busting hardass, didn't I?" I laugh at his stupidity and watch Wave and the others peel out of here just in time as King shouts for us to get inside. Knox and I share a loaded look before we walk side by side into the lion's den, praying we both make it out of here without any new holes in our bodies. As we enter the house, I feel a bit of hope spur to life inside me at the sight of Royal, Sin, Chaos, Artemis, Cronos and London. Knox has grown close with Chaos and the Argyros twins and even Royal. Sin tolerates us but London is a wildcard, you can never get a read on her crazy ass.

"Fuck that! I am not a doctor you can just call on whenever the fuck you want to!" I spin toward what appears to be a living room to see King facing off against his daughter Amelia, who looks like she is about to fuck shit up. It doesn't escape my notice that Cronos separates himself from London and his twin as he moves closer toward Amelia.

"I didn't have a choice!" King defends.

Amelia throws her hands in the air. "You always say that! What part of stop fucking calling me don't you understand? I don't want to be at your beck and call, I made something of myself, even if it is under a fake name. I have a legit fucking life and you can't just keep sending your men to drag me out of my workplace so I'll patch up your men."

"It wasn't just anyone, Meelz, it was Luka," Rook butts in. I frown at the sight of blood on Rook's shirt. Luka is his brother in law and Bishop's right hand man after King.

Amelia looks to her uncle and some of her anger vanishes as she stares at him. "It's because it was Luka why I didn't shoot the fuckers the moment they shoved me in the car," she bites back.

"They laid their fucking hands on you?" Cronos growls drawing all our attention to him, if possible Amelia looks angrier when she meets Cronos's gaze.

"That's none of your business, you and my dad can both stay the fuck away from me and lose my number." She turns back to face her father. "I'm done. I don't want you calling me or showing up at my apartment or where I work." The plea in her tone is clear and I feel kind of sorry for her. I gaze around the room at all the faces to see them all looking guilty, well everyone except for Sin and London. Bishop, Knight and Vincent make their way into the room followed by Kiara, Allison, Koby and Anya, who rushes toward her daughter. Allison moves to stand beside her husband with tears in her eyes as she looks at her daughter.

"Meelz—"

Amelia cuts her mother off before she can continue. "No, Mom. I have done everything this family has asked of me whilst trying to pull away so I can live my life free of the burden of being a Murdoch, but you all keep sucking me back in. Royal, Chanel, Chaos and fuck, even London love this life but Destiny, Nytress, Unique and me don't. Destiny has a chance at a career in the MMA but because of her last name she is limited. I can't use my real name at the hospital or I will lose my job the second they know who my father is. I am begging you, Mom, let me go and make him stop dragging me back into this shit."

"Angel, you can't escape your fate," Cronos pushes, earning a tearful glare from Amelia.

"I can and I will. You know better than anyone what this life can take from you." Cronos's face blanks in an instant at her words.

"Amelia Queen Murdoch, you are hereby granted leave from this family." Everyone turns to Bishop. King rushes his brother but Gage, Knight and Rook hold him back.

"You stay the fuck out of this, Bishop, she is my daughter!" King roars.

"It's because she's your daughter why I am granting her this wish. She hates us, King," he bellows. Amelia flinches but doesn't deny his claim, instead she drops her chin to her chest. "She is not to return here. She is free to live her life without being weighed down by being born into this family." Bishop lifts his gaze to look at his niece. He looks almost pained as he stares at her. "This will always be your home, Meelz. I'm sorry that you have been burdened by the weight of this family's last name. Should you ever wish to return, you know you can, but until then, your freedom is your own. Live your life how you want to and on your own terms."

"Thank you," she chokes out. As she turns to leave, Cronos snaps his arm, blocking her path. King rages but my focus is on his daughter and Cronos. They share a look I can't decipher but no words need to be spoken. You can tell from the way they stare at each other that there is something between them. Amelia sighs and places a kiss to his cheek before brushing past him and not stopping when her parents call for her to come back.

Amelia Murdoch just earned my respect for not bowing to the easy way in life and choosing to live on her own terms.

Chapter Nine

Destiny

Uncle King and Aunt Allison chose to sit out of the debrief and head home. Aunt Kiara chose to go with them and make sure they are okay. I can't believe Amelia just did that, she has always been adamant about not wanting a part of this life and I guess in some ways I want to get away from this mafia life too, but another part of me loves it. I'm a hypocrite. I want my cake and eat it too but life doesn't work like that. I can't have one foot in and one foot out—in this life you are either all in or out, there is no in between.

"Let's get this meeting over with," Uncle Bishop grits out. Dad comes to stand beside me and Mom claims the spot beside him. I look around the living room and take in the faces of my family, each of them is pledged to this life now with no escape. This is what they wanted. I wasn't sure it was what I wanted until this moment. I played God and took the lives of men whose faces I can't even remember because they chose to strip me bare and tried to break me. My gaze lands on Knox and Taylan. My breath hitches when I find Taylan already staring at me with an intense look in his eyes.

A shadow of darkness clings to him like a second skin. Fathers want their daughters to steer clear of the bad boy type for fear of them leading them down a dark path. But I have this urge inside me to walk down the path of darkness and succumb to it, let it drown me in its darkness so it will take away this feeling of guilt. Guilt for killing those men and guilt for fucking a man who used me and led me to think he cared, only to turn around and be the devil in disguise.

"I want you to break down the events of what happened, Destiny." I shake my head to clear it as I look at Uncle Bishop.

"What more is there to say. I got taken, we fought, I got free and that's the end of it." My uncle narrows his eyes.

"Destiny, you need to tell us—"

Before he can continue pushing me, Taylan cuts in. "They were Russian."

"How do you know?" Dad asks.

Taylan looks at me when he answers. "Because your daughter is fluent and played translator, didn't you, Slayer?"

"Is that true?" Mom asks. I grind my teeth forcing my anger to subside.

"Yes. They want your formula and were hoping that I would tell them. Andreas is losing control of Russia and the Crows are rising against him." Everyone begins speaking at once but all their conversations become white noise as I stare at Knox and Taylan. I can tell from the way they are standing at the edge of the room near my cousins that they are hoping if I decide to rat them out that their friendship with Chaos and Royal as well as Artemis and Cronos will save them from my family.

"We need to go to Russia and meet with Andreas," Mom announces.

"No. There is way too much heat on you right now to leave the country," Uncle Knight says.

"Knight's right, until we know who it is, going back home is out of the question. We know firsthand what they do to women, Anya." Aunt Koby's words are laced with an edge of pain and anger. Uncle Knight wraps his arm around her shoulders and draws her into his side. Chaos moves to stand beside his parents and places a hand on his mother's shoulder. I smile at the sight. Ryat looks so much like his uncle, well of course he does, considering his father was Chaos's identical twin.

"Gage, have all our men combing the streets, I want these cunts found. Vin, I need you tracking them." Uncle Bishop turns his gaze to Royal and the others. "I need you back in Miami and shaking down every fucker for any intel. Artemis, you, London and Cronos are to head back to Greece and act like nothing is astray. Right now the only people we can trust are in this room. I'll reach out to Ian and see if he knows anything." I know what he is saying, the heads of the families may not be able to be trusted right now.

The heads of the US are Uncle Bishop and Royal, The head of the Greeks is Artemis, which is fine because he is marrying into the family so he can be trusted but the other four, Andreas, Ian, Knox and Waverly aren't family. They may be friends and they can turn on us at any time.

"Where is the girl that was with you?" At Uncle Rook's question Taylan shoots me a look. He and Knox both shift their stance, waiting to see what I will say but ready to fight if they need to.

I hold his gaze as I answer. "She was a mess, she was one of the women Waverly rescued and was triggered, so Wave took her so she could get help. They thought she was Taylan's girlfriend and wanted to use her against us. They tried to rape her," I add on to silence any other question, knowing the mention of rape in this family shuts down every conversation. It's a shitty thing to do considering how that has affected so many women in my family.

Uncle Bishop turns his heated gaze to Knox and Taylan. "She should have been here." The reprimand in his tone is clear. Knox nods stiffly.

"She wasn't one of mine to order, my sister made the call and I stand by her. I also stand by your family and will vow before you all that the Re Della Strada will stand with you and help however we can to eliminate this threat against your family."

"You've proven to be an ally but given the situation, you can understand how your word won't be enough," Dad adds with an edge to his tone.

Before they can all start arguing, I cut in. "Taylan has

offered to remain here in New York as my trainer. If they try to double cross us, then we have their underboss here within our grasp." Taylan's eyes burn with anger. I shoot him a smug look and purse my lips. The others begin discussing my revelation and move about the room. The moment my parents leave my side, Taylan is in front of me vibrating with rage.

"Within your grasp, huh?" I smile cockily.

"I sold it, didn't I?" I sass back.

"Keep fucking with me, Slayer, and I'll take it out on you during your training."

I feign hurt and bat my lashes. "Oh please, don't make me run laps." I pout.

The dark glint that enters his gaze has me stilling. "Fuck with me and I'll put your ass in the underground fights your family doesn't know are still running." My eyes widen as the bastard smirks and winks at me before moving back to stand next to Knox, while I stand here staring at him.

"Well, I guess you will make that title fight after all." I turn away from Taylan to look at London and Artemis.

"Yeah... I guess so," I mutter.

"Taylan is a good guy and will do whatever he can to help." I want to snort and tell Artemis he is delusional about his friend but I keep my mouth shut.

"Yeah, I'm sure he is," I mutter but suddenly feel exhausted, all the adrenaline is wearing off and right now all I want to do is go home, then sleep for a few days and try to process what the fuck happened. I know it's gonna hit me hard when I finally come to terms with everything but right now, I just want to block it out and pretend that it never happened.

When London and Artemis join in the conversation with Royal and the others, I use everyone's distraction to my advantage and quietly leave the room. I know my dad will want me to stay with them but I don't want or need them coddling me. I just want to be alone so I sneak out of the house like a rebellious teenager. I snag a set of keys off the mantel and make a dash for it. I smirk when I push the button on the key fob and the lights to Uncle King's Audi flash. He loves this R8 and I feel bad about *borrowing* it but not bad enough to turn around and hand the keys back.

I slip into the driver's seat and caress the wheel for a second before pushing the button and smiling when the engine purrs to life. I probably should have been a boy given my love of fighting and cars, but my dad was unlucky and wound up with me. I'm closer to my dad than I am to my mom. He supports my dreams of wanting to fight but mom thinks I'm wasting my life and I'm too pretty to get punched in the face for money.

I bite back a squeal when the passenger door opens, startling me. My shock morphs into outrage when Taylan slips into the seat beside me.

"Get out!" I snarl.

"Unless you want to be dragged back inside by your ear, I suggest you plant your foot and get the fuck out of here because Mommy is looking for you."

Shit!

As if on cue she appears out the front door. Without

second guessing myself, I slam the R8 into gear and plant my foot. I smile when the power of the car has me pushed back into the seat. The pull on this thing is fucking epic. I maneuver the car down the drive, not letting off the gas, knowing mom will be calling the guards to lock the gate. My exit is in sight as I see Tiny with his phone clutched to his ear. At the sight of me he waves to the other guards, signaling them to seal the gate so I plant my foot flat. My breath hitches and my adrenaline spikes, wondering if I will make it through those iron bars and when I do, I squeal in delight.

"Take that, motherfucker!" I shout through my manic laughter that dies off the second I remember I'm not alone on my little jailbreak.

"Don't stop on my account." I grip the steering wheel in a vice-like hold and grind my teeth.

"Why the fuck are you here? I didn't peg you for a stage five clinger, Tay Tay." I can feel him glaring at me and fight to keep my smile at bay, knowing I am working his nerves with my pet name for him.

"If you hadn't snuck off you would have heard that I am your new bodyguard courtesy of your father." I snap my head toward him and find that he looks just as pissed about this as I am.

"What the fuck, why?"

"Apparently since you and I will be spending a lot of time together training it only seems fair that I be the one to guard you. You know, because if I turn out to be a backstabbing asshole then I'm within their grasp to kill, which makes keeping your ass alive my number one priority." His tone is laced with bitterness.

"I didn't ask for any of this. I just want to go home, sleep then train, I don't want all of this fucking extra shit," I admit.

"Too late, you and I are now a package deal whether we like it or not, so suck it the fuck up."

"Kind of like how you sucked the cum out of me?" I retort without missing a beat.

I nearly jump out of my fucking seat when his large hand lands on the top of my thigh. "Or like how you sucked our cum off your finger?" I smack his hand off my thigh and ignore the laughter that comes from him, he's infuriating.

The remainder of the drive is spent in silence, I refuse to speak to him. Even when I park the car and stash the key on the front tire, knowing Uncle King will come for his baby, neither of us utters a word. Even when I enter my apartment and try to slam the door in his face, he says nothing. I head straight for my bedroom and slam the door, locking it behind me. I march over to my bed, snatch a pillow and then press it against my face so it can muffle my screams of anger.

It takes me a good ten minutes to calm down enough to strip out of my clothes and pull on a pair of booty shorts and a crop top before climbing into bed. We both hate being around each other so I have no idea how the fuck him training me is going to work. I close my eyes and calm myself by thinking about my training and going over my moves in my head, that always helps but instead of seeing my moves, I see the vacant eyes of the men I killed.

I bolt upright gasping for air, scrubbing a hand down my

face. I try to push away those images that keep flashing like a movie in my mind. I'm stronger than this, I won't let a little death scare me and reduce me to a shell of a person. I look around my room and suddenly feel... scared. The shadows seem to form shapes and are closing in on me. Before I can scream for Taylan, scarface appears in front of me, silencing me with a hand around my throat.

Chapter Ten

Taylan

I've barely fallen asleep on her hard-as-rock fucking couch when her ear-splitting scream pierces the air, forcing me to leap to my feet and draw my gun. I rush down the small hallway and kick her door open. I dart my gaze around, searching for the intruder but all I see is her screaming and clawing at her throat as she lays there.

She's having a nightmare.

I stow my gun in my waistband, eliminate the space between us and try to shake her but she still continues to scream and won't wake, so I resort to drastic measures and cover her mouth with my hand. It takes her two point five seconds to snap her eyes open. The second they do I remove my hand. She sits upright gasping and darting her gaze around the room.

"Slayer?" She screams and scoots across the queen bed, looking at me with pure fear that has me stumbling back a step and raising my hands. A few seconds pass before she registers that it's just me and no one is here to harm her. I stand here and watch as she feels her chest and throat. Her breathing is erratic, I can tell from the look in her eyes that the nightmare is still fresh in her mind.

I know exactly how she is feeling and how much it must be weighing on her.

"The nightmares won't last forever," I say quietly.

Her gaze cuts to me, a deep groove forms in the center of her brows. "What?" she rasps out.

"I'll bet good money that you closed your eyes and saw the faces of the men who you killed." Shock colors her features. "Was it scarface that was choking you?"

Her mouth is ajar as she studies me like I'm a science project. I can tell she doesn't trust easily and in turn, that is shit for me because I need her to open up about this Koda thing so I can find the cunt, kill him and get Kimber's kid back so I can go home. Gage and Bishop made it clear that I'm the pawn in this and me being here is the only way they are going to trust Knox and believe him not having anything to do with this situation.

"He was here... in my room," she says barely above a whisper, the hint of fear that laces her tone has me softening slightly. I keep my hands raised as I move to sit on the edge of the bed, she stiffens but doesn't pull away.

"The nightmares will consume you if you let them."

She swallows audibly. "How do I stop them?" The hard set of her jaw shows me she hates having to confide in me but she doesn't have any other choice right now.

"Time. I know everyone hates hearing that answer to a question but it's the truth. Over time you will learn to train your mind to block out the faces." Silence encases the room for a while until she clears her throat and draws my attention back to her.

"Who hurt you?" Her question is simple and should be easy to answer but it's a double edged blade for me. Only three people know the truth about me, Knox, Xan and Wave. I've never spoken a word about it to Lake, Mom or anyone else and I sure as fuck don't plan to make her the fourth person to know my story.

"No one, go to sleep," I grit out as I stand, but she leaps across the bed and grips my arm, stopping my escape. I look from her hand to her and raise a brow. The terrified look on her face has me lulling my head back and staring up at the ceiling groaning. "Fine. Move your ass over." She releases me instantly and shifts to the other side of the bed. I peel off my shirt and push the borrowed sweats down my legs and climb beside her in my boxers. I can feel her staring at me but I ignore her. If she doesn't like me sleeping next to her like this I'm more than happy to return to her uncomfortable couch and leave her here to suffer on her own.

I place my arm behind my head and close my eyes, ready to sleep for a fucking week. I'm sore and angry that those Russian fucks got the jump on me. Just as I'm about to cross over into the blackness of a dreamless sleep I feel her cuddle into my side. I remain still and say nothing when she wraps her arm over my waist and rests her head on my chest as she pulls the covers over us.

"Body heat, that's all this is," she declares. I can't help but smile.

"Whatever you say, Slayer. If this position gets you to shut your mouth and sleep, then snuggle away."

The sun beating down on my face is what rouses me from sleep. I arch my back and try to turn but something is weighing my arm down. I snap my eyes open and frown at the sight of a mess of blonde hair splayed over my arm and chest.

Destiny.

I drink in the sight of how peaceful she looks, it's been a long time since I felt like how she looks. After she cuddled into my side we were both out within minutes and she didn't have another nightmare. I look around her room, able to see more now thanks to the sunlight. She has a pin board above her desk in the corner of attractions from all over the world but the one in the center is a picture of the Eiffel tower. I didn't peg her as the type of girl who wanted to travel, all she has talked about is how much she wants to fight and make it big in the octagon.

I reach around her back and wrap my arm around her, liking the way she feels pressed against me. The moment is shattered when the iMac on her desk begins to ring with an incoming FaceTime call. I quickly drop my arm and feign sleep when she bolts upright. I remain still but I can feel her staring at me.

"Fuck," she grits out before she pushes off the bed and stumbles over to her computer. I blink my eyes open and smirk at the sight of her bent over her desk, the bottom of her ass cheeks are hanging out the bottom of her shorts. "Yeah?" she says when she answers the call.

"Clearly you're not a morning person," a girl quips.

"Shit, I'm sorry. I forgot we were supposed to meet up today. Give me thirty minutes and I'll meet you at the gym," she rushes to say and steps aside. The girl's mouth hangs open, on the computer, when she spots me in the bed.

"Dest!" she screams. I dart my gaze toward the wardrobe where she has her back to me and strips off her shirt.

"What?" she calls back as she pulls on a sports bra.

"Who is that hunk of juicy meat in your bed?" Destiny freezes and slowly turns around to face me. Her eyes are wide and she looks like a deer caught in the headlights, but the moment I smile her face morphs into a vindictive mask.

"No one, I'll see you soon," she clips out as she rushes to end the call and finish getting changed.

"Did you forget I'm your new bodyguard and where you go I go?" I ask as I stand and stretch. She stands there running her gaze up and down my body. "Take a picture, Slayer, it will last longer."

"Asshole," she snarls as she crosses the room to enter the small bathroom that is attached. I take my time changing and making use of the other bathroom down the small hallway, I need clothes and a phone stat. As I exit the bathroom, I call out to her but she doesn't answer. I search the apartment for her but don't find her.

"Bitch ditched me!" I snarl. She is going to pay for that fucking stunt as soon as I get the essentials and a fucking phone, I am going to that gym to show her that she is going to listen to me whether she likes it or fucking not!

With no fucking phone I can't even order an Uber. I'm forced to walk and the longer it takes me to get to the store the angrier I become. I don't know why I am so pissed off, maybe it's my abandonment issues or the fact the little bitch was able to sneak past me, whatever it is has me wanting to strangle the fucking life out of her. If she gets taken again, then it's my fucking neck on the chopping block, not hers!

I pull up to the front of the gym a couple of hours later and sling the duffel bag of clothes I just got over my shoulder and nod to the Uber driver. Before entering, I pull out my phone and sigh with relief that the fucker has finally finished uploading all my contacts—losing your phone fucking sucks, let me tell you that. I hit Knox's number and place the phone to my ear as I watch people file in and out of the gym. The place has definitely had a makeover and it turns a good profit judging from the amount of people coming here but we all know this palace is just a front to wash their cash.

"Who the fuck is this?"

I smile at the grumpy fuckers tone. "It's me."

"About time you got a fucking phone."

"Did you miss me, Knoxy?" I tease.

"Shut up, asshole. What the fuck is going on, Taylan? After you bailed last night I was left standing there trying to answer questions I didn't have the answers to."

"Like?" I push.

"Like why the fuck you said you were Royal Murdoch?"

I scrub a hand down my face. "I knew they'd take me with her if they thought I was him, no one knows who the fuck the *Memento Mori* is and they were smart keeping their identities secret." I fill him in on everything that happened and how we got away.

"Who the fuck is this Koda, Tay?"

"No fucking idea, dude, but I plan to make this little bitch talk," I vow.

"Taylan, you need to reign in that fucking temper, you can't treat her like shit and whatever you do, do not get involved with her."

I cringe. "Yeah... Uh..."

"Fuck me sideways, you already fucked her, didn't you?" I rub the back of my neck and scrunch my face up.

"Yeah, but she consented, I made sure."

He sighs and I can picture him tugging on the strands of his hair as he tries to calm his temper. "Tay, she doesn't know you and what happens when things get tough for you. If you plan to sleep with her again, you need to make sure she knows your triggers, be honest with her and explain everything."

I scoff. "She ain't someone I plan to keep around, Knox, I'm good with just fucking bitches."

"Taylan, the only girl you have slept with more than once is my fucking wife!"

"Lake is different and you are always there! Don't throw that shit in my face when you both wanted it. Fuck you for bringing it up!" I snarl as I end the call, my anger from earlier resurfaces as I stomp across the lot to the entrance of the gym, ignoring my phone ringing. He knows about my past and what I went through, for him to bring that shit up and throw it in my face like that is fucked up. The sound of flesh hitting flesh is music to my ears. I look around to see people on the weights, sparring on the mats but my attention is snatched when I see the ring—it's who is in the ring that holds my attention.

Destiny has her hair piled on top of her head, her navy blue sports bra and some tiny as fuck spandex shorts on. She's in the ring with her dad and another girl, the girl from the call this morning! I make my way over to them but keep myself concealed behind a pillar, if I'm going to train her I need to see what she has and judge if she even has a chance to win this fight against Tiana *Prime Time* Lawson. That bitch I've seen fight and she is dirty as fuck. She toes the line perfectly to the point the ref can't call her on any of the moves she makes because it's not illegal in the ring it's just unethical.

"When she comes in and charges you, wait till the last second and then drop down and sweep her legs out from under her," Gage instructs her. He steps back and motions for her friend to come at her but she's too slow and winds up getting a hook to the ribs. "Doll?" Gage shouts across the room. I follow his line of sight and balk at the sight of Kiara Murdoch. I've heard the stories about her and how she used to fight in the *underground* but I thought it was just bullshit stories to make the Don's wife seem tough.

"Yeah?" Kiara calls back as she makes her way toward

the ring with gloves on and a similar outfit to Destiny's, but her long raven hair is loose and flowing around her.

"Can you give me a hand with Dest for a few minutes?" Gage asks.

"Anything for my beautiful niece, plus my class just finished so I'm all yours until Bish arrives." Destiny is grinning like she won the lottery as her aunt climbs in the ring and her friend steps out. I look around and notice that Kiara's presence in the ring has garnered the attention of almost everyone in this place. They all abandon what they were doing and crowd around the outside of the ring.

"I can't hit my aunt!" Destiny says. Kiara and Gage both smirk.

"If you can land a single hit on her, I'll even pay your new trainer and give you Sunday's off." Destiny scowls at her father.

"I never take days off and if I hit my aunt, Mom will kick my ass," she defends.

"Honey, your mother knows what I am capable of and I promise you that I will pull my punches and this will stay between us." Destiny's jaw is slack as she stares at her aunt. I shake my head. She is underestimating her opponent and that is going to be her worst mistake. I grind my teeth knowing I should stay out of this and let her get her ass beat, but I also need to prove to her and Gage that I am an asset and can help her win against Tiana.

Fuck it.

I push my way through the crowd and drop my bag down beside the ring before climbing up, drawing the attention of the three Murdochs in the center. Gage and Kiara look surprised to see me but Destiny looks annoyed that I'm here. That shit makes me giddy, knowing I'm under her skin. I duck down and climb through the ropes and come to stand beside the little shit as I look at her father and aunt.

"Give me two minutes with my fighter." I don't wait for their response as I grab Destiny's arm and drag her to the side of the ring. She tries to break free of my hold but stops when I push her in the corner and crowd her space. To anyone watching it just looks like I am coaching my fighter, but her and I know this is a power move and unless she wants daddy dearest to know I've slid between her sheets she won't make a fucking scene, even though her eyes spit fire at me.

"What the fuck do you think you're doing?" she hisses at me.

"Helping you not get your ass beat by your own aunt."

The defiant little shit rolls her eyes. "That's not going to happen."

"Don't test me right now, Slayer. I'm already pissed off enough about your stunt this morning." Her eyes twinkle in delight, earning a growl from me. I press in closer, brushing my lips against the shell of her ear. She tries to fight her reaction to me but the shiver that works its way down her spine gives away how she feels having me this close. "You will be making it up to me tonight when we get home." I don't give her a chance to respond before I pull back and stare into her eyes. "Your aunt will have you on your ass in two seconds flat if you keep underestimating her. I've heard the stories about how she fights and I'm sure you have to."

Her dazed outlook vanishes and is replaced by a fierce look of determination. "Either help me or get the fuck out of my way."

"One minute," Gage calls out.

"Listen to everything I say and you may just make it out of here with your pride intact," I say.

Chapter Eleven

Destiny

I shoot Taylan one last look over my shoulder before turning back to my aunt, my dad stands on the side of us.

"You have three minutes, that's it. Destiny, your job is to stay on your feet and not get pinned." I shoot him a scathing look that has him smiling before he turns to my aunt. "Doll, show her what you're made of, if she can't put you down then you will be her new training partner until she can pin you." I balk at him but before I can argue my point he steps back and nods to Thomas outside the ring that is crowded with people to ring the bell. I'm not worried about this fight ending up on the internet, no one aside from members of our family are allowed their phones in here so we can train in peace without the worry of people leaking tapes of us.

The second the bell sounds I expect my aunt to go on the defensive but she surprises me when she comes at me with arms swinging. I block her hit and crouch down, Taylan told me not to strike until I can get a read on her or find a weak spot. She's too nimble and fast for me to attack her, her foot work is fucking insane and makes it hard for me to judge where she is stepping.

When she comes at me with a left hook and a right cross over that I narrowly miss I decide to say fuck it to what Taylan said and fight how I always do. My reach is longer than hers, which means she has to come closer. I wait for her to take a swing at me, when she does I push off my back and drop my left arm slightly as I swing out with my right hook. What I didn't anticipate was for her to expect that move, drop low and tackle me to the ground. We grapple on the floor for a minute before my own aunt has me pressed face first into the ring with her knee in my back and my left arm wrenched back. Dad rushes forward and crouches down beside us.

"Tap out." I grit my teeth and ignore the burn in my arm as she tilts it further back and shake my head.

"Never." I growl.

"You're done." Taylan calls out as he enters the ring and stands behind my father looking pissed off. "You could have rolled out from under her if you weren't so cocky and thought your size difference would give you the strength you needed to overpower her." To teach me a lesson my aunt pushes my arm back further, drawing a cry of pain from me, leaving me no choice but to tap out. She releases me instantly. I admit my pride is more wounded than anything. I roll over and stare at my aunt's outstretched hand. If she were anyone else I would smack it away but I can't disrespect her like that.

She helps me to my feet and smiles. "You were over anticipating every move, to get a read on someone you have to play defense," she says.

"I had three minutes to take you down, that didn't leave me much time," I defend.

"All you needed to do was watch closely for thirty seconds, she favors her right side and always tenses before she throws a punch," Taylan adds from beside us. Aunt Kiara and Dad both look surprised at his observation. "You try fighting like how you just did against Tiana and she will have you tapping out in round one." His words hit their mark. I hate that he's right and I did overestimate myself when I know better.

"Hit the showers, take the rest of the day off," Dad says, I ignore all the people crowding the ring as I climb out and head straight for the locker rooms. My ego is bruised and shame is washing over me like a tidal wave. I grab my towel from my locker and head for the showers, sighing in relief when I find them empty. I strip off and turn the water ice cold as my muscles are aching. I should be in an ice bath but too fucking bad, a shower is quicker. I brace myself as I step under the spray and grit my teeth as the cold water soaks me.

I close my eyes and push away all thoughts of the fight with my aunt and try to clear my mind except all I see behind my closed lids is the faces of the men who I killed. I gasp and snap my eyes open only to stumble back a step at the sight of Taylan standing before me. I place my hand over my heart to try and calm it.

"What the fuck are you doing in here?" I snap. His eyes trail down the length of my body, and unlike some girls I'm not ashamed of mine and am proud of what my momma gave me. His gaze is laser focused on my pussy. When he gnaws on his bottom lip, my body begins to heat despite the temperature of the water.

"I came in here to lecture you about being a cocky bitch, but then I saw you naked and *wet* and all the blood in my body rushed south." Without permission my eyes drop to his groin and the sight of his hard length pressing against his shorts has my breath accelerating. Taylan doesn't wait for me to respond as he tosses his phone to the side and moves in closer, eliminating the space between us. His clothes get soaked instantly but he doesn't seem to care or even notice when he grips my waist and pulls me flush against him. He bends down so his forehead rests against mine, our breaths mingling as we stand here staring at each other, breathing the same air.

"What—"

He cuts me off before I can finish speaking. "I've only ever fucked one woman more than once, want to be the second?"

I balk at the bastard. "That's the pick-up line you're going with?" I scoff.

He smirks and wiggles his brows. "I could have said, nice legs, what time do they open?"

Despite my annoyance toward him I can't stop the

chuckle from breaking free. I throw caution to the wind and wrap my arms around his neck, then press in closer so my lips ghost over his.

"I don't like you."

His eyes darken as he shifts his hand from my waist to cup my pussy, drawing a gasp from me. "That may be true, but you like how I can chase the monsters out of your night-mares." I don't have a chance to respond, he meshes his lips to mine, robbing me of air when he pushes a finger inside me. I press up on my tiptoes and cling to him, deepening the kiss when he crooks that finger inside me, stroking that sweet spot. He pushes me back so I'm flush against the shower wall and pulls his finger free. I break the kiss.

"Why'd you stop?"

The cocky smirk on his plump lips annoys the fuck out of me. "As much I would love to watch you come on my hand, we don't have the luxury of time before people come in here, so you're going to come on my cock then we're going to head back to your apartment so you can slam that cunt on my face while you suck my cock sixty-nine style, baby."

My jaw slackens but I would be lying if I said the idea of sixty-nining him didn't have me growing wetter by the second. Taylan pushes his shorts down his legs, his monster cock springing free. It's hard and resting against his shirt, looking angry and in need of me to help relieve the pressure. I lift my leg and hook it around his waist, pulling him in closer.

"Don't make promises you can't keep, Tay Tay," I tease. Instead of answering me he grips the backs of my thighs and lifts me. Reaching between us, he positions his cock at my entrance before looking up at me.

"You want this, right?" This is the second time he has asked me for consent and the voice in the back of my head is telling me that consent was taken from him.

"Yes, Tay Tay." He looks almost relieved by my answer. This time when he slips inside me I'm prepared for his size, it still stings a bit but nowhere near as much as last time. When he bottoms out inside me we both moan, I feel so fucking full.

"Fuck your pussy is so tight," he grits out through clenched teeth.

"I need you to move, Taylan." He grips the globes of my ass in a punishing hold as he draws almost all the way out then slams back inside me. I cry out in pleasure. "Bite down on my fucking shoulder," he demands as he repeats the move making me moan loudly again. "Now!"

"Why?" I rasp out.

"You really want your daddy to hear his baby girl being railed in the shower?" My eyes widen in horror but I don't get a chance to ponder that thought before he's thrusting in and out of me, leaving me no choice but to obey him and bite down on his shoulder through his shirt. He moans when I sink my teeth in deeper. He's fucking me so good my vision turns hazy. My legs tighten around his waist as I scrape my nails down his back, hard enough for him to feel it through his shirt. "Fuck yes, keep doing that, baby."

I dig my nails in harder and whimper when his cock glides against that sweet spot continuously. Fuck, his cock is amazing and the fact he knows how to use it is a blessing. So many guys have big dicks but have no clue how to use it to satisfy a woman but Taylan isn't one of those men, he knows exactly what he is working with and how to use it. I feel my orgasm cresting, my body heat ramping up as I wait for the exhilarating euphoria to crash through me.

"I can feel your pussy clamping down on me, Slayer, don't come until I say." I whimper in response not wanting to wait, I need this release. "Be a good little girl and wait, I'm gonna come with you then eat that dirty little cunt out." His dirty promise has me moaning and melting into him, the sound of skin hitting skin rings out in the empty locker room and I admit, that sound is a turn on.

I feel my orgasm and try to fight it, I want what he promised. Memories of the last time he ate me out and how he tasted our cum was so fucking sexy. His thrusts turn urgent and I pray he is close because I can't hold off much longer, it's too fucking hard.

"Come on my cock, Slayer," he growls, as if he is the master of my orgasms. It obeys him and tears through me like a tornado. My teeth dig deeper into his shoulder but it doesn't do shit to quiet my screams. Taylan buries his face in the crook of my neck as he comes, but unlike me he's able to quieten his cries. The aftershocks haven't even finished coursing through me before he's pulling out and placing me on my feet. When he drops to his knees before me, I widen my stance and cup my tits twirling my nipples between my fingers, earning an approving look from him before he buries face in my cum-filled cunt.

"Hmmmm." I bite down on my lip to remain silent but I'm so fucking sensitive and each time he moans his approval the vibrations from that against my pussy has me shuddering and prolonging my orgasm. I almost pout when he pushes to his feet to stand but he surprises me when he kisses me. I open for him instantly and then gag. I try to pull back but he grips the back of my head holding me in place as he spits the cum he just sucked out of me into my mouth. Our gazes are locked. The instant I swallow and stop fighting, his eyes darken with approval.

Fuck, we taste so good together.

He breaks the kiss and rests his head against mine, both breathless and panting. Sex with Taylan is unexplainable, he takes without asking but he gives you twice as much back. He is infuriating and makes me want to murder him but the moment that cock slips inside me I stop hating his existence and cling to him like he is a lifeline.

"Be a good girl and get changed," he says huskily.

"I need to shower."

"No. You are not washing me out of you, I want to taste my cum when you sit on my face. Get dressed, Slayer, you have a dick appointment to keep."

Jesus Christ, my pussy is fluttering at his words.

Chapter Twelve

Taylan

From the time we walked through her front door we have been all over each other, fucking on the kitchen counter, sofa, against the large glass windows, shower, hallway, bed. We destroyed her apartment and only came up for air because we couldn't ignore our hunger any longer. Destiny being the smart mouth she is said she would order dinner for us as a thank you for my services.

We sit across from each other at the kitchen counter, eating our takeout like a couple of starved kids. The sight of her in my shirt has me frowning. Today started out like shit but she curbed my anger by letting me fuck her six ways to Sunday and it was fun, but that's all this is to me, *fun*. I keep that thought to myself for the moment, not wanting to piss her off.

"So did you get paid?"

I lift my gaze to hers and frown. "What?"

She rolls her eyes. "For the bet you made with that bitch?"

My face slackens. "How did you know about that?"

She shrugs her shoulders trying to act unaffected. "I have my ways."

I take a swig of my beer before answering. "No. It was a stupid thing to do—"

"I'm not looking for a ring or kids or anything like that, if that's something you want then you're with the wrong girl, Tay Tay. I'm here for a good time, not a long time."

Her words are like music to my ears, I know girls tend to get attached if you fuck them more than once. Hearing her admit that she is just having fun as well is a huge fucking relief.

"I'm glad we agree."

"Yeah, well, one bad relationship was enough for me." Her tone is laced with bitterness, I have a hunch she is talking about Koda so I push on.

"Was it some jock?" I ask casually.

She shoots me a deadpan look. "Don't play coy, Tay Tay. You and I both know who I am talking about, so let me break it down for you. He trained at my gym, seduced me, stole my virginity, dated me. Turns out he's an undercover Russian snake. The end."

"How the fuck did he get that close to you? Do they not run background checks at the gym?"

"No, dumbass, I was talking about the gym at my college. He was a TA and I was a student. If you ever tell anyone that I will fucking kill you, seeing how my family reacted to

London fucking her headmaster was enough for me to take that secret to my grave."

Not willing to let this conversation go, I press on. "How did you figure out who he was?"

She sits there studying me for a moment debating whether or not I'm worthy of this knowledge. "Why do you want to know?"

"Because me being glued to your side for the foreseeable future puts a target on my back as well. I need to know why he is coming after you now."

"So, this is about you wanting to stay alive and not get to know me better?" I open my mouth but she waves me off. "It was a joke, Tay Tay, you and I aren't going to become friends that braid each other's hair and paint our nails."

I shudder. "No, just no."

She laughs but it dies off quickly. "I want something in return for me telling you about Koda."

My hackles raise. "What?" I force out through clenched teeth.

"I want to know why you always need consent." Before I can say anything she presses on again. "Don't deny it, we've fucked on every surface of this apartment and every single time you asked me to say I wanted it and I want to know who hurt you."

I try to remain stoic and give nothing away but fail, her eyes soften slightly as she looks at me.

"Knowing the truth won't change anything, my past doesn't affect you," I say in a firm voice.

"Maybe not but if I'm going to give you leverage against

me then I need the same thing from you, it's only fair." I drop my container on the counter and scrub my hands down my face, only Knox, Wave and Xan know the truth about what happened. Reliving that moment in my past is something I avoid at all costs. Fear begins to snake its way up my spine, I push back from the counter and stand turning away from her as I try to gather myself. I try to think of something else to offer up in exchange and keep drawing a blank except for one thing, but I don't know if I can trust her with that information either. With no other choice, I spin around to face her to find her staring at me with rapt interest.

"I can't tell you." This time when she opens her mouth I push on. "I'll tell you something that no one else aside from five people know and if you ever breathe a word about it to anyone, I will slit your throat." My threat seems to pique her interest.

She takes a minute to mull over my words before agreeing to my terms. "You go first."

All the air leaves me in a rush, I'm going to hell for betraying my friends but I can't let her into my past, I just fucking can't.

"I've fucked Knox's wife." Her eyes widen to the size of dinner plates, her mouth opens but no words come out. "Seriously? You have a mouth that could start a war and always have something to say but hearing that I fucked Lake silences you?"

She snaps her mouth closed and narrows her eyes. "You're a fucking pig!" She sneers.

"Girl with the big ass mouth say what now?"

"You are the worst kind of friend and that bitch is disgusting for cheating on her—"

Anger surges inside me as I cut her off. "Don't ever fucking speak about her like that!" I roar, she scowls at me.

"Don't ever fucking raise your voice at me again asshole."

"Don't ever call Lake a bitch!"

"She is and so are you, how could you do that to your best friend?"

It dawns on me then. "Knox knows about me sleeping with Lake." Shock splays across her face.

"And he let you live?"

I snort and shake my head. "Knox is always present when it happens, I would never have touched Lakeland like that behind his back."

Curiosity spurs to life inside her eyes. "Do you still... fuck her?"

"Jealous?"

"Curious actually," she counters.

"No. After Lake got pregnant we stopped."

She studies me again and it's making me uncomfortable at how she is reading me. "Oh my God!" she squeaks out.

"What?" I hedge slightly worried when she grins like a psycho.

"She's the girl."

"What girl?"

"She's the only girl you have slept with more than once, you kept sleeping with her because you didn't need consent to be given." My face slackens. Knox and Lake never clicked onto that but somehow this she devil has.

"No—"

"Bullshit. You kept doing it because they *invited* you into their bedroom which gave you consent. Knox telling you to fuck his wife was all the consent you needed because you knew she wanted it, she even told you to fuck her so it would turn her husband on."

"Shut the fuck up!" I roar, rather than listening to me and taking the hint that my anger was getting out of control she keeps pushing and even comes toward me.

"You liked it because you didn't feel weak about having to have her consent. It makes you feel vulnerable when you ask for consent, doesn't it?" Before I can temper my rage I strike out and wrap my hand around her throat, it takes two seconds for us both to register what I have done before she comes at me fist flying. I block her hits and try to duck out of reach but the bitch is an MMA fighter and knows how to subdue her opponent. She leaps at me and the force of her weight sends me sailing backward, the coffee table behind me not standing a chance against my weight and breaks beneath me. I grunt in pain. She drops her forearm against my throat and presses her knee down hard against my cock, drawing a pained roar from me.

"Slayer!" I grit out in warning as I glare up at her.

"You ever fucking lay your hands on me again, Taylan, and I swear to Christ Almighty I will fucking kill you. Do you understand me?" she screams in my face, now it's my turn to read her.

"He hurt you... he was physical with you." Her jaw locks, she tries to keep her emotions from displaying themselves but I see it in her eyes. "You get off on me asking you for consent because..."

"Shut the fuck up!" Her tone has a pleading edge, making horror surge inside me. I reach up without thought and cup her face between my hands. Her eyes flutter for a second as tears fill them, telling me everything she refuses to say aloud.

"I'm so sorry, Slayer. I had no idea," I whisper. She slams her eyes closed and pushes off me to rest back against the sofa, tucking her legs against her chest and burying her face in the top. I take a deep breath and ignore the pain in my back as I crawl over beside her and draw one of my knees up and rest my arm on top of it. We sit here in silence for so long that nighttime has fallen and the moon is high in the sky, offering us a small amount of light through the windows.

"Koda knew getting his men to strip me down to my bra and panties when they kidnapped us would scare me..." She sounds broken and exhausted.

"Because he had done the same thing to you and wanted you scared and whimpering in a corner," I add.

"Yeah," she says quietly.

I wrap my arm around her shoulders and draw her into my side, offering her comfort. I don't have much experience with comforting a woman aside from Lake, Wave and Mom. River doesn't count because she was harder than me, Knox and Xan, I swear she was more of a guy than the three of us. She rests her head against my shoulder, trying to get closer so I lift her and cradle her in my lap like a child. When she sighs in contentment a surge of protectiveness burns inside me.

"I assume no one in your family knows about him?" She shakes her head against my chest. "Do you want to tell me about him?"

"Not really," she admits.

"Have you ever told anyone?"

"Not a single soul. How do you tell someone that another human being hurt you, my essence is tainted."

"No, your essence is far from tainted. You're strong, fierce and a fighter, Slayer. Don't give that cock sucking cunt any credit."

"I was going to be a lawyer like my mom always wanted. I still trained in the gym, my dad has always supported my dream of wanting to fight."

"I sense a but coming..."

"I also love law and want to be a lawyer."

"Why not do both?" I ask.

"*He* said I would never make it as a fighter because I was weak, too spoiled and sheltered. To be a fighter you have to be hungry, crave the fight and need to win. He said I didn't have those things."

The pieces fall into place. "You dropped out of law school to prove him wrong, winning against Tiana isn't about the title, it's about proving him wrong and showing him that you are strong and hungry, isn't it?"

She takes a shuddering breath and nods. "Pathetic, huh?"

"Don't do that," I scold gently.

"What, say the truth?"

"No, don't brush off what you're feeling and put on that tough girl act."

"It's not an act," she defends. "I am actually a sour bitch and I'm good with that."

"No. You're not a sour bitch, you're just hardened by the events of your past."

I know exactly how that feels.

Chapter Thirteen

Destiny

I can tell he means what he says. I've never spoken to anyone about what happened between me and Koda, not even my best friend Janice knows. I don't even know Taylan, that sounds fucking stupid considering the amount of times we've now fucked but you don't need feel or know someone to have their cock inside you. If my mother knew the way I thought about sex she would have a meltdown. My mom has always preached to me that your body is like a temple and you need to cherish it. Given what she went through, I understand why she needed me to know this stuff from a young age.

"You are the second person I have slept with," I admit. I feel Taylan tense but don't say anything more, giving him time to digest what I just said.

"I want to say thank you but I feel like you would dick punch me if I did." I can't stop the laughter from bursting out of me, he's not wrong, I would have done that. When he trails his fingers through my hair, I melt into him further enjoying the feeling. "If it helps, you're the first Russian-American I have ever slept with." We both laugh at his stupid declaration.

"I guess you're my first Canadian."

"I'll be the only Canadian you fuck, Slayer." His proclamation has us both going silent for a beat until I break it.

"Koda Novikov said all the right things, did everything that would make any girl fall for him and I did." It tastes bitter on my tongue admitting that shit out loud. "He was my TA and off limits. That didn't stop me and my friends from staring at him or picturing ourselves fucking him. One day, when I went to the gym early, he was there. It was just me and him. I remember being so nervous when he jumped on the treadmill beside me that I tried to not look at him, but I couldn't help it, he smiled and butterflies erupted inside me. We began talking, then got coffee. For the next two weeks I went to the gym early just so I could talk to him."

"He was vetting you," Taylan says softly.

I nod. "At the time I didn't realize that, I thought he just wanted to get to know me and hang out. After a month of meeting at the gym he asked me on a date. I agreed. We went to dinner, then he took me to a movie. I thought he would try to bust a move or something but he didn't, he took me back to my dorm, walked me to the door, kissed me on the cheek, then left."

"He hooked you then, didn't he?"

It burns to admit it but he's right. "Yeah. We started hanging out more often, on our fifth date I didn't want it to end so he took me back to his apartment. I thought for sure he would try something then but he didn't, he set me up in his room and took the couch. He never pushed me to sleep with him, we kissed and touched but never took it further until a few weeks later. I wanted to try things and he was eager to teach me, we fooled around but didn't fuck."

I can feel Taylan's breathing accelerate, knowing that he is about to hear my darkest secret soon.

"Your first time was taken from you, wasn't it?" he asks.

I ignore his question and continue on with my story. "One of my friends figured out that we were seeing each other. She threatened to tell and I told Koda about it but he didn't seem worried. Two days after she went missing. I went to his apartment to tell him about Molly being MIA. I let myself in with the key he gave me. I looked for him but didn't find any sign of him but I did see everything I needed to."

"What did you see?"

"Molly's purse was on the counter next to a bloody butcher's knife. I didn't want to jump to conclusions but I couldn't help it. I waited for him to get home, when he walked through the door and saw me sitting there he looked different. I got a glimpse at the man behind the mask. He was no longer the guy I had fallen for—he was a monster. The moment he closed the door and locked it behind himself, I knew I was in trouble." I didn't realize I was shaking until Tay's arm tightened around me.

"I'm right here, Slayer, he can't touch you," he assures me.

I take a deep breath and force myself to carry on. "The

second he put his hands on me I froze, every ounce of training went out the window when he punched me." His hold on me turns punishing as his anger rises, but I don't let it deter me and force myself to carry on. "He beat me. Raped me and then chained me up in his bathroom for two days, trying to torture the information about my mom's business from me. I never broke, no matter what he did to me. I never fucking broke." Taylan releases me and stands. I watch as he begins to pace the living room, feeling belittled and ashamed. I shared my story with him only for him to pull away and not even look at me.

Finally telling someone my story I thought I would feel freed, but Taylan's reaction isn't what I was expecting.

"Am I that disgusting?" I grit out, trying to keep the bitterness out of my tone but failing. He stops pacing and turns to face me with an astonished look on his face.

"Of course not."

"Bullshit, you couldn't get away from me fast enough."

He shakes his head looking all types of out of sorts. "Destiny, your first time was stolen from you and here I am fucking you like a savage. I'm so fucking sorry." I stare at him in astonishment, he doesn't think I'm disgusting.

He's angry at himself.

"I gave you consent, remember?" He tugs on the strands of his hair as he stares down at me.

"You don't deserve the way I have been fucking you! Fuck, the things I've made you do..." He spins around and slams his fist through the wall, pulling a shocked gasp from me. I climb to my feet and slowly make my way toward him.

I reach out and place my hand on his back. He jerks away from me, leaning his back against the wall—he looks like a caged animal.

"I wanted those things. I could have said no at any time and I know you would have stopped. I'm not a broken doll, Taylan. I never told anyone because I don't want them to look at me differently. My mom and some of my aunts have been through something similar and my whole family treats them like glass, I don't want that. I'm okay. I didn't break."

"Destiny, you changed your whole life because of him!" he shouts. I recoil.

"No, I didn't!"

"Yes, you did! You picked up fighting full time to prove him wrong. The course of your life was altered by that cunt. I'll kill the fucker, I swear to God I will break that cunt's essence like he made you believe yours was tainted. I'm going to send the fucker to Ireland where Wave's men can punish him daily for being a rapist. The Irish's form of punishment is just and he will beg for death but they won't allow it."

I look at him in a different light. I hear the truth in his voice.

"Mama had herself a devilish child, didn't she?" His eyes begin to lose some of the darkness in them at my light-hearted joke.

"Get dressed." I reel back.

"What?"

"I need to blow off some steam and you need to train."

"I'm not going to the gym," I say firmly.

"Who said we were going to the gym?"

My interest piques. "Where are we going?"

"To the underground. I need to fight and so do you, we leave in ten minutes."

Butterflies take flight inside me and I shoot him a grin before dashing down the hallway to change.

Taylan drives my car around the city like he knows where he's going. I'm quite surprised since he needed directions to get to the safe house. We head toward the outskirts of the city, neither of us say much but the silence isn't uncomfortable. When he finally pulls the car over I frown as I look around at the deserted lot with a single street light as the form of lighting.

"Is this the part where you kill me and chop up my body?" He turns to me and pins me with a dry stare.

"Ha ha. Get out of the car and keep your mouth shut, do everything I say and you'll make it out of here without everyone finding out who you are." I frown but don't get a chance to question him as he climbs out of the car, I quickly follow after him. Before we can make it two feet from the car he grabs my arm and pulls me to a stop, he runs his gaze over and looks unimpressed as he pushes his lips to the side. Before I can call him out on being a judgmental asshole, he reaches back and yanks his hoodie over his head and tosses it to me. I catch it on instinct and stare from it to him with a raised brow. "Put it on, keep the hood up and keep your head down."

"Why?" I ask as I pull it on and fight not to moan in appreciation when his scent engulfs me, fuck he smells amazing.

"You are the splitting image of your parents." I gape at him.

"Am not."

He rolls his eyes and pulls a gun from his waistband and holds it out to me. "You are. Your family isn't exactly welcome here and if anyone were to look at you long enough they would know you are Gage Murdoch's kid. Take the gun, any fucker comes at you, shoot them and run."

I scrunch my face and shake my head. "I'm not killing another person."

"You either do as I say or you sit in the fucking car and wait, the choice is yours." I sneer at the fucker then snatch the gun from him checking the safety is on before stowing it in the back of my yoga pants. He nods his approval then grabs my hand interlocking his fingers with mine. He leads me through the trees that surround the abandoned area, the only source of light we have to guide our way is the moon. The only reason I'm not struggling or worried he is going to kill me is the fact he gave me his gun. The further we get through the trees I realize we're walking a worn path, I start to hear voices and unknowingly grip Taylan's hand tighter. "I got you, Slayer," he reassures me.

"How do you know about this place?" I ask just as the

voices grow in volume. I see lights through the thick tree branches and sigh in relief.

"Can you keep a secret?" he asks as he peers back at me over his shoulder.

"Yeah?" He comes to a stop and faces me, keeping his hold on my hand as if he is afraid the truth will send me fleeing.

"Since your father stopped the underground fights, we noticed there was an opening in the market for it when we took over the RDS so..."

My jaw unhinges. "*You* run the underground fights!" It's not a question.

He nods. "If you decide to snitch, make sure your father knows that Knox has no idea about this. Him and Xan have their own thing going on so I decided to make something of my own."

"Why did you decide to do this in the US and not Canada?" I ask.

He shrugs. "More money to be made here than back home, a lot of the people that come here have deep pockets and settle scores with rivals. Technically I'm not breaking the laws of the treaty with the families, kind of."

I balk at him. "Yes you are, you're not supposed to enter the US without consent."

"Who said I entered the States?" I frown, not grasping his meaning. "I don't need to be here for this to run smoothly. Put it this way, the guy who runs it for me is someone who is trusted in your family." My face slackens as realization dawns on me, there is only one person my family trusts completely.

"Uncle Luka," I breathe out.

He nods. "Just to be clear, your Uncle Rook knows about this too and turns a blind eye to it because it keeps Luka from hanging out at his house every night." I shake my head, Uncle Rook hated Aunt Clare cooking dinner for her brother nightly, I think it made him jealous since Aunt Carlina never did that for him.

"Don't tell me anymore, the less I know the better." He smiles and nods, then continues leading me through the woods. When we break the tree line, I slam to a stop forcing him to halt from the grip I have on his hand. It's like a scene out of a movie, cars are parked in a large circle in the middle of this field with their lights on, people form a circle around the two in the center that are fighting. Their cheers are so loud I want to cover my ears, being an MMA fighter means if I am caught at an illegal fight ring like this I will be disqualified and never allowed to enter the octagon again.

"Say the word and we can leave now and act like this never happened," he says offering me an out but the truth is, excitement is thrumming through me at the prospect of fighting here tonight.

I turn to look up at him. "I want to fight."

His face morphs from calm to aggressive in a split second. "No," he snaps before pulling me along. I try to struggle but he just keeps yanking me behind.

"Why not?" I shout.

"Because I said so," he snarls.

"You are not the boss of me and you sure as fuck are not my father!" He whirls around so fast I crash into his chest. He grips my chin in his free hand and forces my gaze to his.

"It would be a bit fucking nasty if I was your daddy since you swallowed my cum." I gape up at him, feeling the heat in my cheeks. "I'm the boss here, not you or your daddy. Your last name means nothing in this place, this is the underground. You don't fight tonight, you watch and learn. This is training for you. They might not be paid fighters like you, but these people have no choice but to win. Learn from their determination and watch how they push the limits to win, they will sacrifice anything to win because their life depends on it. Yours doesn't, keep that shit in mind."

I'm sick, his manhandling and dominance has me getting hot and needy for him all over again.

Chapter Fourteen

I keep Destiny beside me as I maneuver through the crowd until I spot Riley, he is the real reason we are here tonight. After learning what I did about Koda, there are only so many places he can hide in this city. Bishop may have men hunting him and all roads out of the city blocked, but the connections you can garner from being a member of the underground gives you extra protection and offers more places to hide that the Don has no idea about. I can't tell her the truth, if she knew the very thing I created could be the reason her nightmare is able to hide would sure as hell seal my coffin closed after she ratted me out to her family.

When Riley spots me his eyes widen with surprise. "I expected more of a crowd," I tease him. He smiles and shakes my hand. Riley was picked by Luka to manage the fights when he couldn't make it.

"I never thought I would see you here in the flesh. Is everything okay? I swear all the books are up to date—"

I cut him off before he can continue. "Everything is good, I'm just here to blow off some steam."

HIs brows jump to his hairline. "You want to fight?"

I shrug and act uninterested. "Got nothing else to do."

"Man, this shit is going to go crazy when I announce you as a fighter." He cuts his gaze to Destiny. I shift blocking her from view and glare at him. "You keep your eyes off her," I snarl.

He raises his hands. "I wasn't looking at her like that, boss, I swear." I narrow my eyes in warning. "When people realize who you are and see your girl it might not be... safe for her."

I grind my teeth as I dart my gaze around. "Got a ride here?" He nods and points to a blacked-out Dodge pickup, three cars over. "Give me your keys." He hands them over without any questions. I drag Destiny behind me as I make my way toward the truck. I tug the passenger door open and turn, lifting her by her hips. I place her on the edge of the seat and force my way between her legs. She crosses her arms over her chest and stares down at me with an annoyed glint in her eyes.

"I'm not a child you can lock in a car, Taylan."

I smirk up at her. "Be a good girl and stay in the fucking truck."

"Or what?" she snaps.

I grip the tops of her thighs—she sucks in a sharp breath. "Want me to fuck you against this truck where anyone could see?" Her eyes darken and her breaths turn choppy, she fucking loves the idea. I brush the tips of my fingers across the top of her pussy loving how she trembles from that simple touch. "Stay here and be a good girl and I'll reward you when I get done."

She darts her tongue out to moisten her lips and nods eagerly. "O-okay."

I fight the smirk from breaking free at her breathless response. "Watch, learn and absorb everything you see." She nods again. I step back and wait for her to shift, then close the door clicking the fob to lock it. She shoots me a glare through the window, so I blow the little shit a kiss just to piss her off some more before heading back to Riley.

"You're up next," he says when I reach his side.

"I need info," I say keeping my gaze focused on the fight in front of me.

"On who?"

I peer at him from the corner of my eye. "I need to know everything about Koda Novikov." He frowns and purses his lips.

"Doesn't ring a bell but I'll ask around."

"Anyone who has intel on him gets 20k no questions asked, wired to their account." His eyes widen.

"I'll spread the word." He pulls his phone from his pocket and fires off a text. I pull my own phone out and bring up the group chat I have with Knox and Xan.

ME

I need any information you can find on Koda Novikov, he was a TA @ her college.

Their responses come in almost immediately.

KNOX

I'll get Mase on it now.

XAN

I'll get Trey and Nano to start digging.

KNOX

He the fucker that napped you and the girl?

It pisses me off seeing him refer to Destiny as *the girl*.

ME

Her name is Destiny!

KNOX

And????

XAN

You hitting that?

ME

None of your fucking business, asshole!

ME

She has a name, use it!

KNOX

Fucking hell, did you go and catch feelings for a Murdoch? *heart eye emoji*

ME

Grow up, dickhead, no one uses fucking emojis!

XAN

The little fucker went and caught feelings!

KNOX

He's been fucking her.

XAN

Before or after they got napped?

I grind my teeth and try to control my temper over these cock suckers talking about me like I'm not in the fucking chat!

KNOX

After!

XAN

crying face emoji This fucker is going to get got when her daddy finds out.

ME

Knox let you live after screwing his sister *Eyes emoji*

KNOX

Fuck you, asshole!

XAN

Talk about my girl like that again and I'll break your fucking jaw.

ME

Step up to the plate anytime, baby boy, you know I'll lay the both of you fuckers out.

ME

Get me the intel I need, assholes.

KNOX

I always liked you better than Taylan, just so we are clear, @Xan.

XAN

I only tolerated him because of you.

I roll my eyes at these dumbasses, the older they get the more immature they become. Ever since they both got locked down by their girls, they have become soft and suddenly joke around now. Joking and giving everyone shit was my thing and now they think they can come in and take that title from me, not likely.

ME

Taylan has added Lakeland, Trey and Waverly to the chat

KNOX

You fucking cunt!

XAN

You're fucking dead, motherfucker!

ME

@Lake, @Wave, your boys are being mean to me.

ME

@trey, I have always liked you the most man, straight up I hope the baby looks like you and not that ugly fucker.

TREY

Crying face emojis Amen to that brother!

XAN

Fuck off, @trey

LAKELAND

Knoxville Bronson!

KNOX

Fuck! I'm out.

WAVERLY

Grayson, get here now.

XAN

I'm gonna fuck you up you little snitch bitch, @taylan

XAN

Coming, babe.

I shove my phone in my pocket and frown at the sight of three guys carrying one of the guys from the makeshift ring. "Give me two minutes to hype the crowd, then come out. Give your shit to Nole, he'll hold it for you." I look at the guy beside Riley and nod, tug my shirt off and hand him that, my phone and wallet. I bounce on the balls of my feet and shake my arms out while cracking my neck from side to side. I can feel the adrenaline beginning to course through my body as I hype myself up.

"He's got brass knuckles on." I spin around and stare down at the blonde demon with wide eyes.

"What the fuck are you doing out of the—"

She cuts me off before I can continue. "The driver's window was down. That's not the point, his hands are strapped, he has brass knuckles. Taylan, you need to stay out of his reach." I glare at Destiny for a second longer before following her line of sight. A large bald-headed guy with pale skin stands across the lot staring right at me. The crowd begins to go wild when Riley announces I'm fighting. "The guy beside him is Allen Rhodes, he used to train at our gym but was kicked out when we found out he was juicing his fighters and cheating. All his fighters wear brass under their tape."

"Shit." I have at most thirty seconds before I have to enter the ring. I look around trying to find something to use but I can't see shit around all the people.

"The keys!" I scrunch my face in confusion. "Use the fucking keys, Taylan!" she snaps before pushing me forward. I pat my pocket and sure enough, Riley's keys are in there.

"You stay right fucking there!" I shout, she rolls her eyes and pulls the hood further over her forehead and waves me away like I'm a pesky fly. I make my way to the center of the makeshift ring to stand beside Riley. The juiced-up fucker saunters toward us with a broad grin on his face, he has at least a foot of height on me and is broader but that doesn't mean shit.

The bigger they are, the harder they fall.

Unlike this bastard, I'm not here fighting for cash, I'm here to release my demons from their cage so I can focus and clear my mind until they pull me back under their blanket of darkness.

"You know the drill, fight until one taps or you knock the other out." Riley looks between me and the fucker as he finishes speaking. "There are no kill shots, am I clear?"

"Clear," I grit out through clenched teeth, not taking my eyes off the fucker who is clearly pinging on some shit right now.

"Yeah, sure thing." The smug tone of his voice tells me he doesn't plan to stop, he wants me dead. Taking out the underboss of the Re Della Strada would earn him a lot of points in the streets.

"Let's make this a clean fight, Kevin," he says while shooting the fucker a hard look. "On my mark," Riley says as he steps back a few steps. "Fight!" he roars, sending the crowd into a chorus of screams and cheers. Kevin and I begin circling each other. The fucker stops moving and crouches down against the hard dirt. I stop and watch him closely expecting him to launch himself at me.

"Die, you Canadian scum," he snarls, then the cunt throws a handful of dirt in my face blinding me temporarily. The wind is knocked out of me when he takes me to the ground, all I can do is cover my face and weather the blows right now. I know this is a no rules fight but no one fights dirty like he just did to win. Pain riddles me, my already tender ribs scream in pain when he lands a solid punch to my side, pulling a pained groan from me. I try to buck my hips to knock him off, knowing I can't take too many hits with his fucking brass knuckles.

"Tag team!" I hear someone scream a second before Kevin grunts and flops to the ground beside me. I drop my guard and look up with wide eyes at the sight of Destiny standing there with her hands taped and no hoodie to hide her identity. Kevin's growls forces me to clear my mind as I push to my feet and hide Destiny behind me, but it's pointless as a jar head looking fucker comes to join Kevin.

"No mercy, bitch!" the cunt sneers at her.

"Touch her and die, motherfucker," I vow.

"Fuck this," the woman in question snaps before rushing

forward, closing the space between her and them before I can stop her. Just before she is within reach of their hold she drops to her knees and slides along the dirt leaning back slightly. Before she can skid through the gap between them, she punches them both in the dick!

I cringe, both of them howl in pain and drop to their knees cupping their cocks. She's quick on her feet and spins around landing a roundhouse kick to the side of Kevin's head before maneuvering the opposite direction and doing the same to his partner. I stare at her, utterly fucking stumped. Her gray-blue eyes are alight with hunger. She flips Kevin onto his back and leaps on top of him delivering blow after blow to his face. He grabs her waist, prepared to throw her off him.

I dart forward and lift my foot, stomping down on his face. I feel the bones of his nose crunch beneath my foot. His partner tackles me from the side, this time I manage to roll out from under him and jump back to my feet. There is no pause or hesitation when we both rush each other, delivering blow after blow to the other, my adrenaline keeping me from any type of pain as I release every ounce of pent up rage I have inside me on this cunt.

My demons have escaped their cage and are wreaking havoc.

Chapter Fifteen

Destiny

The bastard bucks his hips and sends me forward. I tuck and roll quickly jumping to my feet so I'm not at a disadvantage. His nose is fucked, blood is smeared over his face from my hits. I smirk at the size of the large lump on the side of his bald head from my kick.

"I'm gonna break your fucking neck," he vows.

I lift my hand and wave him toward me mockingly. "Come at me, big boy," I taunt. He releases an ear piercing roar before he runs at full speed toward me, there is no way I would be able to take a full-forced shoulder blast from him. I force myself to remain planted where I am, I can see the gleeful look in his eyes as he gets closer thinking he has this fight in the bag. A fraction of a second before he can make contact, I take a step to the side and drop down doing a leg sweep, taking his legs out from under him. He hits the ground hard with a loud grunt and skids along the dirt. I press forward and jump on his back but the fucker shifts at the last second. Panic thrums through me when he takes me to the ground.

I force all my fears to the back of my mind and allow my instincts to take over. I feel like I black out for a second when his fist clips me across the cheek. Before the pain has a chance to register, I shift beneath him and get my arm around the back of his neck and throw all my weight backward as I get him in a guillotine choke hold. It takes every ounce of my strength to keep this hold on him. He pushes up from his knees and uses his upper body to slam me back into the ground, using every ounce of strength he has.

They might not be paid fighters like you but these people have no choice but to win, learn from their determination and watch how they push the limits to win. They will sacrifice anything to win because their life depends on it. Yours doesn't, keep that shit in mind.

Taylan's words from earlier play out in my mind. This is life or death, if I slip or release him there is no doubt in my mind he will kill me. If the sacrifice I have to make is my humanity, then so be it, I will not allow this bastard the satisfaction of taking my life from me. I close my eyes and release a scream so feral a wild animal would be proud of me. My hold on him tightens. I can feel his strength depleting as I continue to cut off his oxygen supply. I see the faces of the men I killed flash behind my closed lids and pray to anyone who is listening that I don't have to add this juice head's face to the list I see when I close my eyes.

"Slayer!" Taylan's voice sounds so far away, I can't let him distract me. Another wild scream tears from me.

"Tap out!" I scream.

"He is! Let him go, baby." I feel hands gripping my cheeks. I snap my arms open to see worried blue eyes peering down at me. "He's tapping, baby, let him go." I frown for a minute until I feel the weak tap of a hand on my back. My eyes widened in horror. I release him and crab crawl backward away from the juice head. He coughs and gasps for air as he flops forward against the ground. I sit here staring at him, I made him tap.

I made him tap out!

"Slayer?" I look at Taylan who is looking at me with worry in his eyes. "Come on," he prompts. I look to his outstretched hand and hesitantly take it, letting him help me to my feet. I sway slightly. He pulls me against him wrapping his arms around me. "Deep breaths, take a second to ground yourself."

I take his advice and breath in and out allowing the rush of the fight to work its way out of my system. I always get worked up when I fight but I have never in my life felt this powerful. Whenever I fight I always go in with a clear, level head but at some point through the fight I black out and this other person takes over. My dad says I have an alter ego and gave her a name.

The very name Taylan calls me.

"I'm okay," I say after a minute and push back from him. He runs his gaze over me, then reaches up and brushes his fingertips over my cheek. His eyes darken, then he pulls back ready to go beat Kevin again but I reach out and pull him back by his arm. "Take me home," I say quietly. I see him warring within himself, he wants to oblige me but that caveman part of him wants to beat the shit out of Kevin for laying his hands on me.

"You never come back here, am I clear?" He's voiced it as a question but he and I both know he isn't asking me, he's telling me.

"Okay." At my agreement he interlocks our fingers and walks us toward Riley. When I see all the phones with their flashlights on, I cringe. There is no doubt that they are posting that fight, I would guesstimate I have at least an hour tops before my dad is blowing up my phone. Taylan stops in front of Riley who hands us our things. Taylan never releases my hand.

"You ever let her in that ring again and I'll snap your fucking neck and deliver your head to your mother." Riley's face pales, he swallows loudly and nods.

I feel bad for the guy so I cut in. "It wasn't him who helped me strap my hands." Taylan frowns, I flick my gaze to the group standing behind him. He spins around and I watch as all the muscles in his back tense in anticipation.

"Ohhhhh, you are my new favorite because you have so pissed my dad and grandpa off without even trying," London singsongs. Royal, Chaos, Sin, Kacey, Artemis, Cronos and London all stand there staring at Taylan, all of them except for London and Sin look like they are ready to break every bone in Taylan's body. I move forward so I'm standing beside him, ready to protect him against my family if I need to.

"You let her go out there against them?" he shouts, garnering the attention of the crowd around us. Chanel steps forward with a cold look on her face.

"She is a skilled fighter and can hold her own, did she not just prove that?" Her tone is laced with venom.

"She could have been killed! They are twice her fucking size," Taylan snaps back. London's face becomes a picture of outrage as she comes forward, stopping beside Sin.

"You think she's weak because she has a pussy?" The five guys groan and mutter between their breaths, they should all know by now that London has no filter and will say whatever is on her mind.

"I never said I thought she was weak," he says in a firm tone.

"The more important thing is why the fuck you brought her here?" Royal says in a deathly calm tone that is fooling no one.

"How did you even know about this place?" I ask my cousin.

He cuts his gaze to me for a second before looking back at Taylan. "Did it cross your mind that her car has a tracker on it?" I gape at my cousin.

"You put a fucking tracker on my car?" I yell.

"Yeah, I did," Chaos answers, giving no fucks that he just invaded my privacy.

"Stay the fuck out of my business!" I snarl.

"Let's move, too many eyes and ears," Kacey says. I look around and notice we have every single person's attention on us. No one argues as we follow Kacey, heading back the way we came. Taylan refuses to let my hand go when I try to pull it free. He shoots me a warning look that has me relenting and allowing him this small win. Royal, Kacey, Chaos and Sin lead the way while Cronos, Artemis, London, Taylan and I hang back a bit.

"Dad is so pissed off and it is fucking epic to see," London says happily. I shake my head, she is batshit crazy, there is no debating that.

"Does Uncle Bishop really know?" I ask her.

She smiles and shakes her head speaking low enough so only we can hear. "No, I just said that so I could blow my dad's bubble. He thinks Grandpa is on his way and it's pissing him off because he wanted to be the one to deal with this situation." I can't hide my smile.

"You're a little shit, you know that?" She beams at me and nods.

"Artemis loves it." The man himself wraps his arm around her shoulders and draws her into his side, placing a kiss to the top of her head.

"Yeah, I fucking do." I can't help the sigh that works its way past my lips, I envy what they have. I look back at Taylan to find his gaze laser focused on me, the look in his eyes has me turning away from him before he can see more than I am willing to share.

"Heads up," Artemis says ,drawing our attention to him as we near the edge of the woods. "Royal has no idea about who runs the underground."

Taylan's face is a mask of indifference. "And you do?" he claps back.

Artemis pins him with a dry stare. "I have my ways, your secret is safe with us but you better have a good fucking reason why you took her there." Our conversation comes to a halt when we break through the tree line. Three SUV's are parked by my car that I can't help but glare, I can't believe Chaos put a fucking tracker on my car. Taylan brings us to a stop a few feet away from my cousins. Chaos and Royal stand there with their arms crossed over their chests while Kacey stands behind Chanel with his arms wrapped around her waist and his chin resting on her shoulder.

Fuck, I never thought I would ever envy Chanel, but I do.

"Start explaining before I start tearing you apart," Royal threatens.

Taylan scoffs, earning a glare from the three guys while Chanel just smirks. "You could but we all know you won't do that because you would violate the treaty and that would start a war."

"Did you miss the part where you are here because we can't trust the RDS or the DCF?" I roll my eyes, the Re Della Strada and the Da Luca Crime Family have proven themselves trustworthy but my family has their heads up their asses and refuse to see that.

"Nope, but I got a tip that intel on the Russian fucks could be found here tonight so I put my feelers out." I whirl on Taylan staring up at him in outrage.

"Are you kidding?" My tone is layered with betrayal and anger.

He doesn't take his eyes off my cousins when he answers me. "No. I would never have brought you here otherwise but it's not like I would've left you behind." His words sting more than I want to admit.

"You could have called," Chaos says.

"Yeah, probably, but I was under the impression you all were supposed to be in Greece and Miami. I got skin in this game, I want that fucker more than your family does," he answers firmly. I admit I thought the same thing, I never expected to see them here tonight.

"Destiny is *our* family, we get those fuckers, not you," Chanel rebukes.

"She's my—mine to protect. I find them, I'm killing them. End of story. Now, if there's nothing else we're leaving." He doesn't wait for a response as he drags me toward my car. I look over my shoulder to see them all staring at us.

"We leave for Miami in two days, anything happens before then you call," Royal calls out. Taylan waves his hand over his shoulder, dismissing my cousin. I want to laugh but refrain, no one dismisses Royal Murdoch except for his father and mother.

Chapter Sixteen

Taylan

Three weeks later...

I've been in the States for a month and I'm still no fucking closer to finding Koda. Riley managed to find some intel on his whereabouts but when I checked it out the intel proved to be bullshit, the fucker lied just so they could get the 20k. I have a routine now and I fucking hate it, I don't like keeping to the same schedule, it makes you predictable and in my line of work that is never a good thing. I always make sure Knox and Lake's schedules are never the same two days in a row. Lake is always changing shifts at the hospital. When she goes on maternity leave that is going to make my life so much easier.

She's three months pregnant now and I'm missing it. I love watching her belly grow bigger. That shit fascinates me how a baby can grow inside their mother.

Destiny is still holding a fucking grudge for keeping her in the dark about why we went to the underground. She constantly gives me the cold shoulder while the sun is up but the moment darkness falls she is on me with a vengeance, fucking me like she hates me. In those stolen moments under the cover of darkness she changes from the cold bitch persona she exudes during the daylight and becomes a seductress.

Fucking her is becoming an addiction and it's not just fucking her. Spending every minute of every day with her is not what I expected. I tire of the same people, except for my brother's and the girls, and I hate to admit it but I… don't hate being around the Slayer.

"Come on, move your ass," Gage snaps at her from outside the ring. I bite down on my tongue to stop myself from biting back at him, he constantly oversteps. I'm her trainer, *not* him! "You're being sloppy!"

She throws her hands in the air and spins away from me to glare at her father. "You want to get in here and try it?"

"Destiny, he's just trying to help." She spins toward the entrance of the gym to see her mother walking toward us. Over the past month I have learned a lot about Destiny Murdoch without her having to say a word. She adores both her parents and loves them dearly, but her mother doesn't agree with the path she has chosen.

"No. He is forgetting that I fired him as my trainer and made him my manager." I shoot Gage a toothy grin when he scowls at me. "I can't do this with him breathing down my throat, Mom."

Anya's features soften as she climbs up by her husband who places a kiss on her cheek and wraps his arm around her waist. "He just wants you to win."

Destiny scoffs. "No, you swayed him to your side," she mutters bitterly.

Anya purses her lips clearly upset. "Baby girl, I will support you no matter what."

"Then support my dream of wanting to be in the ring, Mom," she pleads. I drop my gaze to the floor suddenly feeling like I am intruding on a private moment.

"If I truly believed that this was your dream, I would be the one in that ring training you." I snap my eyes up to stare at Anya, never expecting that to come out of her mouth. "You know I had to fight in a cage daily for my life. I know what it's like to need to fight but I also know what it's like when you hide behind your pain and use fighting as your escape from reality." I watch Destiny slowly shutdown as her mother gets closer to the truth that she continues to hide from them. I'll be honest, it's getting fucking harder and harder to keep lying to everyone and hide the truth about who kidnapped her. I can't even give my brothers the intel they need to track Koda better without giving away Destiny's secret.

"This is what I want," Destiny snaps before spinning around to face me and giving her parents her back. "Let's go again," she snaps angrily.

I shake my head and remove the pads from my hands. "You're done for the day, hit the showers and cool off."

"Fuck you, I want to go again," she pushes.

I force more bite into my tone. "I said you are done, get out of the ring, now!" Her nostrils flare in indignation.

"Asshole," she mumbles as she storms away. Gage shoots me a look that tells me to tread carefully with his daughter before following after her. I grab the discarded pads from the ground and hop out of the ring. I place them all back on the shelves and turn to leave, but come to a stop when I see Anya standing a couple feet away with a scrutinizing look on her face.

"Can I help you?" I ask.

Her eyes crinkle at the corners. "Are you screwing her for fun or because you care?"

I choke on my own spit. "Lady with the jacked up idea, say what now?" I wheeze out.

Her eyes harden. "Don't deny it. I can see it in the way you subtly touch her and follow her movements with your eyes when you think no one is watching."

I cross my arms over my chest and smack my lips. "You've come in here like six times, how the hell would you know that?"

She comes closer leaving a few inches of space between us. "She doesn't like me watching her train but this place has cameras everywhere." I gulp and tense, a cocky smirk touches the corner of her mouth. "So, have you been screwing her since you followed her into the locker room or..."

Fuck!

I grip the back of my neck and cringe at the knowing look in her eyes. "Honestly, I don't know what we are doing. We're glued to each other's sides for the foreseeable future. She doesn't speak to me unless it's to do with training or—"

"Yeah, that's enough details." I nod eagerly to end this conversation. "Let's be clear about a few things. I watch every training on the cameras daily. She is mine and Gage's world. You hurt our world and we'll blow yours apart. Look after her." She turns on her heel, leaving me standing here gaping at her until she stops and looks back at me. "She needs to stop dropping her left arm when she strikes, it's a tell. She also needs to work on her arm bar, her grip isn't strong enough." I stand here with my eyes, mouth hanging open and nod like an idiot. "Before her fight with Tiana she isn't going to fight Kiara to prove to her father she is ready, she is going to fight *me*." My jaw is practically hitting the fucking floor at her declaration. I don't know how much time has passed when Destiny comes to stand before me with a weird look on her face.

"Close your mouth, you look like a dead dog." I shake my head and snap my mouth closed, sending her a filthy look as I brush past her.

"No more slacking or Sundays off," I call out as I make my way toward the exit with her racing after me.

"Why?"

"Your mother just told me the fight with your aunt is out."

"She can't do that—"

"She can and she did."

"No, I am going to fight—"

"Oh, you are going to fight before the match with Tiana, but it isn't against your aunt."

She grabs my arm and pulls me to a stop, I blow out a frustrated breath as I turn to face her. "Who am I going to fight?" The happiness in her tone is clear.

"Your mother." Her face slackens and her mouth parts on a gasp, she looks like she's seen a ghost. "Close your mouth before I shove my cock in it." Her shock is quickly replaced by a heated look as she stares up at me, she takes a step forward and I take one back shaking my head.

"Scared?" she teases.

"Fuck no. But I also don't like the idea of your mother watching me fuck you on the cameras since she watches every one of your trainings." I could fist bump the air right now, I've managed to stun her silent twice in the span in five minutes and fuck it's a glorious feeling.

I dip my finger into the sauce I have simmering on the stove and nearly groan at the taste. Mom taught me, Xan and Knox all how to cook. She said she refused to let the three of us go off into the world without being able to fend for ourselves. Destiny comes bounding into the kitchen, peering around my shoulder to get a look at what I'm cooking.

"That smells so good," she moans. I can smell her shampoo and inhale again, cementing that scent to memory. When we got home, she was punished and forced to suck my cock like a good girl but I had to punish her again because the greedy bitch swallowed my cum without sharing a drop, so I fucked her against the front door and then ate that perfect cunt until she gave me what I wanted. She gripped me by my hair and yanked my head back, kissing me until I shared what we both wanted. I've never met a girl who was into cum swapping before and fuck me it is a huge turn on that she is just as into it as I am. She promised to let me try sucking it out of her ass tonight.

"Your salad is in the fridge," I say as I gently push back against her so she shifts out of my way as I pour the sauce over the pasta. I look over at her and she is practically salivating at the sight of my pasta. "Get your greedy eyes off my prize."

"Just a little taste, please," she whines. I shake my head and turn around to rinse the pan. At the sound of a moan behind me, I spin around and glare at the thieving devil.

"Hey! Get out of it," I scold as I shoulder her out of the way and rescue my pasta. Her eyes are shining with need but not for me, for the fucking pasta I have clutched in my hands. "You look like a rabid dog."

"I don't care. I need that pasta, hand it over, Tay Tay."

"You are out of your fucking mind, this baby is mine." I spin away from her, making my way to the sofa when her words have me freezing on the spot.

"I'll suck the sauce off your dick," She says in a sultry tone. This is the most we have spoken outside of training and fucking, granted she is offering to suck my dick over dinner. "The carbs are in the pasta, I just want the sauce," she adds on.

Be strong, say no!

"Fuck, your cock would taste so good with that sauce…"

I'm weak!

I turn to face her. Balancing the bowl in one hand, I push my shorts down with the other, her eyes shine with triumph as they keep darting between my plate and my hardening cock.

"If I let you suck my cock and have the sauce, I still get that ass though, right?" The corner of her mouth tilts into a smile as she lazily makes her way toward me.

"How about, I suck some of the sauce off your cock and you can use the rest to smear over my ass when you eat it out?"

Jesus take the fucking wheel. She is perfect!

"Deal!" I shout so loud I make myself flinch. Her satisfied smirk would spur my competitive side to life any other time, but she is mistaken if she thinks she is the one winning this game. She stops a foot away from me and grips the hem of her tank top and peels it over her head, exposing those dusty-pink nipples I've come to crave sucking on. Some nights when she puts a movie on I just sit there sucking on them, driving her insane with need. She cups her tits and tilts her head back, releasing a low groan when she tweaks her nipples.

"Fuck." I swallow and force myself to remain silent and act unaffected but my cock gives me away, it's now rock hard and jutting against my abs. She hooks her thumbs in her shorts and pushes them down her legs, her baby-blue thong does absolutely fucking nothing to cover her pussy, I can see it through the thin lace.

I'm no longer starving for pasta.

"Hand me the plate, Tay Tay." I nod like a good boy and hand it to her, then peel my own shirt off. My body ramps up when she slowly lowers to her knees before me. I step forward, loving the way her pupils dilate. She purses her lips and looks between the bowl and my cock for a few seconds. "The only way this is going to work is if you fuck the pasta for a bit."

I snort. "Hold the bowl, Slayer." The look on her face gives away the fact she thought I would decline her, fuck no! I am getting my cock sucked. I grip the base of my dick and slowly press it into the pasta making sure to coat it in the sauce, after a minute I pull back. She places the bowl on the ground and locks her arms behind her back like I have shown her how to and opens her mouth waiting for me.

Fuck the sight of her naked with her mouth open waiting for me is better than staring at the *Mona Lisa*. She's never looked more beautiful to me than she does at this moment.

Shit.

Am I catching feelings?

I push that stupid thought out of my mind as I push the tip in her mouth teasing her. She moans and licks her lips when I pull back. "You gonna let me fuck that pretty face how I like?"

"Yes."

"You sure you can take it?"

She flicks her gaze to mine. "I can take it, you have my

consent to do whatever the fuck you want." That's all I needed. I push forward and throw my head back, groaning when she wraps those perfect fucking lips around my cock. She is a goddamn pro at giving head. She bobs up and down in a quick rhythm. When she sucks me all the way to the back of her throat, I fist my hand in her hair.

"Fuck yes, baby, suck it like that." I keep her in place by her hair as I begin thrusting my hips. The sound of her gagging sends shudders down my spine. I rip her head back by her hair, loving the vision of her spit coating her chin and running down her throat all the way to those perfect fucking tits. "I wonder if Daddy knows his baby girl is a fucking freak and loves to suck my cock." She barely has a chance to moan before I'm shoving my dick down her throat again. She gets off when I tell her how dirty she is and how her father would have a conniption if he knew just how freaky his daughter is.

"Hmmmm." Her moans send vibrations through my cock to my balls and have me shuddering and wanting to cum. I rip her off my cock before I can do just that.

"Get up and lean over the arm of the sofa, spread those fucking legs and keep your arms behind your back." She climbs to her feet and eagerly obeys me. When she tries to rid herself of her thong I smack her hands away and force her over the arm of the sofa by the back of her neck. "Did I say to touch?"

"No," she purrs. I draw my arm back and smack her ass, loving the imprint of my palm on her skin. She wiggles her ass wanting more.

"Greedy bitch." I release her and grab the bowl off the

floor. "Open that ass up for me, baby." She grips the globes of her ass and opens it for me, my cock twitching at the sight. I smear my fingers through the pasta and coat them in the sauce before running them through her crack.

"Shit."

"I've barely touched you," I scold. She whimpers in response. I repeat the process twice more before discarding the bowl and dropping to my knees behind her. My eyes widen at the sight of how wet her panties are. I press my nose against her pussy and inhale her musky scent, groaning.

"I'm so wet for you, Tay Tay," she rasps out.

"Who does this pussy belong to, baby?"

I jerk back horrified that shit came out of my fucking mouth!

"It's yours, Tay, now eat my ass and make me come." I shake off my stupor and do as she asked. Gripping her thong I pull it up so the string is pulled taut against her hole before licking her from top to bottom. "Holy fuck, Taylan," she cries out when I swirl my tongue around that puckered hole I have been dying to sink my cock into for a month.

I alternate between tongue fucking her ass and fingering it, the second I add a second finger she cries out forcing me to still.

"Don't stop, it feels so good," she begs. I pull my fingers free and slide the ruined thong down her legs, then bury two fingers in her ass again while I eat her weeping pussy, loving the scream that rips out of her. "Oh fuck, Taylan, I won't last," she cries. I continue stretching her ass while I tongue fuck her greedy little cunt. When I feel her grow tense I pull back and stand, she glares at me over her shoulder. "What the fuck?" she growls.

I narrow my eyes and land a swift slap to her ass. Her glare melts off her face instantly and is replaced with a lustful look.

"Open that ass and don't move those fucking hands." She does as I say but keeps looking back at me. I know she's scared so I force myself to go slow. "Try to relax and breathe, baby, I didn't let you come because it would have been more painful for you. I promise this is going to feel so good and I'll make you come so hard."

"Okay," she whispers. "I trust you." Those three words give me pause, she shouldn't trust me. She shouldn't feel anything for me! The thoughts slip my mind when she presses her ass against my cock, drawing me back to the moment.

Chapter Seventeen

Destiny

The second he pushes the head of his cock in my ass I cry out and try to leap forward. He keeps me in place by the grip he has on my hips. It fucking burns like a bitch! I try to breathe through the pain and relax like he said to but it's hard when you have a monster-sized cock in your ass.

"Relax, baby," he coos as he reaches around me to circle my clit, drawing a moan from me. He uses that moment of distraction to press in further. I cry out, but this time it hurts less, thanks to him playing with my greedy little pussy. I can feel my own wetness coating the insides of my thighs. This man has turned me into a wanton whore for his cock. We fight daily and can't stand each other but the moment we get home, we are all over each other and fucking the frustrations out of the other. It's toxic but it's perfect.

"Keep going." He draws back and eases back in, slowly fucking me and inching further every thrust. After a minute, the pain starts turning into this sensation of need I have never felt before.

"Fuck, baby, this is the perfect fucking torture."

"I want it all, Taylan, fuck me hard. I need it." His responding growl sends a shiver down my spine. He draws back, leaving only the tip inside me before slamming forward, burying his cock balls deep inside me. I scream so loud I swear the windows rattled. "Fuck!"

"I got you, baby," he reassures me as his strokes on my clit grow faster, taking my attention off the pain I'm in. He gives me time to adjust to his intrusion before slowly easing out and back in, letting me adjust again. "Fuck, your ass is so tight, Slayer."

"Taylan, I feel…" I don't know how to explain this feeling, I have never felt this before. I feel so full. A slow burning sensation is forming inside my belly, my moans grow louder as my pussy starts clamping down on air. My orgasm is right there, but this one feels different. It feels like it has the power to rip me apart.

"Let it happen, baby, it's going to be intense," he vows.

"I need more," I cry.

"Play with your clit." I do as he says, pinching my clit between my fingers. He grips my waist in a punishing hold, losing control and fuck me, it's perfect. His thrusts are so hard the sofa screeches along the floorboards.

"Fuck, yes, like that, Tay. You're gonna make me come so fucking hard," I scream.

"Give me that climax, I want it. I'm gonna come so deep in this ass. You want to taste it, baby?"

His words are my undoing, I come harder than I ever have before. My throat is hoarse from screaming, shudders continuing to rock me as he chases his own release. When he comes, it's my name he calls out. It's the first time he has ever said my name while he comes, hearing that shit for the first time has me warming.

He has barely finished coming inside me before he's ripping his cock out, parting my cheeks and suctioning his lips to my hole. The feeling of his warm tongue prodding that hole has me crying out, it feels so strange feeling the cum being sucked out of me. When he pulls back, I don't wait for his instruction, I spin around and drop to my knees in front of him and wrap my arms around his neck before smashing my lips to his and opening for him like always. The taste of his cum fills my mouth. I moan into the kiss as I swallow every last drop of him.

Realization crashes into me like a ton of bricks and it robs me of breath.

I'm addicted to him.

I break the kiss and stare into his eyes. He smiles cockily but it slowly fades when he registers the look in my eyes. Horror fills his gaze as he cups my cheek tentatively.

"Don't say it. I'm not worthy of you. I'm a good time type of guy, not a long time. I'm tainted and broken, baby. Your ever after is out there but he isn't me."

Find em, feel em, fuck em, forget em.

That was his motto from the start, he warned me and then I had to go and be stupid and catch some type of feelings for him when I knew I shouldn't have. I've always said you can fuck without feelings being involved but the truth is, there is only so many times you can sleep with someone without feeling something.

"I know. I need a shower, thanks for whatever that was." He drops his gaze in shame as I stand and rush to my bedroom, slamming the door behind me. I refuse to allow the tears burning the backs of my eyes to fall as I make my way into the bathroom and climb inside the shower stall. I let the water cascade over me and hope that it can wash away the shame of being rejected.

I cover my face with my hands and growl in frustration. How the fuck did all of this happen over a stupid plate of pasta?

The feeling of shame mixed with my hurt is crippling. If I allow it to consume me it will pull me under, so I fight it. I choose to lock away those feelings and play along. As soon as we find Koda, Taylan will be free and able to leave and return to Canada. I'll never have to see him again and I'll be able to move on with my life. I'll fight Tiana, claim the title and then... What happens next?

I step out of the shower and dry myself as I ponder my future. I have been so fixated on this fight that I haven't even given myself time to think about what comes next. Do I want to keep fighting? Do I want to go to law school?

What the fuck do I want to do with my life?

I growl and toss my towel in the hamper, annoyed at myself for allowing Taylan to get in my head, him suggesting that I am only fighting because Koda told me I couldn't do it plays on my mind every time I step in the ring. I want to say he is full of shit and that isn't the reason I fight, but ever since Koda told me I was weak and couldn't do it, I have trained harder, pushed myself to be the best. Even going as far as taking a title fight against the best who I know is fucking amazing at what she does. Tiana may be a dirty fighter but no one makes it to the top without dirtying themselves a little.

I step out of the bathroom and come to a halt at the sight of Taylan sitting on the edge of my bed, the very bed we both sleep in each night. He doesn't want to admit he feels anything for me but for the past month we have been living, working and sleeping together like a couple!

"Slayer–"

"Stop." His brows form a deep groove in the center of his forehead. "I don't need you to say anything. I crossed a line. You made your boundaries clear from the beginning, I respect that. Let's move on and act like that moment of error on my part never happened, 'kay?" I don't wait for a response as I cross the room to my wardrobe and pull on an oversized T-shirt and some sweatpants. I don't bother brushing my hair, instead tying it up in a messy bun and walk out without looking back at him.

I fucked up, not him.

Unlike last time when we didn't speak aside from training or when we fucked, it's not like that this time. For two weeks since I went and screwed things up, Taylan has put a country of space between us. Did that shit sting? Fuck yes! Am I dealing with it and making sure he doesn't know how much it has affected me? You bet your fucking ass, I am playing the role of bad bitch!

"You're not focused!" Dad scolds, drawing my attention to him. He stands on the outside of the ring with his forearms resting on the top ropes. "Where is your head at?" I dart my gaze from him to Taylan who stands in front of me shirtless and panting. I turn back to my dad and shrug. "Seriously? You're twenty-five and think shrugging your shoulders is the answer?"

I throw my gloved hands in the air. "What do you want me to say? I'm just off today, that's it. No excuse, I'm just... off," I snap in frustration.

"You are never off! What the fuck is going on, Dest?" he pushes.

Taylan tenses but says nothing as he drops his gaze. Pussy. "Nothing, Dad. I'm just having a rough day."

"Is it that time of the month? Do you need a day off? Want me to call your mom? Do you want me to get snacks—"

I cut him off before he can keep rambling and embarrassing the shit out of me in front of Taylan and whoever else can fucking hear him talking about my period!

"No! I'm fine, I'm calling it a day," I huff out as I ignore him calling after me and heading straight for the exit, fuck the shower I'll have one at home! Before I can get two steps out the door, Mia's car comes to a stop in front of me and I have to jump back before I get clipped by her bumper. I glare at the bitch through her windshield, she just grins.

"Get in, your man is chasing you!" she calls out. I look over my shoulder and sure enough, Taylan is charging toward me. Without thinking, I yank the door open and climb in.

"Go, go, go!" I scream just as Taylan makes it to the exit. She plants her foot on the gas and burns rubber getting us the fuck out of there, like we have the po-po on our asses. A minute later the both of us are laughing at our stupidity. "How did you know I needed an escape?" I ask.

"I didn't. I was leaving as you came barreling out the door and then I saw your boyfriend coming in hot after you."

"He's not my boyfriend," I grumble as I slouch back in my chair and cross my arms over my chest. She side eyes me with a look I know too well from my friend. "Save your judgment, I don't want to hear it."

"Girl, no man chases after a woman he isn't either fucking or related to. Spill the beans now and give momma the tea." I normally don't share stories or allow others to know my shit but I can't stop it. As soon as I open my mouth all of my secrets come spewing out and I tell her everything about Taylan, minus the shit that involves my family and anything to do with that side of my life. By the time I have finished telling her everything, I only then realize we have stopped moving and are parked in front of her house. Mia still lives at home with her parents and older brother. Her mom and dad are both great and have busted their asses to provide a great life for their kids. "That was... wow."

I cringe. "Seriously? After everything I have just told you, *wow* is all you can say?" She swivels in her chair to face me and immediately I groan at the look on her face, if she was an emoji she would have heart eyes.

"He is perfect. Equal parts broken and damaged but also caring, attentive and fucking freaky in the sheets." I feel my cheeks grow warm, I never should have told her about how Taylan likes to fuck. Out of all my friends Mia is the one with the kinky side and is all about trying everything once.

"He's not broken or damaged!"

Her face breaks out into a satisfied look with a smile to match. "Look who is all defensive over someone who isn't her boyfriend."

"Shut up," I snap before climbing out of the car, she meets me around the front of her Audi and places her hands on my shoulders.

"Hear me out?" I shoot her a bored look. "Come out with me tonight and take your mind off the fight and everything Taylan related. I'll call Peyton, Missy and Britt and we can go out for a girls night."

I gnaw on my lip, debating her offer. The idea is appealing but with Koda still out there I don't know if it's a good idea. No one has been able to find him and it's actually starting to freak me out—Uncle Vin can track anyone and the fact he hasn't located him yet really has my hackles up.

"Don't make me beg. One night of fun and then you can go back to no carbs and training until you die of exhaustion."

I roll my eyes. "You are so freaking dramatic."

She wags her brows in response. "So, is that a yes?" She sounds like a child pleading for an extra cookie before dinner.

"Fine." I reel back and cover my ears when she starts screaming. She is like a fucking energizer bunny, the girl has so much fucking energy bottled up she can start selling it off.

A few hours later Missy, Peyton, Britt, Mia and I are all dressed to the nines but unlike my friends I feel self-conscious. I'm not one to wear revealing shit like the dress I am currently suffocating in. My tits nearly touch my chin and my ass is practically hanging out of the bottom of the dress. I spin around in front of the mirror and take in the sight of myself. My gray-blue eyes are highlighted with smokey eye makeup, the thick eyeliner has them popping. My long blonde hair is straight and falls down my back, while the skin-tight red dress hugs me like a second skin. It's a corset style strapless dress that has my tits almost spilling over the cups, the hem ending just below my ass. I tried to pair it with a pair of flats but my friends refused and handed me a pair of red stilettos that makes my legs look like they are longer than they are.

"You look beautiful, Dest, stop overthinking this and enjoy yourself." I meet Britt's gaze in the mirror and force a smile.

"I feel like a fraud," I admit.

Her face contorts in outrage. "You are no such thing! You, my friend, are fucking stunning and deserve this night out more than any of us. We're going to have drinks, dance and forget all about the pesky boy who has you all up in your feels." I pull my gaze from hers, unable to stand the sight of pity in her gaze. Mia filled them all in about what was going on with me and Taylan before they even got here. I have been friends with these girls since high school, even when I was sent to Blackwood we stayed in contact. They were under the impression that I was sent away to boarding school and I hate that I can't tell them the truth but this is just one of the burdens of being in the life of the mafia.

"Come on, bitches, we need shots, then it's off to the club!" Peyton hollers, bringing a smile to everyone's faces.

"Come on, Dest, we got you. No more thinking about him or the fight, it's time to focus on having a fantastic fucking night with your girls." Britt's words have me smiling, it's the first real one I have smiled in what feels like months. The only times I have smiled lately has been when Taylan is around and I hate that, he has become a comfort that I didn't know I needed. He chases away all my nightmares and makes me feel safe.

He's become my favorite hello and I know he is going to be my hardest goodbye.

Chapter Eighteen

Taylan

I've been pacing the length of her apartment for hours!

After she sped away from me outside the gym, I was left to deal with a million fucking questions from her father. None of which I could answer without implicating myself. I was grilled on everything from my training techniques to being a mooch. That shit ground my fucking nerves, I am no fucking mooch! I have been busting my ass teaching her everything I know so she can win this fucking fight in a few months' time.

My phone begins to vibrate in my pocket, pulling me from my thoughts. I fish it out of my pocket to see it's Knox calling. I debate letting it ring out but I decide against that and answer it.

"This better be good!" I clip out.

"Where the fuck are you?" The worry in Knox's tone has me freezing mid step and turning rigid.

"What's wrong?" I snap. "Is Lake okay?" I begin to worry something has happened to her or the baby.

"Where are you?"

"At Destiny's! What the fuck is going on, Knox?" I snarl.

"Where's the girl?"

My blood turns cold, I dart my eyes around the empty apartment as dread begins to fill my veins.

"She ditched me," I grit out through clenched teeth. I can feel my stomach knotting as I wait for him to explain why he is panicking.

"Get the fuck out of the apartment now!" I don't question him, I grab my jacket and gun and snatch my keys off the counter as I make my way to the door. "Find her, do not go back to her apartment, Taylan!"

I freeze in front of the door. "Why?" That one word holds so much weight to it.

"You need to find her now! He has been stalking her and you, watching your every move."

I jerk in surprise. "How do you know this?"

"Kimber got a call, we haven't been able to locate him or find the cocksucker because he's been there with you the whole fucking time watching!"

A cold shiver works its way down my spine, I turn around slowly and scan the empty place. "Knox, where is he?"

"He's been living in the apartment above her for months. It wasn't a random snatch and grab that night, he knew where she would be and her movements. We traced the call, Tay, he's been above you this entire time."

"Fuck!" I roar. I end the call and race out of there taking the stairs to the next level. I don't hesitate as I draw my gun and ram my foot against the door, the wood splinters and gives under the pressure of my boot. I dart inside scanning the entire place but it's empty sans the plethora of photos that are scattered across the counter in the small kitchen.

Disgust, fear, anger and a range of other emotions race through me as I stare down at the still shots from a video feed. My phone keeps ringing but I can't move to answer it. My gun falls from my limp grip and clatters against the hardwood floors, when my phone starts ringing again I swallow and blindly answer it without checking the caller ID knowing exactly who it is.

"Get our guys onto tracking her phone," I whisper.

"Taylan, what the fuck did you find?" I open my mouth but no words come out. There are photos of me and her fucking all over her apartment, pictures of her in the shower, me and her sleeping in her bed. There are even pictures of us walking into the gym, her and me at dinner at the restaurant down the road. "Taylan!" Knox's voice snaps me out of it.

"He's been stalking her, there's pictures of *us*," I grit out.

"Fuck! You need to get rid of them."

"Why?" I clip out.

"Because her father and uncles are on their way now, I texted them when I called you." Just as I reach for the images to hide them so her father doesn't find out, they all barge into the room. I look up and inhale what I'm sure is going to be my last breath. Gage, King, Bishop, Knight, Rook, Vincent and Luka all stand there with their guns raised and pointed at me.

"Too late brother, they're here," I say before I end the call and shove it in my pocket. I bend down and retrieve my gun. A wise man would keep it in his hand to try to defend himself but there are seven of them so I stash it in my waistband. If I'm going down, then I'm gonna go down like a man, I'm no bitch. The seven of them creep in closer as my phone continues to ring incessantly but I don't move to answer it even when Gage steps and stands on the other side of the counter staring down at the images before us of his daughter being fucked by *me*.

He darts his gaze from the images to me then back a couple of times before his face morphs from shock to murderous. He raises his gun and presses it against my forehead, his brother's don't move to intervene and neither do the other two. They can see the photos from where they stand and from the looks on each of their faces, they agree with what Gage is about to do. I knew this would happen if I touched her but I ignored his warning the night we went to their house after we escaped.

"What did I tell you?" The deathly calm tone of Gage's voice let's everyone in this room know he isn't letting me walk out of here.

"To keep my good for nothing hands off your daughter or we would end up in this very position," I answer.

"Correct. Now this is where I start a war for killing the underboss of the Re Della Strada." I nod, I knew I wasn't destined to live a long life and I came to terms with that years ago when I did what I did and became the Taylan everyone knows today.

"Don't leave a body for them to find, I don't want my family at war because I touched the forbidden fruit."

"Is that all my daughter is to you?" he roars in my face, I take a deep breath and shake my head holding my gaze so he can see the truth in my eyes.

"No. She was never some chick, she was... something more but I... hurt her." His face contorts in hatred, his finger itching to squeeze that trigger and splatter my brain across this apartment.

"You hurt my little girl?" He pushes the gun against my head to drive his point home.

"With all due respect, either kill me or let me fucking go so I can save your daughter from the man who hurt her worse than I ever could," I grit out. Before Gage can respond, Bishop steps forward.

"Why weren't we informed about Koda Novikov before?" Power wafts off Bishop in waves, it's easy to see why he is still the Don and has gone this long without being challenged.

I keep my gaze on Gage as I answer his brother. "She didn't want anyone to know. Call me crazy but I respected your daughter's wishes. It wasn't mine or Knox's story to tell. Kill me if you want but make your mind up fast because he knows exactly where she is and he knows we are on to him." I see the hesitation in Gage's eyes so I push on. "I think I know where she has gone. I hurt her but I do... care about her. Let me help you save her... please," I plead. Gage and Bishop share a look before turning back to me.

"This isn't over, you little shit," Gage vows. I don't stick around, I rush out of the apartment with all of them hot on my heels.

"Where is she?" Rook shouts as we rush down the stairs.

"At your daughter's boyfriends club," I answer as I continue down to the parking garage while they run out the lobby doors to their cars. Unlike them, I won't be stuck in traffic. I jump on my matte-black Dodge Tomahawk and pull my helmet on. The engine purrs to life and I almost groan at the sound of this. This baby can hit 420 mph at top speed. I kick the bad bitch into gear and burn rubber out of there. It takes me a minute of hitting the main road before I'm flying past the three blacked-out cars that hold the Murdoch family. It's dark and the road is slick from the rain earlier but none of that registers to me as I head straight for the club, praying that I'm right, if she isn't there I don't know what I'll do. My phone begins to ring and I answer it through the Bluetooth in my helmet.

"Yeah?" I say breathlessly.

"Where are you?" Knox demands.

"Track my location," I tell him.

"Are you okay?"

"I'm alive so that has to count for something," I say without missing a beat.

"Don't joke, Taylan. Wave, Xan, Trey and their crew are on their way. I'm coming, brother." Warmth rushes through at his words, this is why I chose them. They are my family for this very reason. I never have to ask, Knox and Xander know I need them but would never ask for their help.

"Knox—"

"Shut up, Taylan. You'll get to your girl. I'll be there as soon as I can."

"Thank you."

"Thank me by not dying." He ends the call right in the nick of time, I slam to a stop out front of the club, not caring about the bike being parked illegally. I hang my helmet on the handlebars as I rush through the crowd gathered outside and push my way to the front. The bouncer tries to stop me from entering. I throat punch the cunt without missing a step as I jump over him, patrons follow my lead cheering but I ignore them as I rush through the crowded club trying to find my Slayer.

"Fuck!" I snap, I look around but I can't spot her. I leap onto the bar ignoring the bartenders, needing a birds eye view. The dim lighting makes it fucking hard to see anything but I don't give up. I can feel it in my bones that he's here, he cleared out that apartment and left those pictures on purpose. The call to Kimber was staged, he knew we would track it and wanted us to find him.

He's going to make his move tonight!

I catch a glimpse of red in the center of the dance floor, her blonde hair flies around her as she spins, dancing with her friends. I jump off the bar and run toward her shoving every cunt out of my way, I have tunnel vision for the beautiful blonde and no one is going to stop me from getting to her.

The moment I break through the crowd she spots me and stops moving, her eyes widen for a fraction of a second before she takes in the look on my face and closes the space between us. I'm drunk on the sight of her perfect body in that red dress, her tits look edible.

"Why are you here?" she asks with an edge to her tone. I don't waste time, I grab her wrist and start dragging her toward the exit. Her friends protest but the second I pull my gun from my waistband they scream. I lift it and fire a shot up at the ceiling. People drop to the ground screaming, I use their second of fear to my advantage and drag Destiny through the throngs of people. We have a mere two seconds before they come to their senses and begin rushing for the exit.

"Taylan!" she screams my name so loud I freeze and face her. She points toward the back of the room and I curse at the sight of Koda and his men. The crowd comes to their senses finally registering their flight instincts and everyone begins rushing for the exits. Destiny is shoved forward, I wrap my arms around her and hold her close so she isn't dragged away or knocked to the ground in those fucking heels she's wearing, she won't stand a chance against a crowd this size. More shots ring out from the back of the club. I wrap my arm around her waist and turn us so she is in front of me and push her toward the exit.

"Keep moving, your dad will be here shortly," I shout in her ear. We're knocked from both sides but my hold on her doesn't lessen. I can see the exit over the heads of the others and grit my teeth as I try to push her faster but she keeps tripping in those fucking stupid shoes. "Unless I'm fucking you in those heels, you are forbidden to ever wear those things again," I growl in her ear, now isn't the time for her to shiver with lust but she does and I can't help but smirk.

The exit is just there, we're so close!

"Move and she dies." I don't move a muscle when I see the gun pressed to her temple. The crowd screams and moves away from us, giving us a wide berth as they run to the exit. I flick my gaze to the side and glare, the bouncer I throat punched smirks back at me. "Try anything and I shoot," he declares as one of his buddies comes forward to snatch the gun from hand. "Release her."

"Suck my dick, cunt," I snarl. I grunt in pain and drop to my knees when I'm pistol whipped across the back of the head. Destiny whirls around and hooks the fucker behind me but stops moving when the bouncer shifts his gun to me. Her eyes fill with fear at the sight of me on my knees with a gun pointed at my temple.

"Both of you move, now!" the cunt barks. I climb to my feet and grip her hand in mine as he keeps the gun pressed to my head and forces us to move toward where Koda is. With the stampede of people rushing out of the club there is no way her family can make it inside against the crowd, we're on our own.

We walk down a hallway that is dimly lit but is lined with armed men, they form a barricade around us like we're the fucking president as we are led out a service exit where a van idles. I want to roll my eyes at how fucking cliché this is. The side door is open and we're shoved inside, I push her behind me against the back doors and use my body as a shield. Six guys climb in with us and keep their guns pointed at us as one of them bangs on the side to signal the driver to move. The windows are spraypainted black, so I can't see out to try gauge our direction.

"Phones, hand them over now." The bouncer sneers. I slowly raise my hand and reach into my pocket pulling it out and tossing it to the cunt. He looks over my shoulder at Destiny. "You too." He flicks his gun in a hurry up motion but she snorts.

"Look at the size of this fucking dress, where the hell would I be able to hide it?" She holds her hands up and motions down her body forcing me to grit my teeth and not rip these cunts eyes out for looking at her like they want a taste.

"Don't push me girl, the boss will be doing an *intimate* search to make sure you ain't lying." She shudders behind me. I reach back and pull her flush against me, she buries her face in my back. I fucking hope her father is smart enough to figure something out, I think when the cunt opens the door and tosses my phone out. Knox would have been tracking it so he would know an estimated circumference of where they would be taking us.

Chapter Nineteen

Destiny

I'm ashamed to admit that I'm scared.

Taylan hasn't let me go but I'm worried when we get to where we are going they are going to rip him away from me. Being alone scares the shit out of me now. Before him I was fine existing and just living to fight but not now. Now, I want more, no, I need more from my life.

My fear spikes when the van comes to a stop. I jerk forward and crash into his back but he doesn't budge. One of the guys slides the door open and three of them jump out, the other three keep their guns trained on us as they order Taylan and me out of the van. He grips my hand in his and helps me out. I use my free hand to pull the hem of my dress down, hating how all of these guys are staring at me with hungry looks. Taylan releases my hand and pulls his shirt off, they all cock their guns but he ignores them as he pulls his shirt over my head. When our gazes collide I see it.

He lied!

He does care about me!

He places a kiss on my forehead that says so much more than his words could ever explain. He reclaims his hold on my hand as we are ushered forward to another car, this one looks sleek and expensive. The back door opens and I just know who is inside the car. Before I can warn Taylan, I'm yanked out of his grasp. I scream. He spins around ready to fight but five of those fuckers jump on him. I scream and plead for them to stop hurting him but they don't stop punching, kicking or even using the butts of their rifles to injure him.

"Fucking stop!" I scream as tears trek down my cheeks. "Koda, please!" I wail. At the sound of his name, the man himself emerges from the back of the car wearing a suit that looks a size too small for him, his cold green eyes land on me and I tremble in fear.

"Enough," he says in a calm tone. I know the evil he can inflict and I refuse to allow him to hurt Taylan because he tried to help me. "Take them," is all he says before I'm being carried around the back of the large shed—no, not a shed, a hanger. I gape in horror at the sight of the plane that sits there with men standing on both sides of the staircase that leads to the open door. I struggle in the bastard's hold trying to get free. "Keep fighting and your friend pays the price." At Koda's chilling threat, I stop moving and allow the fucker with his arm wrapped around my waist to carry me up the stairs. I almost throw up in my mouth when I feel his hard length pressed against my back.

He places me in a chair at the back of the plane, I remain seated not wanting to fight and have them inflict more pain on Taylan. He is thrown into the seats across from me, grunting in pain and I flinch at the sight of him. His face is bloody, bruised and busted up but the smirk he shoots the guy that threw him in his seat would have you thinking he's having a grand time!

"Get this plane off the fucking ground, now!" Koda clips out as he makes his way toward me. I look to Taylan who pushes to his feet but is immediately punched in the face by the cunt of a guard. Koda smirks at the sight of him spitting blood on the floor when he claims the seat beside me. I tense and shift as far away from him as I can. "Keep him seated," he orders the guard who drops down beside Taylan and rests his rifle across his lap, making sure to keep it pointed at him with his finger on the trigger. I nearly jump out of my skin when Koda places his hand on the top of my thigh.

"Don't fucking touch her!" Taylan roars. He's answered with a punch to the side of his head. I want to cry at the sight but I bite back the tears, even when Koda trails his hand up my leg. Koda's men begin talking in Russian as they prepare the plane for takeoff. A small part of me prays that my dad gets here in time, I may seem like a fool but after the first time I was kidnapped, I started wearing the ring Uncle Vin had made for each of us girls, when you twist the diamond it starts transmitting your location. I know my family would have been tracking us this whole time since I activated it in the van.

"Give me what I want and I'll stop all of this," Koda

purrs as he leans in and runs his nose along the side of my neck. I keep my eyes on Taylan the entire time. His face is etched in pain at the scene before him, but he can't do a fucking thing to stop this. As long as he is here with me I'm sure I can take whatever Koda does because he'll ground me, he'll chase away the nightmares, right?

My hope begins to flee my body when the plane starts moving down the small tarmac, we're going back to Russia. My family may have a truce with the Russians but even I am not idiotic enough to believe that Andreas has control of the country. If he did, Koda would have been found weeks ago and dealt with. The plane begins to gain speed as we prepare to take off and that's when I see the headlights of cars, I know it's my family coming for me but they're too late. They try to chase the plane but they won't stop us and they won't risk firing at it in case I'm hurt. My stomach drops when we take flight, I press my hand against the cool window and close my eyes.

I'm so sorry, Dad.

Please find me before it's too late.

Koda grips my chin and forces my gaze to him, the elation I see in his eyes angers me. He's a fucking monster!

"*Pora domoy, moya babochka.*" (Time to go home my butterfly.)

I shake free of his hold and glare at the bastard. "*Rossiya ne moy dom! Ty umresh'.*" (Russia isn't my home! You are going to die.)

His eyes widen in surprise. "You speak Russian?"

I school my features. "*YA svobodno govoryu, tupitsa.*

Russkiy — moy rodnoy yazyk." (I'm fluent, you dumbass. Russian is my native tongue.) I see the proud smirk on Taylan's face and that bolsters my bravado until Koda's gaze darkens and he punches me in my mouth. Taylan rages and fights to get to me but his guard and two others subdue him with a beating. I taste the metallic tang of my own blood and rather than spitting it on the ground. I spit it right in his arrogant face. My moment of triumph is short-lived when Koda wraps his hand around my throat and then starts punching me. I try to fight him off but the fucker overpowers me. I feel my cheek split a second before I bite through my lip, I cry out when he lands a powerful hit to my right eye.

"Stop! Leave her the fuck alone, you bastard!" Taylan screams. I can feel the anguish in his voice. Koda stops hitting me but doesn't draw back, the sight of my tears just fuel his triumphant smile.

"You will give me what I want. Mark my words, *Suka* (bitch)," he sneers before shoving me back against the wall hard enough that I grunt when my head bounces off it.

"I'm going to peel the fucking skin from your bones and wear it as a suit for that," Taylan promises but Koda ignores him as he grabs a handful of my hair and pulls me to him, then smashes his lips against mine. I shove against his chest but it's fucking futile. My mind goes back to being chained up in his bathroom and being at his mercy for those two days. The depraved things he did to me still robs me of breath when I spiral. Fighting is my escape, it's my outlet to let all my pent up rage and anger out for the injustice I suffered at the hands of a man I thought I could trust.

He breaks the kiss and looks into my eyes smiling. "I can't wait for you to show me everything you have learned, I've been watching how good you perform for him." Horror fills me and my eyes widen as disgust rolls through me. He laughs at the horrified look on my face. "Oh yes, butterfly, I have been watching you for a long time." I gag, unable to control my reaction.

"Y-you've been watching m-me?" My bottom lip quivers.

"We all have been." I look around to see the leering looks and proud smiles on his men's faces, then swallow the bile that rushes up my throat. "The way he bent you over that couch... hmmmm." He moans as he runs his nose along my chin. I lock gazes with Taylan who looks just as sickened by this as I am. I feel violated all over again by Koda. "You're going to perform just like that for me and my men."

"No!" I cry out as I reel back, shaking my head, unable to keep my tears at bay.

He wraps his hand around my throat, squeezing. "Tell me what I want to know and I will end this all quickly. Defy me and you will be punished."

Fear grips me in its clutches. I can't speak, I can't form a coherent thought let alone voice it. I picture all of these men defiling my body and I choke on a sob. Koda seems satisfied by my reaction and releases me. I slump in my chair, keeping my gaze on my lap. If I give him what he wants, Taylan and I will die. If I defy him and keep my mouth shut, he'll rape me and so will his men.

He's doing all of this over a formula my mom came up

with years ago, all of this pain and suffering is over fucking drugs!

I'm still lost in my own thoughts when the plane lands. I don't know about you, but when my anxiety is high everything takes forever. Andreas has done his best to change things but he's too soft, he grew too lax and now he is faced with an uprising. My only hope is that he has men willing to fight alongside my family to save me. There is no doubt in my mind that my family will be coming and as soon as they realize where I have been taken, my mom will be leading the hunting party. This is her domain, her turf and if anyone can find me in this fucked-up place, it's her.

Koda drags me off the plane by my hair, literally. Taylan screams and issues threats but is ignored. I don't fight or protest when he throws me in the back seat of a car. It's snowing and my body feels cold to touch but I don't register it, I'm too lost in my own head. Koda slips in the back seat beside me while I watch Taylan being dragged to another car. He tries to fight but is met with another beating but this time, I can't form words of protest. I remain silent the entire drive, I don't even fight off Koda when he pushes his hand between my clenched thighs. Each time his fingers brushed against the lace of my panties memories of how he raped me over his bathroom sink played out like a movie on repeat in my head.

When we finally stop driving, he drags me by my arm

this time. I stumble and trip in my heels but he doesn't care, he just keeps yanking me after him. I don't look around the house as I'm led through it to some type of internal garage where I'm forced into a metal chair, my ankles cuffed to the legs of the chair. Taylan's shirt doesn't cover enough so my panties are seen. My wrists are cuffed behind my back, the metal biting into my skin but I remain silent. Even when they bring Taylan in and cuff him to the chair in front of me, I remain silent unlike him who vows to kill all of them and their families.

"Scream as much as you like, I own this part of Russia and no one will aid you if you escape, not even your precious Andreas," Koda taunts. I knew that already. I'm not stupid, for Koda to have a plethora of men and the means to do what he has done shows me Andreas never had full control of Russia like he thought.

"She doesn't know anything," Taylan snaps.

Koda scoffs. "She knows everything, her mother is a Volkov. Men in that family were ruthless, Gods amongst men. My father was an adviser for Vladimer Volkov. No one would have dared to rise against that family but her mother ruined Russia when she sided with those American scum."

I snap my head up and grind my teeth. "Eti amerikanskiye podonki pridut za mnoy, i kogda oni eto sdelayut, oni budut medlenno ubivat' tebya, poka ya smotryu." (Those American scum are coming for me and when they do, they are going to kill you slowly while I watch.) Koda eliminates the space between us in two steps. I expect him to hit me again and brace for it but instead, he grips the front of Tay's shirt and shreds it. I open my mouth to scream at him when he grips the front of my dress but it's too late, he tears it down the middle exposing me to him and all his men who are in here.

"You fucking cunt, stay away from her!" Taylan bellows but it's too late. Because of the style of the dress I wasn't able to wear a bra and only have nipple shields on and a thong. Koda smiles viciously as he peels the nipple shields off me and steps back laughing. His men move in closer to get their fill. They whistle and laugh, some even lick their lips and grab their cocks but I refuse to cower.

"Your mothers will bury their sons before I kill them and anyone related to you. I won't stop until your existence is wiped from this earth," I say. My threat is met with laughter from everyone except for Taylan and Koda, the latter sneers at me before barking at his men to get out. When Taylan and I are finally alone in the room I release a breath I didn't realize I was holding.

"Look at me," Tay demands.

I slowly turn to face him and the devastated look in his eyes almost has me crumbling. "I'm gonna tell you the truth right now and you will hate me for saying it but you need to hear it—"

I cut him off before he can finish. "My family were at the tarmac, they wouldn't have boarded a plane until they knew where ours landed. They won't reach us in time before Koda starts torturing and raping me. I know, Taylan." Pain bursts to life in his eyes.

"I'm so sorry, Slayer, I promise—"

"Stop making promises you can't keep," I snap angrily, I know this isn't his fault but I can't stop my anger from rising. If he hadn't rejected me then I wouldn't have been at that fucking club!

"I can keep this one," he implores me to believe him with a loaded look.

"I don't believe you."

"Want to know my story and why I need consent?"

Even the predicament we are in can't stop me from gaping at him and the curiosity inside me from breaking free.

"You finally gonna tell me?" I press.

"Only when you need to be distracted, it isn't a happy story or one that will make you swoon." I search his gaze for any sign of deceit but see none.

"Why would you tell me? You said only three people know this story, why would you trust me with it?"

He smiles sadly and drops his chin to his chest and peeks up at me through his lashes. "That's precisely the point, I do trust you, Slayer." His words hit me in the chest and have warmth spreading throughout my body.

"You can trust me but not be more than my fuck buddy?" The words spew out before I can stop them. He takes a shuddering breath and stares down at the floor. I snort, even with our futures facing uncertainty he can't be honest about his fucking feelings.

Chapter Twenty

Taylan

I can feel the betrayal wafting off her in waves. I can't say what she needs me to even with our lives hanging in the balance. I may feel something for her but that doesn't mean I can make myself say what she wants to hear. If I give in and allow her to consume me, then I could end up like the bitch who gave me life. There's a reason I was never taken by child services, no one cared enough to search for me when the bodies were found. I have no idea who my father is and even if I did, I don't think he would have cared.

A thought hits me, pulling me from my thoughts. I dart my gaze around the room and frown.

Where the fuck is Kimber's kid?

Not once has anyone uttered a word about Kimber's kid, if he had the girl surely he would have said something. That's when the truth slams into me like a ton of bricks. Holy fuck, the realization is more crushing then I want to admit. She never knew who the father was but now she knows. He does have her but she isn't a slave.

"Why do you look like you just got sucker punched?" Destiny asks. I open my mouth to answer but snap it shut when the internal door opens and Koda and four of his men enter. I have a newfound hatred of this cocksucker, I'm going to enjoy killing this cunt.

"Ready to begin?" he taunts her.

"Where's your daughter?" I ask. He snaps his gaze to me and narrows his eyes. I smirk. He just confirmed my suspicion. "Did you tell Kimber after we escaped or before?"

He marches toward me, wraps his hand around my throat, forcing my head back as far it can go. "Shut your filthy mouth." Spittle smacks me in the face but not even that can stop my smile from breaking free.

"Kimber searched for her for years. She thought her daughter would suffer the same fate as she did. She didn't though because her daddy rescued her from Karl." His grip on my throat tightens but I force the words out. "You thought you fucked up after hurting Destiny, but when you learned the mother to your child was working alongside the DLCF you saw your way back in," I wheeze out. He releases me with a hard shove.

"You think you're so smart," he sneers.

"Smart enough to know *no* is a full sentence, which you seemed to have ignored when you raped your daughter's mother." He whirls around and clips me across the jaw, the pain doesn't register. "When you learned about Kimber you had to find a way back in. You were at the club tonight because your cousin is your partner. You own the club with him."

Destiny gasps. "Oh my God, Unique!" she breathes out in worry for her cousin.

"Well done, you figured it out. Yes, I own the club with my cousin, that idiot is too stupid to know when he's being used." Hearing that his cousin has no idea about what Koda's true intentions are, Destiny relaxes slightly knowing her cousin isn't in danger. "Kimber was a faceless whore, someone I fucked on the regular when dealing with Karl but I knew the moment she gave birth that baby was mine. The DNA test proved that." Hearing him confirm it makes it real. "Kimber's too stupid to know I'm Lila's father. A couple of pictures were sent to her and she was eating out of the palm of my hand wanting to do whatever it took to get Lila back."

"You have a daughter?!" Destiny screeches drawing his attention back to her, the disgusted look on her face is clear. "How the fuck could you do this to me when you have a child, a daughter, what would you do if someone did this to your baby?"

"Don't try to analyze me and don't think for a second that you can try to manipulate me. Unlike your fucking stupid parents, I know who I am and also know the risks that come with the life I lead. My child is nowhere near me and this life. Don't worry, butterfly, she won't ever know you existed."

This guy is fucking delusional.

If I didn't want his blood coating my hands so badly I would admire his smarts, instead of running for his life after he hurt Destiny, he plotted. He used what he had and wormed his way back into her life without anyone knowing. No one looked at how close he already was to her because she didn't tell them the full story, so he was free to amass an army and grow because he made her feel ashamed because of what he did to her!

"You are sicker than I thought!" she spits out. I take in the sight of her shivering and loathe the sight of the bruises covering her beautiful face—her right eye is swollen and almost shut completely, her lips have crusted blood on them.

"Hold him, I want him to watch," Koda orders. Before his men can reach me, I speak.

"No need, I won't look away." The painful regret in my tone has him smiling. Destiny shifts her gaze to me when he steps between her legs forcing her knees to widen as much as the cuffs on her ankles will allow. Her lip begins to tremble when he cups her tits. My breaths come in rapid pants as I grind my teeth so fucking hard my jaw protests. I clench my fists and pull against my cuffs when he trails his hands down her body, the metal biting into my skin, drawing blood. I sound like a rabid dog growling and grunting as I try to break free, even though I know I can't but it doesn't stop me from trying when he cups her pussy.

"Taylan," she whimpers my name like a plea, and that right there crushes me more than I can even admit.

"Eyes on me, baby," I say softly. I fight to keep my face blank of rage when he pushes a finger inside her. I watch her body stiffen and her eyes fill with tears as she begs me with her eyes to save her. "Kill me!" I scream. Koda keeps his fingers inside her as he looks over his shoulder at me.

"Where would the fun be in that? I want to torture you both. You seeing me break her will crush you. Her knowing you are right there, within reach but unable to save her will destroy her more than anything I do to her body." I hate that he's right, she's right in front of me and I can't save her.

I'm weak.

"You're fucking useless and weak just like your mother. You can't save that bitch, fuck, you can't even save yourself. Now bend the fuck over before I get the belt." Vance's words slam into me, for years his words haunted me more than the pain he inflicted on me.

Koda drops to his knees and forces her knees wider to accommodate his size. He grips her red lace thong and rips it off her. She cries out and I die a little inside.

"Destiny, look at me!" I roar when that cunt buries his face in her pussy, tears roll down her cheeks and the cock-suckers around me laugh and cheer on their boss like this a football game. Her tearful gaze meets mine and I'm transported back to the time I was a weak starving kid living in a trailer, helpless and unable to save myself.

"Please," she whimpers. Koda pulls back and smirks at his men, thinking she is begging him to make her come but that plea is for me, she wants me to distract her and I am powerless to deny her.

"I need consent because Vance took it from me. My mom let her boyfriend beat her and do whatever he wanted to me just so she wouldn't be alone." I keep talking to distract her from Koda eating her pussy and the jeers from his men, encouraging him to get her wet enough to take them all. "She was more scared of being single and unable to get her daily fix than facing a beating when Vance was on the come downs. She offered me up to her boyfriend and friends as payment for a fix." Her eyes widen in horror. "He would beat her unconscious and then fucked her while I was made to watch. He said it wasn't classified as rape because she wanted it and knew she had to pay for her hit."

"Pinch her tits!" one of the cunts beside me calls out. I see him rubbing himself through his jeans from the corner of my eye. Koda obliges and reaches up to pinch her nipples, drawing a pained cry from her but her gaze never leaves mine.

"My mom made him angry one day, real fucking angry, when she didn't let his friends fuck her. Three of them held her down while Vance gave her a hot shot. She died with that needle still embedded in her fucking vein!" I yank against my restraints when I see her begin to tremble, she's trying so hard not to come. "I grabbed a knife from the counter and stabbed Vance in the neck, his friends took off and left me there. Knox and Xander found me two days later. The police ruled it as a murder-suicide, they thought she killed him then took the hot shot."

"Taylan..." she whimpers, her face contorts in agony and I hate myself so fucking much right now. I can feel her self-loathing and pain just from the look in her eyes, that look will haunt me for the rest of my life.

I stare deep into her eyes and force every ounce of anger out of me so all she can see is my feelings for her in my gaze.

"Let go, Slayer, it's okay," I barely say above a whisper. The fuckers around me laugh but I don't care, she needs me to tell her that it's okay to come and that I'm still here. "Let go, baby."

And she does. I slam my eyes closed, unable to look at her when she cries out as her orgasm takes hold. The fuckers around me grunt and groan, making me feel sick to my stomach.

I'd rather burn in hell for eternity than watch her come on someone else's tongue.

"This time, I want you to look right at him when I fuck you." Koda's words have me snapping my eyes open. He uncuffs her ankles and I fight with every ounce of strength I have to break free. I won't fucking let him rape her, eating her out was bad enough but fucking her, that will destroy her.

"I'll kill all of you cunts, don't you fucking touch her! You hear me, you don't touch her!" I roar as I fight to get free. The cuffs biting into my skin is almost painless opposed to the pain radiating inside my chest. When I watched Vance beat my mom I was weak and did nothing. When he raped me and let his friends take turns, I took it. I never fought back or my mom would be beaten for my resistance and now, I feel exactly like that but ten times worse because Destiny didn't ask for any of this. She doesn't want him... she wants *me*.

Chapter Twenty-One

Destiny

Taylan fights to get to me. The four guards don't bother to try to stop him, instead they all stand there laughing and mocking him in Russian. When my ankles are free of the cuffs, Koda moves behind me to remove the cuffs off my wrists. I see the feral beast inside Taylan that he keeps hidden, he told me once before that out of him and his two best friends he has the worst temper. After hearing his story, I understand why. I'm not the only one running from the demons of my past, he has just been out running a lot longer than I have.

I feel dirty and used but I refuse to allow Koda to touch me again. My dad won't get here in time, so that means I have to woman up and find the strength and courage within myself to save us both.

Don't let them break your mind, you will want to give up

and allow them to win but you can never stop fighting or they win.

My mom's words play on a loop as Koda slips the key into my cuff, and the second my left wrist is freed, I strike. I jump forward and spin around using Koda's second of stupor to my advantage and grip his hair in one hand while using the clip of the cuff in my other hand to press against his neck. The four guards shout and draw their weapons but it's white noise as I shift so the chair is no longer in my way, Koda is still crouched on the floor gazing up at me with a sinful smile.

"Kill him," he barks. I snap my gaze to Taylan just as one of the guards turns his gun on him.

"Pull that trigger and I bury this in his throat," I warn. I feel conscious and at a disadvantage because I'm naked but I push every single one of those thoughts out of my head as I dig the open cuff harder into his throat, loving how he winces in pain.

"You kill him, we kill both of you," the guard on the right with a neck tattoo threatens as he presses the barrel of his gun against Taylan's temple.

"You kill me, you will be running for the rest of your life. I may be a Murdoch but I am also a Volkov and that means my name still holds power here in Russia. Everyone knows who my mother is, they fear her name alone. Do you think the people in this country would hide the man that killed the daughter of the woman who gave them their freedom?" I see my words have them all considering another outcome. I'm bluffing but they don't know that. It has been years since my mother has come back here, for all I know no one here will even remember her but judging by the looks in the guards eyes they believe me.

"Kill him now," Koda roars. I press the cuff in harder, relishing the sight of his blood running down his neck.

"You can kill him but make no mistake, I will hunt the four of you down. He is the underboss to the Re Della Strada. You kill him and you will have the Da Luca Crime Family, Re Della Strada, *Memento Mori* and the Murdochs coming after you... I give you my word on that." Before a decision can be reached a bomb goes off outside of the house, rocking the foundation and taking my feet out from under me. My ears ring from the loud explosion and parts of the ceiling give way and land on me, knocking the wind right out of my lungs. I push the broken plaster off my legs and take in the sight of the room. Taylan is still cuffed to his chair with pieces of plaster stuck in his hair. The guards have their guns raised. The one with the neck tattoo comes at me, and before I can defend myself, he smacks me in the face with the butt of his rifle.

I fall back against the cold concrete floor, black spots dancing in the corner of my eyes. I'm on the verge of passing out, I don't even register him dragging me along the floor by my hair. Pain filled whimpers spill from my lips but I'm too dazed to fight him off when he forces me back into my seat and cuffs my hands. My chin hits my chest and remains there as I feel blood trickling down my fore-head. I try to center myself and keep from succumbing to unconsciousness. The ringing in my ears is painful and the fact I can't rub them to try and alleviate the pain is frustrating.

"Slayer!" I try to lift my head but it's futile, my right eye is swollen shut now from Koda's punch. "Destiny, focus on me, baby!" he pleads. I try to lift my head but a pain erupts in the back of my scalp and my head is ripped back by my hair. My neck is craned so far back it burns in pain. I lock eyes with the monster above me.

"When I kill your attempted rescue party, you are going to watch as I torture him slowly and then I'm going fuck you next to his dead body," he promises ,then spits right in my face before releasing his hold on my hair and rushing out of the room with his men following after him, as he barks orders in Russian for his men to spread out and take out whoever is trying to save us.

"Slayer?" I lull my head forward and stare at Taylan. He looks like a broken little boy. I see so much torment in the depths of his eyes, the demons inside him are strong. It's probably a bad time to come to this realization but I know he will never allow himself to fall in love with someone because he's scared to death that he will wind up like his mother and put someone else before his own sanity and safety.

"I'm fine," I rasp out.

"If you get another chance to escape, you run. Don't you dare try and save me, you get the fuck out of here, do you hear me?" I scrunch my face only to cringe in pain, blood slowly trails down my cheek.

"I won't leave you behind," I vow. His features harden

but the sound of the gunfire growing closer has us both pausing with bated breath,

"Destiny." Whenever he uses my name I know he's serious, I'm starting to hate the sound of it coming out of his mouth, I prefer him calling my Slayer or baby.

"Yeah?"

He shoots me a small sad smile. "If there was ever a woman I would want to try with, it would have been you, baby." If my eyes could widen in shock they would have but all I can do is stare at him in stunned silence. "You don't need to fight to prove anything, the only person you have to prove anything to is yourself. Remember that." His words have a lump forming in my throat.

I swallow past it. "When he comes back—"

"That's your family out there, he isn't coming back if they have anything to do with it."

I shake my head. "I can hear them yelling and understand what they're saying," I say as the shouts reach us through the thin walls of the garage.

"What are they saying?"

"Crows," I answer.

Disappointment shines in his eyes. "It's Andreas," he mutters.

"My family isn't here," I say dejectedly. "Don't watch when he comes back, I don't want you to see it." I try to keep the bitterness from coating my tone but fail.

His eyes darken as he leans forward as much as the cuffs will allow. "You fight that cunt every step of the way, you don't give in no matter what they do to me. You get the fuck out of here and get back to your family, don't look back."

Tears prick the backs of my eyes when I hear more shouts, Koda's winning against Andreas and we are running out of time. "I'm sorry you're in this mess because of me," I choke out, feeling disgusted with myself for putting him in this position. If he had stayed away from me and never came to the club that first night, he would have been free and I would have been some blonde he met once at a random party.

"I'm not," he bites back.

"If it's any consolation, I would cry for real at your funeral." Shocked laughter rips out of him and quickly dies when the pain in his ribs rears to life.

"Don't cry over me, I'm not worth your tears."

I shake my head, denying his claims. "You're worth more than you think. Don't let your past define you. Fight your demons and I'll fight mine." He darts his gaze away from me, I sigh knowing that I can't help him get free of the clutches of his past. He has to save himself.

A strangled scream tears out of me when the internal door is kicked open, both Taylan and I snap our gazes that way. A sob forces its way past my lips at the sight before me.

"Mom," I choke out. She looks like a badass in leather but the shattered look in her eyes almost has me crying out. She rushes toward me, dropping her guns to the ground in front of me as she reaches out and gently cups my face.

"I'm here, baby, I'm right here," she reassures me as she looks me over, only then noticing for the first time that I am naked. She slams her eyes closed and takes some deep breaths as she conjures up the worst possible ways her daughter was harmed.

I feel like I let her down, she warned me about ending up in a situation like this. I thought I knew better but I was so fucking wrong. I made her worst nightmare come true.

"Mom?" She snaps her eyes open and I hate seeing the unshed tears in her eyes.

"Let's get you out of here," she clips out as she moves behind me and unlocks the cuffs. I sigh instantly as she rushes toward Taylan and uncuffs his ankles first before moving to free his wrists. I try to stand and stagger forward, but Mom catches me before I can hit the ground. "Shit, he can barely walk and I can't carry both of you out of here."

"Take her," Taylan grits out as he attempts to stand.

"No, I'm not leaving you," I snarl, he looks at my mom and nods.

"Anya. Get her the fuck out of here now," he says as he pushes to his feet and reaches out to tentatively cup my cheek. I press my cheek into his touch. "Go, don't look back, Slayer."

"No!" I cry out as my mom throws my arm over her shoulder and wraps the other around my waist and begins to pull toward the exit. "I'm not leaving him!" I scream as she uses my own weakness against me.

"He's armed, I left him a gun. You are my priority, Destiny. I can't lose you!" I peer back at him, he stands there clutching his side looking right at me.

"Look away," he mouths as Mom pulls me through the

door. The house is littered with bodies, and gunfire sounds out all around me as Mom leads me toward the back of the house. She snags a throw off the back of the sofa and does her best to wrap it around my body. We duck as low as we can as Mom leads us out the back door, I flinch when she fires two shots to the left and a man drops to the ground.

"I need you to move, your father and uncles have the front covered." She releases me and pushes me forward while she walks backward, covering my back. She really would die for me and I have been nothing but an ungrateful bitch to her. I press myself against the house as I limp along, trying to make my way to the front where my dad and uncles are. Mom fires another two shots and I quicken my pace, scared to death that she will be shot or injured because of me.

When I reach the edge of the house I stop, Mom pulls me back a step and slips in front of me. She pokes her head out fast before pulling back.

"How did you get here so fast?" I ask.

"We knew they would think we would wait until you landed to track you. But the moment you turned that tracker on, Vincent knew you were heading to an airstrip, so the guys split up and I met your father at our hanger. We followed you on the radar from a distance, we would have been here sooner but we couldn't get off the ground quick enough." She sounds angry.

"Thank you," I whisper. She whirls around and pins me with a stern look.

"I will never not come for you. I thought being a mother

was something I would never get the chance to experience but here you are. You are my everything, Destiny. All I have ever wanted is for you to be happy and live a life full of love and happiness and I failed you."

I gape at her. "No, Mom. You gave me everything, I just thought I knew better and I was so selfish—Mom!" I scream as I grab her arm and shove her to the ground just as one of Koda's men round the corner with their gun raised. Time stands still as I stare at the barrel of his gun. I can hear my own breath over the chaos around us, and feel a sense of peace wash over me when I see his finger shift to the trigger.

"Destiny!" Mom screams in pure fear but I can't appease her, it was a choice between me and her and I chose her. I won't allow her to be hurt because of me.

"Move!" the guard clips out, surprising the fuck out of me. "Unless you want to fucking die, move, because Andreas and your father are being overpowered thanks to the M2's Koda has." Mom leaps to her feet and grabs my arm, yanking me into her side as she raises her gun and points it at him.

"Why the fuck are you helping us?" she grits out.

"Because I know exactly who you are, Anya Volkov. I may hate Andreas but I don't hate you. Head back the way you came and follow the trail at the back of the property, it will lead you into town. Go, now!" Mom hesitates for a second before nodding tand pulling me after her. We find the trail easily enough but when I see the house I can't do it. I pull free of her hold and run back, ignoring the pain radiating throughout my body and her calls as she chases after me.

"I can't leave Taylan," I shout as I break through the back and immediately drop to the ground when shots are fired at me. I army crawl along the ground as more shots ring out around me.

"Destiny!" Mom screams when she makes it inside, firing off more shots before diving behind the sofa near me, dropping the clip from her gun and slamming another mag in. "You are in so much fucking shit when we get home!" I cringe. "Move!" She slips out as she raises her gun and fires blindly over the back of the sofa giving me a chance to crawl toward the garage. The moment I make it through the open door, I climb to my feet only to pause at the sight in front of me.

Taylan and Koda are on the floor, beating the shit out of each other. I look around for a weapon and spot a bench on the wall, I rush forward and push around the contents until I find a screwdriver. I grab it and turn back to them. Tay is on top raining down blow after blow but Koda manages to flip them so he is on top. He lands a hit to Taylan's face followed by a sucker punch to the ribs. Taylan shouts in pain and that's what snaps me out of it. I rush forward and bury the screwdriver to the hilt into Koda's back. He throws his head back and roars in pain. I yank it free and stab him again. He falls to the side and stares up at me in surprise before that look quickly morphs into an anger filled look.

"Suka!" (Bitch!) He tries to stand but stills when Mom pushes her gun into the back of his head.

"Nazovi yeye thuck eshche raz, yi ya snesu tvoyu

grebanuyu golovu, suka." (Call her that again and I'll blow your fucking head off, bitch.) Koda glares up at my mom.

"Anya Volkov," he spits.

"In the flesh," she snarls, then tosses me the throw blanket I dropped in my haste. I wrap it around myself and knot it, then turn to Taylan. He sits there, clutching his side and winces in pain but I see blood soaking through his fingers. I smack his hand away and gasp at the sight of the knife wound.

"He stabbed you?" I shriek before using my own hands to apply pressure to stop the bleeding. He howls in pain.

"Who the fuck are you?" Mom snaps. I keep my gaze on Taylan who looks pissed off at the sight of me.

"Kortov Novikov's son," Koda answers smugly. I look back at them to see shock plastered across my mother's face.

"You father was a piece of shit and so are you."

"Coming from the bitch who smuggles drugs for a living?" he counters.

"Is that what this is about? You want my formula?" She laughs but there is a manic edge to it. "I sold that formula to Andreas five years ago, he's the one who has been running the coke, not me, you stupid fucking fool."

"You lie!" Koda screams. "He told me it was you who runs it, you think you are better than the rest of us because you fuck some American scum—"

"I am better than you!" Mom yells right in his face. "I never allowed my father or Vlad's bullshit to cloud my judgment. I fought for my life and won. I was the first woman to ever be Pakhan of the Bratva and if reclaiming that title means it keeps pieces of shit like you from coming after inno-cent girls, then so be it." I stare up at my mother with a wicked smile on my battered face.

She's my fucking hero!

"A bitch can never lead." I flinch at the icy tone of Koda's voice. The sight of him has my heart racing and my fear spik-ing. My adrenaline is starting to wear off. Now I am faced with the aftermath of what he has done to me. I can't break down here, not in front of my mom. I've always made sure that she has seen me as strong, resilient and able to handle anything life throws at me, I refuse to allow her to see that a man destroyed my self-worth.

"This bitch can and will. I'm taking Russia back and you won't be around to see it!" Mom vows.

Chapter Twenty-Two

Taylan

Carnage.

That is the best word to describe the sight as Destiny and I walk... well she walks and I limp outside. The moment Gage spots his daughter, the fearful look on his face evaporates. He rushes forward and rips her away from me. I stumble but manage to catch myself on the hood of the car beside me. I keep my hand pressed against the wound on my side where that little bitch Koda stabbed me. I can feel the cold sheen of sweat over my body and feel myself growing weaker by the second.

"You look rough, kid." I flick my gaze up to see Vincent standing before me strapped to the hilt with weapons. Blood splatter is visible on his face and arms, but the sight that holds my attention is the three bullets lodged into his Kevlar vest.

"I thought you were a sniper?" I wheeze out.

He claps me on the shoulder and I flinch in pain. He withdraws his hand and shoots me an apologetic smile. "I was the one who fired the missile. Be glad it was me and not Gage because he can't aim for shit." I crack a smile at his teasing of his brother-in-law.

"Fuck you! My aim is perfect," the man himself defends. I peer over at him and see Destiny tucked under his arm and nestled into his side. Everything becomes white noise as she and I stare at each other, this is the second time we have been kidnapped together and come out the other side to tell stories about it.

I can't remember everything we said in there but something is telling me this thing between us isn't over yet.

"You need to go with Andreas and get patched up." I tear my gaze from Destiny to stare at Vincent.

"Yeah, okay," I mutter as he signals for a guy to come forward and help me into the back of the car. The tinted windows are too dark for her to see me in the back seat but I can see her perfectly fine. She's putting on a brave face for her family's sake but I see the cracks in her armor. The moment she is alone she's going to fall apart and I won't be there this time to pick up the pieces.

Koda has been apprehended, which means my job here is done, we've proven the RDS and DLCF are allies to the Murdochs, *Memento Mori* and Godfathers. With Anya taking Russia back, this means their family will now control three countries. Fuck, if they manage to get control of the English they will have the majority vote and could potentially come for us.

Andreas and one of his guys climbs into the front of the car. The second the engine starts, Destiny pulls free of her father. I roll down the window in time for her to grip the frame as she peers inside the darkened car at me. Her features are etched in pain, her eyes plead with me not to leave her and stay. When I open my mouth she shakes her head, forcing me to remain silent.

"You aren't your mother, you are far too strong to lose yourself in someone else. I wish you every ounce of happiness, Tay Tay, because you deserve it. You are someone's happy ever after..." Her bottom lip begins to tremble, she closes her eyes and sucks in a deep breath before slowly blinking those beautiful gray-blue eyes open again and pinning me in place with that look. "You're just not mine," she whispers, then places a kiss to the tips of two of her fingers and then presses them against my lips before stepping back.

Andreas begins reversing out of the driveway but my gaze is still locked on the blonde-haired beauty sandwiched between her uncle and father, who both glare at me but I ignore them. The broken look in her eyes has pain spurring to life in my chest.

"I wish I could be your ending," I whisper as we drive away from the only woman who I think actually really gave a damn about me, and was willing to help me slay my demons just so I would remain by her side.

Spending three days in Russia recovering wasn't something I enjoyed but today is the day I finally get to go home and I'm itching to get the fuck out of here. Andreas and his men have been good to me. Being here did give me insider information though. At the next meeting with heads of the families, Anya is going to announce that she will be reclaiming her birthright as Pakhan of the Volkov Bratva. According to Andreas, Gage is pissed that she is choosing to rule under her maiden name and not Murdoch, but in this country, the Murdoch name doesn't mean shit, it holds no power and the Murdochs can't call the shots.

Anya earned the respect of her people and in turn they will remain loyal to her and her only. I haven't seen any of the Murdochs or the one Murdoch in particular that I wanted to see the most. I was told by Kyros, Andreas's second, that once the remainder of her family arrived the night we were rescued they returned to the states. Knowing she is so far away hurts but this is for the best. We both knew that I was only stationed with her until the threat against her life was eliminated and it has been.

I snatch the phone Andreas got for me off the bedside table and scroll through the list of contacts until I find the person and hit call. It rings three times before she answers.

"Hello?" I hate that hearing her voice still brings a smile to my face even after all the shit she has done.

"Miss me?" I tease.

"Taylan?"

"How many stunningly handsome guys do you have calling you, Kimmy?"

She chuckles but I can tell it's forced. "Just you." There's a beat of silence before she breaks the awkwardness. "Do you still hate me?"

A whoosh of air escapes me as I mull over her words for a minute. "I hate what you did, but I don't hate you."

"Thank you," she says barely above a whisper.

"There's something I need to tell you."

"What is it?"

"Your daughter's name is Lila." A harrowing sob comes through the phone. "She's at a boarding school in Romania." I tell her everything Koda told me and how for the past three days I have been searching for her daughter. Andreas sent his tech guy to me so we could both hunt down Kimber's daughter. Koda was telling the truth, a quick call to the school proved that she is indeed a happy kid and hasn't been harmed. He may be more worthless than dog shit but at least he didn't harm that poor girl.

"D-does she know who I am?" Kimber chokes out.

"I don't know, Kimmy," I answer honestly, the school wouldn't provide me that type of information. "Wave has a plane standing by for you to go to Romania and get your girl. I will personally cover the costs for you and her to see a therapist so you can both reconnect and work through the trauma you both have suffered by her being separated from you."

"I didn't even recognize him, Taylan. I had no idea he was her father, I swear—"

"I believe you, Kimber. Now, go get your girl and I'll see you both real soon."

"Taylan?"

"Yeah?"

"I'm sorry I forced you to make that stupid bet and betrayed you."

I scrub my hand down my face. "I know you are, but without that bet I wouldn't have got to hang out with one of the coolest chicks I have ever met."

"You really like her, don't you?"

"We just started talking again, Kimber, don't push your luck. Go get your kid," I say, ignoring her laughter as I end the call and head out to meet Kyros so he can take my bruised ass to the airport.

Saying goodbye to Russia is fucking easy, if I never stepped foot back in this country I would be totally okay with that. Canada may be cold and small but it's nothing like this place. I'm the only one on the private plane aside from the crew, so I use the alone time to close my eyes and dream about the blonde-haired beauty that I refuse to admit hasn't been far from my thoughts for the past three days.

"You look comfortable." I snap my eyes open and stare up at the woman who gave life to the woman I was currently envisioning, bending over the arm of a sofa as I sank my cock into her perfect ass.

"What are you doing here?" I blurt.

Anya rolls her eyes as she peels her coat off and hands it to the flight attendant before claiming the seat opposite mine. She crosses her legs and rests her hands on top of them. Guards file onto the plane and claim seats around us but none of them even look at the two empty seats on either side of us. Anya and I don't utter another word until the plane takes off and levels out in the air.

"I had business to attend to here."

Unwarranted anger unfurls inside me. "You don't think that could have waited? You know, maybe your daughter might have needed you after what she went through."

Anya's face reddens in anger. "You think you know what my daughter needs because you spent mere weeks with her? Or is it because you were sleeping with her?"

I school my features making sure to give nothing away. The men in their family may be ruthless, cunning and powerful, but the women are just as bad if not worse. I know Anya is baiting me and I need to make sure I play my cards right.

"Why are you really on this flight?" I dodge her question and from the twitch of her upper lip I can tell she isn't pleased by that.

"I thought you and I should have a chat."

"About?"

"My daughter."

I scoff. "No thanks."

"You don't have a choice. You answer my questions and I may allow you to leave this aircraft breathing."

"What the hell is it with your family and always threatening to kill people?" I am fed up with always being threatened by them.

"You don't get to where we are by keeping your hands clean. Unlike Kiara and Clare, who don't enjoy inflicting pain, Allison, Carlina, Koby and myself, we all enjoy getting down and dirty with the guys."

"My mind just went to the gutter and I am fighting back the gag that wants to break free."

She purses her lips and narrows her eyes, clearly unimpressed with my joke at her expense. "She's a twenty-five year old girl."

"And your point is?" I clap back.

"You're thirty-three, established and have a life you've built for yourself in Canada. Destiny will never give up being in the ring, her father is her everything—"

I scoff. "You clearly don't know your own daughter well," I grit out.

"Be very careful here, Taylan, I won't tolerate being disrespected."

"You don't like me? Cool. Then kill me," I taunt, then push on before she can speak. "Instead of sitting here trying to analyze me, you should think about trying to get to know your daughter better, Anya. She fights because she was told she couldn't do it. She does love her father but she idolizes *you*!" Her face scrunches in confusion. "She also fights because she wants to prove to you that she is just as strong as her mother, she is trying to show that she is worthy of you."

"You fool! She never has to prove anything to me."

"Yes, she does!" I roar, gaining the attention of her men. They shift in their seats ready to strike me down if I make the wrong move. "You constantly work at those shelters with your sister-in-laws, you work with Gage and the others and she feels like she is just an afterthought. You never spend time with her, she thinks you hate her fighting—"

"I do!" she yells. "Being a fighter is dirty, you have to hunger for the win. It's life or death in the ring. I never wanted her to fight like I had to. Being a lawyer is safe, she would be free of being hurt."

"She's a fucking Murdoch and a Volkov! You are the Pakhan now, Anya. Her father is always going to be a target and now her mother has a bright red bullseye on her. She will never not be in danger. Fighting is her escape."

"Escape from what?" I snap my mouth closed and slink back into my seat, tearing my gaze from her. "Answer me!"

"It's not my story to tell. Speak to your daughter, Anya. You might be surprised by what she tells you, the both of you are more similar than you think." I slowly return my gaze to hers. "She has walls built so high so you can't see the broken little girl that hides behind them. Smash those fucking walls down and save her before you lose her to the demons in her mind. Trust me, the demons of your past can destroy anything good in your life."

"I know better than most what demons of your past can do, don't misjudge me. Much like you and your friends, I had to fight for everything in my life. I was ruthless, I was a killer without any remorse."

"Well, in that case congratulations because your daughter is your twin. You spent so much time trying to force her to be someone she isn't, that you lost sight of what was directly in front of you. She is dying inside and you are too blind to see it for yourself. Fuck Russia, it will still be there in years to come but your daughter might not be."

Chapter Twenty-Three

Destiny

Two weeks later...

I'm drowning.

I am suffocating.

A gut-curdling scream tears out of me as I bolt upright in bed. A few seconds later my bedroom door bursts open to reveal my mom and dad, rushing toward me but I flinch away. Dad wraps his arm around my mom's shoulders, both looking worried and hurt—not for themselves but for me. When we first got back, I tried to return to my apartment but when we pulled up in front of it I couldn't get out of the car.

Knowing he was spying on me and saw everything that Taylan and I did makes me sick. He's still alive. Dad gave me a choice that night to end his life or keep him alive to suffer. I chose to let the cunt suffer. He's locked in the bunker out back of Uncle Bishop's where he is tortured daily by Uncle

King and Aunt Allison. There have been days where I wanted to go see him, just so I could prove to myself that I am strong enough and that he doesn't have a hold over me. But every night I close my eyes, I see his face and relive every moment spent with him and how he violated me.

"Baby, we can't help if you don't speak to us," Mom pleads. I shake my head and lay back down, rolling over so I can face the window dismissing them. "Destiny, please."

"I'm fine, go back to bed," I say. They both sigh but do as I ask and leave me alone, wallowing in a hole of despair. How I could kill three guys and sleep like a baby is a mystery but having Koda's hands on me again reduced me to a crying mess who can't even sleep. I know why I can't sleep, and between knowing why and not being able to remedy that hurts more than my nightmares.

Taylan.

He's the reason I didn't have nightmares. Each night he held me as I slept I felt safe, protected and knew Koda couldn't get to me but he did. He was there the entire time and we had no fucking idea. I roll over and stare up at the ceiling, refusing to allow the tears that prick the backs of my eyes to fall. I've had no outlet for my anger. Dad won't let me train until I'm fully healed physically. But what he doesn't understand is that I will never be healed, the damage inside me is unrepairable. I thought I was strong after the first time, I put the pieces of myself back together and carried on with my life, but not this time.

This time, he won.

I don't know how long I lay here before I finally give up

on sleep and change into some sweats, an oversized T-shirt and some sneakers, before tip-toeing out of the house so I don't wake my parents. I want to snort at myself, twenty-five and back home with dear old mom and dad because I'm too scared to stay in my own apartment. I'm pathetic, I know and I think they are starting to realize that as well. I'm not the strong, fearless daughter they thought I was. I'm a fraud.

The crisp morning air hits me as I exit the house and inhale a deep breath, relishing in the freshness. Before I can talk myself out of it, I take off and jog around the compound. I want this fight with Tiana more than ever now. Before I wanted it to prove that I was good enough and I could do it to prove Koda wrong but now, I want it because I want to show *myself* I can do it.

Every couple hundred feet I pass a guard manning the fence line. They each nod their heads and go back to standing like a statue. I feel ashamed that just the sight of them frightens me at the moment, that at any given moment they could say fuck it to human decency and drag me into a dark corner and rape me—they are twice my size and could overpower me if they wanted to.

I slam to a halt, gasping for air as I hunch over and rest my hands on my knees. Two weeks and already I'm beginning to lose my fitness.

"You're up early." I shriek and nearly fall to my ass. I turn around and realize then that I'm in Uncle Bishop's back yard. The man himself sits on one of the pool loungers with a cup of coffee and his tablet in his lap.

"You scared me," I breathe out as I make my way over to

him and claim the seat beside him. I frown when he retrieves a fresh cup of coffee from the ground and hands it to me.

"I have cameras all around the compound, each time they catch movement an alarm goes off." My eyes widen.

"I woke you," I say guiltily.

He shrugs. "I barely sleep anyway. My men stand in the blind spots so they don't trip the alarms."

I cringe. "Sorry, Uncle B," I mutter as I grab the cup from him and allow its warmth to seep into me when I take a sip. "How did you know I would come here?" I ask.

He smiles lovingly. My uncle looks like a badass gangster and to his enemies he is but not to us. All we have ever seen is his soft side—well, everyone except Royal. He always gets to see his father's gangster side.

"I had a feeling you would find your way to that bunker," he says, flicking his gaze behind me to where the bunker is. My shoulders droop and I drop my gaze to the ground as I gnaw on my lip. "There is no time frame on when you will heal and be okay, Destiny." I lift my head and look up at him. "It's okay not to be okay, sweetheart."

My lip begins to tremble and my eyes fill with tears and his face falls. He places mine and his cups on the ground, then wraps his large arms around me holding me while I cry. It seems all I fucking do is cry these days! I can't seem to get a hold on my emotions, they are running rampant inside me and I am nothing but a passenger to them. He places a kiss to the top of my head. I clutch his shirt in a vice-like grip, not wanting him to let go.

Each and every one of our aunts and uncles helped raise

each of us kids. We all love our parents but our family is so tight-knit because we were all raised by the same group of parents and that's why we are so close. Well, everyone except for Chanel, she is only close to Royal and the twins.

"I don't know how to be okay," I choke out.

Uncle B slowly pushes me back and places his hands on the tops of my shoulders as he stares into my eyes. "And that's okay, Dest. I wish I could take the pain away. I would give anything to have traded places with you so you wouldn't have had to suffer." The conviction in his tone is awe inspiring and I don't doubt for a second that he doesn't mean what he says. "I built this compound to keep all of you safe, I never wanted this life to touch any of you kids. I clearly fucked up with Royal since that little prick wants to live in my shadow." I crack a smile at that. "But you, Nytress, Unique and Amelia are the only ones who don't want to be a part of this life and that makes me so happy."

I reel back. "Really?"

"I granted Amelia's wish because you all deserve to live a life without the burden of being a Murdoch. Meelz has never wanted this and I'm proud of her for wanting something of her own. Nyt and Neeks are off touring the world and being young and free. I won't pretend to know what you went through but I can see it in your eyes that this life has taken your innocence from you." I immediately drop my gaze but he clucks me on the chin forcing my eyes back to him. "You want out, then get out. I'll help you like I am helping Amelia behind her father's back."

"Oh my God!" I breathe out.

He smiles and winks. "I may be the Don of this family and rule over thousands but make no mistake, my girl, the eight of you kids and your children but especially my granddaughter rule over me. Your happiness is the most important thing in the world to me and if I can help you achieve that, I will regardless of what my idiot brothers say." It warms my heart that he still includes Havoc when he thinks of all us kids.

"Thank you, Uncle B," I say, meaning it. Speaking to him has lightened the burden I have been carrying around me lately.

"You never have to thank me. Gage did a good job raising you."

I smile proudly. "Yeah, he did."

"But thank God you look like your mother because your father is fucking ugly." Laughter bursts out of me, I haven't laughed like this in weeks and it feels so good.

"God, I missed that sound." I jump to my feet immediately at the sound of my dad's voice. I expect him to look angry that I'm here talking to my uncle and not him but he just looks... happy to see me smiling.

"If it helps, hearing how ugly you are was what made her laugh," Uncle B says as he climbs to his feet and winks at me. "This conversation stays between us, I promise," he says low enough for only me to hear, then places a kiss to the top of my head and heads back inside, but not before shoving my dad first, bringing a smile to my face.

"You know he was a mistake, right?" Dad says as he comes over to me and claims the seat Uncle B just vacated. I reclaim mine and sip my coffee. Dad and I sit here and stare up at the slowly lightening sky, not saying a word but just enjoying being together.

"I want you to train me," I say, breaking the silence after so long.

I feel his gaze boring into the side of my head. "Are you sure?"

I take a deep breath and lull my head to the side meeting his gaze. "Yeah. I want this fight against Tiana and then..."

"Then what?" he pushes.

"I don't know, I think I want to try law school for real this time."

His eyes widen. "Don't let your mother sway you—"

"She hasn't. I've been thinking about this for a long time now, I don't know if I want to fight for the rest of my life."

"If this is what you want, then you know I will support you." Hearing him say that means so fucking much to me. I jump up and shove him so he shifts over and climb in beside him. He wraps his arms around me and sighs in contentment.

"I missed this," I admit.

"So did I. It's been a hot minute since you wanted to hang out with your old man outside of the gym."

"Yeah, I guess I didn't realize what was really important to me until..." I clamp my mouth closed, unable to finish that sentence.

"Do you want to talk about what happened?" I close my eyes and mentally facepalm myself, of course he would think that I was talking about Koda when in truth, I was talking about someone else. Someone else who hasn't even texted, called or sent a fucking email!

"No."

"Your mother and I just want to help." I sit up and throw my legs over the side giving him my back.

"You can't help me," I force out through gritted teeth. "This is my demon to kill."

"We can help if you let us," he begs.

"No, you can't!" I snap before I stalk off, ignoring him calling out to me, I round the front of Uncle Bishop's house and break out into a sprint. Maybe Taylan was onto something, if I keep running I might just be able to outrun the darkness of my past.

Chapter Twenty-Four

Taylan

Find em, feel, em, fuck em, forget em.

That was the motto that I have lived by for as long as I can remember, but somehow I feel like that doesn't apply to me anymore. It's been a month since I left Russia and yet I still don't feel whole. Something is missing. I have been trying for weeks to convince myself that it's because I lost my pride or ego or whatever the fuck you want to call it when I wasn't able to save her, but the piece of myself I am missing is her!

Knox and Lake both tried to convince me not to move out but their pleas fell on deaf ears. I need my space to think and try to regroup. Don't get me wrong, I like my new house, it's big enough for me and has ample enough space but it's... empty. Xander and Wave even flew over to spend a couple of days with me. Hanging out with them, Lake and Knox like the old times was great, but was bittersweet because River was missing... but it wasn't just that. Seeing them so in love and watching how the guys found any excuse to touch their girls, whether it was a simple brush of their fingers down their arms or running their fingers through their hair, it had a pang of longing hitting me in the chest.

Knox is worried that I will fuck up tomorrow at the meeting with the heads of the families, he's an idiot. He should know better than anyone that I am a master at compartmentalizing shit. My phone rings and I roll my eyes at the sight of the devil himself calling.

"Yes, darling, I packed those panties that you like," I say when I answer.

"Ha-ha fucker! We'll swing by and pick you up in an hour."

"Sweet. I'm packed," I say before I end the call. I'm about to toss my phone back onto the sofa when it rings again, but this time it's an unknown number. I debate letting it ring out but curiosity gets the better of me.

"Who dis?" I snap.

"So mature." I tense at the sound of Gage's voice.

"What can I do for you, Gage?" I clip out in a firm tone. I haven't spoken to any of them since I landed in Canada and left Anya on the plane.

"Just so we are both fucking clear, I wouldn't be making this call if I didn't have to."

"Then why are you?"

"Because my wife says you can help." This piqued my interest.

"Well, please carry on then."

"I don't like you!"

I snort. "And I won't lose sleep over how you feel about me, now either get to the point or I'm hanging up."

"I'll beat your fucking face in, you little punk!" he snarls.

I roll my eyes. "Kay, well nice chat—"

"Train Destiny for the fight against Tiana and I won't snap your neck when I see you tomorrow."

I splutter. "Guy with all the threats, say what now?"

He growls and that gives me great satisfaction, knowing I'm working his last nerve. I enjoy pushing people's buttons. "She has three months to be ready."

"And?" I press.

"With how she is training, she wouldn't be ready in six months."

"Tell her mother to jump in the ring with her and not to hold back, break her and she will break down all her walls and then you will both see the real beast your daughter hides from the world. Catch ya on the flip side, Gage." I end the call and slouch back into the sofa scrubbing a hand down my face. "She's haunting me without actually haunting," I growl in frustration.

By the time Knox picks me up, I'm in a sour mood, I barely mutter two words to him on the flight to Switzerland. When we get to our hotel, I snatch my key from him and head straight for my room, needing to be alone. I decide to take a shower and try to calm myself before I go looking for a fight in the wrong place. Right now fighting is my only option because my cock seems to be broken. The fucker won't get hard unless I'm thinking about a certain blonde who is a huge pain in my fucking ass.

I step out of the shower and wrap the towel around my waist, before walking out only to slam to a halt at the sight before me. "Don't you fucking people have boundaries?" I snap. I'm fucking fuming right now and I don't give a fuck who she is or who she is married to.

"She's here, room 201. Go to her." I stop digging through my duffle bag for some clothes and look at her in shock.

"Crazy woman who broke into my room, say what now?"

Her face morphs into a pissed off look as she climbs to her feet and drops a gold room key on my bed. "201, say goodbye or agree to train her but either way, *she* needs to see you. She has no idea I am even here speaking to you."

I shake my head. "You are out of your fucking mind, Anya. The person who needs to help her is you—"

"The minute we land back in the States, I will be in the ring with her. I may be the one who can break my daughter and force her to feel but you and I both know you are the only one she wants to put her pieces back together." I say nothing as she slips out of my room like a fucking ghost.

"Fuck my life!" I snarl into the empty room as I quickly change, then lean against the wall, staring at the stupid card like it might attack me if I get too close. I stand here tugging on the strands of my hair for the better part of an hour debating what the fuck I should do. I check the time on my watch and cringe, it's nearly one in the morning. "Fuck it," I snap before I swipe the card off the bed and stalk out of my room, making my way to her room. The entire way my heart beats rapidly, like it's trying to burst free of its cage. My palms are slick with sweat when I finally come to a halt outside her room.

Should I knock?

I shake my head. No, I don't want to wake her up if she's sleeping. Maybe I could just sneak in and stare at her for a bit? I nod like a mad man, slip the card into the slot and wait for the green light to flash, then quietly slip inside her room. I close the door softly and pad through her room, following the soft glow of light coming out of the bedroom. The room is set up the same as mine so it's easy to navigate. I creep forward and slip inside the room, the sight of her fast asleep with the covers tangled around her has me wanting to drop to my knees and thank God for creating such a masterpiece.

I silently move toward the chair in the corner that is shrouded in darkness, telling myself I'll just sit here for a while and stare at her until I get my fix, then I'll slip out before she even realizes I am here. If she sees me, that would be bad for the both of us. Just the sight of her has my cock growing hard. I look down at the traitor and glare at it. The fucker couldn't even get hard when I tried to rub one out to porn, but the mere thought of her has me rock hard.

Would it be creepy if I got myself off right here?

I push that thought away because yes, yes that would be fucking creepy!

I tense when she whimpers and begins to stir. Her tiny hands clench the sheets, her head swings side to side. "No, no, no, stop it. Don't touch me." A strong sense of protectiveness washes over me knowing she is having a nightmare about what she went through, what I witnessed her go through! "No!" she screams so loud I reel back into the chair as she bolts upright in the bed panting. She clutches her throat and then looks down at her lap. She sighs in relief when she realizes where she is.

I remain still and hold my breath, praying she will fall back asleep so I can slip out of her room but she suddenly stiffens like she feels my eyes on her. She closes her eyes for a second and swallows audibly then snaps them open and slowly turns toward me. Panic flares to life in her eyes, her mouth opens to scream but I lean forward the panic slowly fades as she drinks in the sight of me like she can't believe I'm here.

"Wake up," she says aloud, then smacks herself across the cheek. "Ouch!"

"You're not dreaming, Slayer," I say quietly so as to not spook her. She runs her gaze over me, taking in every inch of me. A deep groove forms between her brows that has me wanting to smooth out the lines with my fingers.

"You're really here?" she whispers. I nod.

"I am."

"Why?" That one word is laced with an immense amount of pain and confusion.

I open my mouth and close it a couple of times trying to find the right words. "I... I don't know."

"You have to leave, Taylan," she pleads.

Her words spark me to life. I slowly stand and look down at her, wishing more than anything that I could be what she needed me to be. I want to give her that security and make promises to always remain by her side but I can't...

"I never meant to hurt you, Destiny."

She rolls her lips over her teeth and inhales sharply through her nose before blowing it out slowly. "I never meant to feel anything for you. I never wanted more than a bit of fun but then..." She lets her sentence trail off.

"Shit changed. I get it," I say honestly.

"No, you don't get it." Anger drips from each word.

"Yes, I do!"

"You walked away so easily, you felt nothing when you drove away and left me there after... after what h-he did to me." When tears brim her eyes, I lose my self-control and eliminate the space between us and climb on the bed, pulling her to me. She climbs on my lap and wraps herself around me, burying her face in my neck. My hold on her is strong and protective. Her scent invades my senses, pulling memories from my mind that I tried to keep buried so the anguish of not being near didn't pull me under.

"I felt your pain like it was my own," I admit.

She pulls back and stares down at me. "You left me behind like I was nothing. You may not be able to say the words, but I know you feel something for me, Taylan. I can see it in your eyes."

I take a shuddering breath and try to turn away from her, but she grips my chin forcing my gaze back to hers. "I can't give you what you want, Slayer, I told you that from the start. I am not the guy you get a happily ever after with."

"Then don't give me after, give me *now*."

I search her gaze, trying to decipher her meaning, but draw a blank. When she presses her lips to mine, then when I open for her, she takes control and plunges her tongue into my mouth, moaning. The taste of her has a haze of need washing over me and my cock leaping to attention. She rolls her hips, drawing a groan from me. My hands take on a mind of their own and begin touching her everywhere before finally landing on her ass and gripping her cheeks in a bruising hold.

She breaks the kiss, resting her head against mine as she holds my gaze. Lust and love swirl inside those gray-blue eyes. "I need you." Three words, that's all it takes for me to snap and flip us so she is pinned beneath me. Her blonde hair is fanned out around her, her lips swollen from my kiss and her chest rising and falling quickly as she waits for my response.

"Tonight, that is all I can give you."

"Then give me all of you while you can." She's never let me see this side of her before, vulnerable. She is letting me see everything she feels for me and it's breaking my chest open, my heart wanting to burst free and bury itself inside her because it knows the truth, she owns it. I hate the fear I harbor because of my past. I've never wanted a different life until now, and if I wasn't so fucked up and broken I could have this incredible woman, who has shown me she loves me without uttering those three words.

I shut off my inner voice and capture her lips, needing her to distract me before I self-combust. She wraps her arms around my neck and holds me close so she can deepen the kiss, her nipples pressing through her cotton shirt and rubbing against my chest. The soft whimpers that escape her drive me crazy with need, my hips move on their own accord and grind into her pussy. She breaks the kiss, crying out. I growl, needing to hear more of those sounds. I rip the shirt down the middle and salivate at the sight of her dusty-pink nipples. I bend down and capture one in my mouth, she cries out and arches her back off the bed.

"Yes, Tay." She moans when I bite down, I release it with a wet pop before latching onto the other one and paying it the same amount of attention. I love how responsive she is to my touch. She thrusts her hips up trying to gain some friction, if this is going to be the last time I get to have her like this then I want to savor every fucking moment. I trail kisses down her toned stomach. When she rests forward on her elbows to watch me, I flick my eyes to hers and keep them there as I slowly peel her sleep shorts down her legs. I toss them over my shoulder as she bends her legs at the knees and opens for me. I groan at the sight of her beautiful cunt, it's perfect.

"I need to taste you, baby, you good with that?" I ask, needing her consent. She nibbles her bottom lip and suddenly looks worried, that's when I remember. *Koda.* "Shit, I didn't think—"

"I need you to go slow and keep looking at me, I want you to take away that horrible memory and replace it with this one." The vulnerability in her voice pains me.

"Are you sure?"

She nods. I quirk a brow waiting for her to say the words.

"Yes, I'm sure." I do as she asked and keep my eyes on her as I press forward between her legs. She darts her tongue out to moisten her lips. I press a kiss to her inner thigh and shoot her a smile.

"Keep those pretty eyes on me, baby. It's just me, he'll never touch you again, I made sure of that." Her face contorts in confusion, but before she can ask questions, I swipe my tongue through her folds, distracting her.

Chapter Twenty-Five

Destiny

I bite down on my lip to keep from screaming when he sucks my clit into his mouth, he's barely touched me and I can already feel my orgasm cresting. I try to fight it off, frightened that when it does crash into me I'll see Koda between my legs and not Taylan. He pushes a single finger inside me and I lose the fight to remain silent, I moan so loud. His tongue matches the tempo of his finger, the rhythm is punishing.

"I can't," I cry out when I feel my orgasm wanting to break me in half.

"Eyes on me, baby, I got you," he reassures me, then sucks on my clit again. I lock my gaze onto his and trust that he will put me back together again if I break a part. Unable to stave it off any longer, the orgasm tears through me with such power that it robs me of breath for a second before a gut wrenching scream works its way out of me. I scrunch my eyes shut and throw my head back as the aftershocks take control of my body as he slowly works me down, lapping at my clit gently and easing his finger out.

I flop back against the bed panting and watch him rid himself of his shirt and pants. The second he pushes his boxers down his legs, his cock smacks against his abs, thick and hard. My mouth waters at the sight of it, knowing I'll get to taste him shortly. He crawls up my body and uses his weight to pin me in place, his lips hover above mine.

"Taste yourself on my tongue," he orders. I close the sliver of space between us and kiss him. The instant his tongue intertwines with mine I moan, loving the way I taste on him but it's missing his cum and I need to taste us both together, one more time. He deepens the kiss as he lines himself up with my entrance. I feel his head press against my opening and my breathing turns erratic as excitement thrums to life inside me.

I break the kiss and stare up at him, emotions so strong slam into me. "I love you," I whisper. I thought he would be shocked at my declaration but no, all I see is pity in his beautiful eyes. I refuse to allow him to withdraw inside himself so I press on. "I need you to make love to me, just this once. I need you to do this for me, Tay Tay, so I can let you go." I hear the pain in my own voice. He closes his eyes for a second, taking a deep breath and then slowly pushes inside me as he blinks his eyes open and presses his forehead against mine.

"You have me," he says against my lips as he buries himself inside me. We both cry at the feeling of being joined once again. Fuck, he stretches me perfectly. The burn of having him inside me again after so many weeks slowly eases as he begins to move inside me, while keeping his gaze locked on mine the entire time. This feels different compared to all the other times we've slept together, we're letting our bodies say what our mouths can't.

Pain and pleasure begin to burn inside my chest. I want the pleasure to outweigh the pain but it can't because the pain inside me will always be present, knowing I can never have him. I would give anything for this to be a Disney movie where the girl gets the guy but it isn't a movie, this is real life and sometimes you have to lose.

It's better to have tasted love for a fleeting moment then to die never knowing.

"Taylan," I grit out through clenched teeth.

He rests his elbows on either side of my head and pulls almost all the way out before slamming inside me again.

"You wanted slow, soft and vanilla."

"What?" I gasp out around his next thrust.

"We don't do soft, we do hard, feral, all-consuming sex. Your pussy is punishing you for denying it what it really wants."

"What does it want?" I gasp out as he skims that sweet spot inside me.

"It wants me to fuck it like a starved man. You can't come because you don't really want me to fuck you this way, you want me to own you, consume and use you, don't you, baby?" I'm ashamed to admit that his dirty promise has my pussy growing wetter at the thought of him slamming into me so hard that I'll feel the ghost of him between my legs for days.

"Own me." His eyes blaze. "Consume me." He stops moving. "Use me then make me come so fucking hard on that cock, then come inside this pussy so you can suck it out and spit it in my mouth."

Unbridled need unfurls in his eyes as he pulls out of me, flips me onto my stomach and grabs my hips, forcing me to my knees.

"This what you want?" he snarls as he slams inside me without warning. I cry out and slip forward. He grips my waist in a bruising hold as he fucks me. Fuck, this right here is what I *needed*—I thought making love would be special but I was dead wrong. Him dominating me and using my body for his pleasure is what I need. I can already feel my pussy clenching around his cock, I'm two seconds away from coming. "You take my cock so fucking good. baby."

"Taylan, I'm gonna come," I scream out, his next thrust sending me hurtling over the cliff. I come so fucking hard I almost black out, my throat hoarse from screaming but he isn't one to be deterred. He gives zero fucks that my body is still trembling from that release or that my body is about to give out.

"Don't you fucking dare," he snarls when I try to shift forward. He yanks me back onto his cock, drawing a sharp cry from me. "This is me owning you, now fucking take it and come on my cock, I want to taste that cum." Fuck, his words must possess magic powers because I can already feel heat pooling in my belly as it tries to obey its master. "Give it to me, Slayer," he roars over the sound of skin slapping against skin. Without warning a wave of pleasure slams into me, robbing me of air. I scream his name so loud that the rooms surrounding us would have heard. "Destiny!" he cries out when he follows me over the cliff of pleasure. He has barely finished coming before he pulls out of me and twists around so his face is between my legs. He grabs my waist and pulls me down onto his waiting tongue. I stare down at him between my legs moaning when his eyes turn hazy as he sucks our releases out of me.

I push his hands away and slide down his body before sealing my lips to his and swallowing every last ounce of cum he spits into my mouth, moaning the entire time. Fuck, tasting both our releases together is a taste I have begun to crave.

I break the kiss and roll off him with my head resting on his arm, both of us breathing frantically like we have just ran a marathon.

"That was incredible," I mutter.

"I told you I was good." I smack him playfully on the chest as we both laugh. All too soon the sound dies down and the heat of the moment passes, bathing us in a tension-filled silence. I'm trying to delay the inevitable when I throw my leg over his and wrap my around over his stomach, trying to hold him here. I rest my ear against his heart, listening to it beat and fooling myself into thinking that it beats for me.

I don't want this moment to end.

To my surprise, he begins trailing his fingers through my hair. I sigh in contentment, loving the feeling of him touching me again. I didn't realize how lonely I have felt these past few weeks without him until now. I close my eyes and savor this moment because when he does leave it is going to destroy me.

"How did you get into my room?" I ask.

"I have my ways." I roll my eyes, he's such an asshole.

"Do you regret coming here?" I hold my breath, waiting to hear his reply, while his heart still beats the same rhythm, offering me some comfort.

"No. I should but I can't regret a single moment with you." I shift and rest my hands under my chin on his chest and look at him.

"Why should you regret it?"

His brows draw in and a flicker of regret flashes in his eyes. "Because I shouldn't have touched you, not touching you meant you wouldn't be hurt when I walk out that door." His honesty is refreshing but it doesn't stop it from stinging to hear him say that.

"Would you have ever come to me without that bet you made with Kimber?"

He mulls my words over for a second before nodding once. "Yes."

"Why?"

"You were a challenge, you didn't drop to your knees and beg me to notice you. You brushed me off and acted like I was an annoying bug you couldn't get rid of and that attracted me to you instantly. I had to have you."

"You have me now, why can't that be enough?" I beg. All emotion melts off his face and is replaced with an emotionless mask. He shifts, forcing me off him as he climbs off the bed. I clutch the sheet to my chest to hide my nakedness, as I sit here with my stomach in my throat and watch him pull his clothes on as I fight back tears. Once he has his shirt and pants on he reclaims the seat he was in when I woke up and begins putting his shoes on.

I want to say more but I can't, twice now I have tried to make him stay but he still leaves. I refuse to be that girl who begs the guy she loves to stay when he doesn't want to, so I climb off the bed and snatch some tights and a shirt from my suitcase, fuck panties and a bra. I pull my trainers out of my duffle bag near the end of the bed and pull them on, keeping my back to him the entire time even though I can feel his eyes burning into the back of my head. I snatch my hair clip off the side table and pile my hair on top of my head. I steel my spine and slip my own mask into place before I turn and face him, he looks confused but I refuse to dwell on that.

"When you leave, don't come back." He opens his mouth but I push on. "I won't have you fucking with my head, I'm already messed up from everything and I don't need you adding to that." He rests his forearms on the tops of his thighs and hangs his head. "I'm going to let you go." He snaps his head up and looks perplexed and slightly hurt.

Fuck. Him!

"What if I don't want you to?" His words have me wanting to crumble but I refuse to allow him to have that power over me.

"If you meant that, then you wouldn't be running away

right now, you would stay and prove to me you mean what you say."

"I want to mean them—"

I raise my hand, cutting off his bullshit. "No, you don't. I may be the Havoc Slayer but I am not the slayer of your demons, you have to be the one to do that. I'm going to walk out that door and out of your life for the last time." Pain blooms to life in his eyes. I force myself not to succumb to the need to comfort him. "I meant what I said, Taylan. I do love you but not enough to be someone you can visit and fuck when you feel like it. Find a way to conquer your fear, you are not your mother."

It takes every ounce of strength I possess to walk out of that room and leave him behind. I fight back the tears as I make my way to the elevators. I need to hit the gym and take out my frustrations there before I destroy my hotel room. Pain is radiating inside my chest but I refuse to allow it to consume me, I'll channel it and use it to help me win this fight against Tiana.

Chapter Twenty-Six

Taylan

All the heads of the families sit around the circular table. There are the Murdochs, Re Della Strada, *Memento Mori*, Godfathers Of The Night, Da Luca Crime Family, The Crows and the Falcons—the English led by Ian but his daughter has just been announced as his heir at the meeting. Andreas and his crew stand behind their chairs with Anya standing in the middle of the four of them.

"The Crows move to announce that I am stepping down as Pakhan," Andreas announces, everyone already knows this but it's just formality for Ian who is the only one who didn't know. "A new Pakhan has been selected, Anya Murdoch will now head the Bratva under its former name, the Volkov Bratva. All in agreement?"

A chorus of yeses sound out around the room. Ian looks irritated at this but he is smart enough to know that the Murdochs don't make a play until they have a power move in place and right now, they hold half the power. With Knox and Wave being related there is no worry about those two going against each other but the one to watch now is Ian, he is the only solo member at this table and his face shows he is thinking the same thing.

"Is that all?" Bishop asks as he prepares to stand, but I speak for the first time garnering everyone's attention but my focus is solely on the new Pakhan of the Bratva as I speak.

"I want Koda Novikov handed over to the Da Luca Crime Family where he will receive the same punishment as Karl for what he did to…" I clamp my mouth closed and choose a different way to word it. Anya's eyes study me and I can feel Gage's glare boring into the side of my head but ignore him. "I want him to suffer for years, torture isn't enough. I want him begging for death and suffering for years to come for what he did." The hatred in my tone is clear.

Anya looks to her husband who stands from his chair and moves to join his wife. Andreas shifts so he can fit beside his wife. Not wanting to be seen as weak, I push back from the table and stand, placing both my hands flat against the wooden surface. I took a leaf out of their book and made a power move, the tension in the room growing thicker by the second as everyone waits with bated breath to see what will happen between me, Gage and Anya.

"You act like you know something we don't know about… *that* situation." He can word it however he likes but everyone in this fucking room knows we are talking about Destiny.

"I do know." I make sure to announce each word slowly so there is no chance of him misunderstanding my meaning.

"Believe me, when I tell you this is the best option for *that situation*," I tack on just to be an asshole.

His upper lip twitches but he keeps his composure. "You don't have a say in what happens with Koda, that problem has been resolved by the Russians as is their right since what happened transpired on their turf." He sounds like a cocky fucker and my anger seizes control of me.

I slam my fist into the table. "Fuck the rules!" I roar and tear my gaze from him to look at Anya. Knox rises and places a hand on my shoulder trying to get me under control but I shrug him off. "She is dying inside, you asked for my help and this is me giving it to you, Anya." Understanding flares in her eyes.

"What the fuck is he talking about?" Gage asks his wife but she ignores him and keeps focusing on me.

"He *hurt* her, didn't he?" She may have spoken softly but the weight of those words slammed into me as if she shouted them. I take a shuddering breath and drop my gaze to the table. "Answer me!" she screams.

I slowly lift my head and look between both of them, Gage looks like he's on the verge of having a panic attack, Anya looks like a pale ghost. "Give him to me, let me take him to Ireland where Wave will make sure he suffers for... what he did." Anya gasps and stumbles back a step, Gage begins shaking his head.

"No, no, no fucking way, not my little girl," he yells, hoping that if he denies it out loud it will make it true. I may not have told them directly but they can read between the lines. I cut a glance to the rest of her family to see them all sitting with mixed looks of shock, anger, guilt and wrath etched into each of their features.

"You have my word that he will suffer daily, he will have a guest every hour to make sure he is serviced. He will get medical treatment so he doesn't die, we'll keep him alive for as long as you want but make no mistake, he will be treated like all the other traffickers we capture." Wave says as she stands, Xan and Trey following her lead and flanking her on either side.

"Why?" Anya asks her.

"He hurt one of mine and for that he will meet the worst of punishments." Anya nods and looks around the table until her gaze finally lands on me.

"He is to suffer, and I want access to him whenever I want." I nod my agreement knowing Wave will agree to the terms as long as she can take him home so Kimber can get her pound of flesh. "He's being kept at the Murdoch compound—"

"You and I are transporting that low-life piece of shit," Gage snarls at me before storming out of the room. I nod my agreement.

"You can transport him immediately," Anya says in a flat tone.

"I'll fly back to the States with you all, then take him to Ireland." Once she nods her agreement, everyone starts to file out of the room. I turn to Knox to find his hard unyielding gaze focused on me already.

"All of this for a girl you claim not to be able to care for."

I glare at my best friend. "Stay out of it," I grit out.

Knox snaps his arm out, grips the back of my neck and pulls me forward so our foreheads touch. "Listen to me, you little shit. The past doesn't define who we can become. If it did, I wouldn't be with my wife and wouldn't have two amazing fucking sons. Let. Go. Taylan." My breathing grows loud. "Let it all go, brother. Jump head first into whatever it is you have with her and try because if you don't, you won't just be hurting yourself."

"I can't."

He presses his head harder against mine. "You can! Stop being a pussy. You aren't that bitch and never will be, Xan and I won't let you become her."

"Promise me you will save me if I do?" I beg, his eyes soften.

"On my life, Taylan, I will never let you lose yourself." I close my eyes and take a deep breath.

"I'm scared," I admit.

He smiles and nods. "This will be the scariest thing you will ever do in your life but if you don't try you will regret it."

"Okay." He smiles victoriously and pulls me in for a hug before slapping me on the back twice and shoving me toward the exit so I can catch up with the Murdochs. I wave to Xan, Trey and Wave as I run after the others.

Picture the most awkward situation you have ever been in and then times that by ten, that's me right now. I am sitting between Rook and Knight with Bishop, King and Gage in front of me with Vincent standing in the aisle with his arms crossed over his chest. I thought Royal and the others would be on this flight, but turns out he and the others have their own plane and so does London and Artemis, which left me alone with the Murdochs.

Yippee.

I try to discreetly look around for Anya but Gage's growl draws my attention back to them. I shoot the three in front of me a grin which they don't return.

"There is a lot of testosterone in here," I say, trying to break the tension filled silence but fail.

"You want me to break your fucking jaw, don't you?" Gage snarls.

I scrunch my face. "Why would you do that?"

"Because we all saw what the fuck you did to his daughter, *our* niece." I cringe at Bishop's admission. I try to move and rub the back of my neck but Knight glares at me from the side so I drop my arm back to my lap and sigh.

"So, what happens now?" I ask, losing all traces of humor to my voice.

"You take that cunt to Ireland after we say our goodbyes and then you never come back," King says.

Fuck this!

I shift forward and rest my arms on the tops of my thighs and lock eyes with Gage, ignoring the others, this is between me and him not the rest.

"I'm not leaving her."

"Yes, you are," he grits out as he mimics my position trying to taunt me into losing my cool.

"No, I'm not. You want me to tuck tail and run like a scared little bitch, then you are going to have a do a lot fucking better than this." I motion with my hands toward his brothers and brother-in-law.

"You think a little shit stain like you is good enough for *my* daughter?" It's a rhetorical question but I answer it anyway.

"No, I'm not." He tries to mask his surprise but fails. "You all know what I do for a living, you know firsthand what Knox, Xander and I have done to get to where we are. We fought for everything we have, clawed our fucking way out of the gutter and fought any fucker who got in our way. I have a temper unmatched by my best friends and will lose it sometimes, but never at *her*. I am a street rat and I'm fucking proud of that. I wasn't born with a golden spoon in my mouth. I'm a piece of shit and I can admit that but there will never be another person in this fucking world who will care about her as much as I do."

"*Care*, not love?" Gage taunts.

I scoff. "No offense but none of you ugly fuckers will be the first to hear me utter those words for the first time in my life, she will be." I see Bishop fighting to keep from smiling out of the corner of my eye. Unlike his older brother, King fails to hide it as he turns to look out the window.

"Not only did the universe bless me with a granddaughter to fuck with my son, she also blessed me with someone who can fuck with you," Bishop says as he claps Gage on the back, the latter just continuing to glare at me like I am the bane of his existence.

"I'll make you a deal, honor it and you just may get what you want." His tone sets my nerves on edge and the sparkle in Gage's eyes tells me that's exactly what he wants.

"Name your terms," I counter. When he finishes laying out his terms, a part of me does want to tuck tail and run but my Slayer is worth every ounce of pain this is going to cause me. I can feel his brothers and Vincent staring at me, waiting for me to deny his offer but I won't. "I agree to your terms but you will agree to mine as well." His nostrils flare but I push on. "When her mother gets in the ring with her, I *need* to be there."

He opens his mouth to deny me, I can see it in his eyes but he doesn't get a chance. Anya appears beside Vincent and speaks. "Agreed. She returns back to the States tomorrow with Luka, we fight then."

Chapter Twenty-Seven

Destiny

I feel bad for Uncle Luka being stuck with me but I didn't want to head home with my parents. I need a day to myself and being the great guy that Uncle Luka is, he offered to stay back with me. When London learned I wasn't going home with the others, she ditched her stage five clinger fiancé and came and hung out in my hotel room with me. It sucked having to say goodbye to her but she had to go back to Greece to help Artemis since Cronos was nowhere to be found.

Honestly, I was avoiding the inevitable. I knew going home meant that shit was final, after leaving him the way I did I know there is no coming back from that. I talked a big game and said things I didn't really mean but it wasn't like he objected and said I was wrong. He let me leave and that was the sign I needed, I wasn't enough for him to fight for and that's okay. One day someone will fight for me and it just fucking hurts that it won't be *him*.

"We going home, kid?" Uncle Luka asks from his seat beside me. I shake my head.

"I have too much energy after sitting on the plane for so long, can you take me to the gym, please?" He smiles and shakes his head.

"You and your mom are so much alike it's actually scary." I smile and relish in the compliment. It's not often I'm compared to my mom, normally I always get told I'm so much like my dad. We travel in comfortable silence, that's the greatest thing about Uncle Luka, he never pushes but he's always there if we ever need him. I've always wondered if he had a special someone in his life, none of us have ever seen him with a woman, but he's really private and says he likes it that way so Uncle Rook can't give him shit. "You know with your mom being the new Pakhan, you will have a guard on you 24/7?"

I sigh and press my head against the cool glass. "Yeah. I figured as much, let's hope this one is a female."

"Why?" he asks curiously.

I turn and pin him with a dry stare. "Don't play coy. I know you all got to see the evidence of what happened with my last guard." He shudders in revulsion.

"That is something no uncle *or* father wants to see, thank you very much."

"Well, it won't be happening again," I say bitterly.

"This life can take a lot from you if you let it, don't let it rob you of happiness because of what your last name is. If you want to sneak out and go to a college party, call me, I'll drive and not utter a word to anyone."

I smile. "Uncle B said he has cameras all over the compound." He lulls his head to the side and shoots me an eye roll.

"Who do you think installed those cameras and setup the system?"

I gape at him. "Damn, that is some spy level shit."

He chuckles and shakes his head. "Not really, I watched a YouTube video and then upgraded the system so it couldn't be breached." We talk the rest of the way about lame shit really but I clamp my mouth closed when we pull into the gym carpark and I see my mom's car parked out front.

"What's she doing here?" I mutter aloud.

"No idea but I'm walking you in." I nod and slip out of the car. Uncle Luka walks by my side and keeps looking around as if he suspects someone is going to jump out at us. I've never seen him relaxed, he's always on edge and ready to strike. We enter the gym through the staff only door, finding all the lights on which is odd for this time of night. The gym closed three hours ago. We walked past the offices, then hit the main area, only for me to slam to a halt at the sight of my parents in the ring sparring. My jaw practically hits the floor, I've never seen them spar before. Dad always refuses, saying mom can whoop his ass without needing to be in a ring to do it.

Uncle Luka and I remain planted to the spot as we watch them. Mom moves like a snake, so quick, so sure of her every move. Dad is lethal, even at their ages they look good.

It's gross that my dad still sports a six pack and my mom has abs just as defined as my own. They begin to circle each other and I expect Mom to be the first to make a move but I'm proven wrong when Dad does this weird side step thing and then strikes out at my mom who ducks just in time to not get hit in the side of the head.

"Come on, baby, I'm just getting warmed up here!" Dad shouts through his laughter, earning a glare from my mom.

"Your pussy footwork won't save you."

"Oh, but you love when I play with that pussy."

Oh my God, eww!

"Yeah, I'm out!" Uncle Luka announces loud enough for them to hear. Mom and Dad both turn toward us, neither of them looking remorseful about me hearing that disgusting shit my dad just spewed! Uncle Luka taps me on the shoulder and wishes me luck before he vanishes out the way we came.

"Dest, I knew you would come here first." I scrunch my face in disgust and look away from my dad, utterly disgusted by what I just heard. "Are you blushing?"

I scoff. "No!" I snarl as I stomp across the gym and drop down on the bench seat by the ring.

"Don't be grossed out, you should be proud that your parents can still get down and dirty."

"Oh my God, eww, Dad!"

"Gage!" Mom and I both say at the same time, Dad just stands there with his arms resting on the ropes shaking with laughter. I huff and cross my arms over my chest.

"You both are nasty as fuck, you know that, right?" Dad

laughs louder while Mom uses my dad's body as a shield so she can laugh out of sight.

"Get changed and get your gloves, if we're doing this I'm not doing it bare knuckles." Dad's laughter dies off immediately at my mom's admission. I stare at her, thinking she is pulling a prank but the firm set of her jaw shows me she isn't bluffing. I leap to my feet, grinning and dash into the locker room to change into my spare clothes I leave here. I change in record time, then run back into the gym and gag at the sight of my parents making out in the middle of the ring.

"Stop that shit!" I shout. They break a part but not before I catch the lustful looks they shoot each other. "Jesus, why couldn't I have parents that hated touching each other?" I grumble as I climb into the ring ignoring their laughter. Dad comes to grab my hands, I hold them out for him to tape.

"No, she won't need it," Mom says stopping him. I shoot her a look over his shoulder.

"Why?" I ask.

"You won't need it, baby, this isn't about winning or losing." I frown, not understanding what she means, but I don't argue. Dad helps me get the gloves on but the tension in the room starts to shift and I don't like it.

"You both are acting weird, why?" I ask once Dad finishes gloving me up. Instead of answering me, he cups my face and places a tender kiss to the top of my head. When he pulls back the look of anguish in his eyes has me utterly confused. "Are you okay?"

He tries to smile to reassure me but it doesn't meet his eyes. "No matter what, we will always love you, Destiny."

I frown. "I know, I love both of you too." He nods and steps back, facing my mom they share a loaded look before Dad nods and then steps out of the ring.

"Don't make me regret agreeing to allow both my girls to fight each other... please." I look at each of them utterly perplexed. I can feel they are up to something but neither of them is giving up any information.

"Come on, baby girl," Mom says. I shake off the unease and move to the center. We touch gloves, then I jump back going on the defense. I know from years of training and watching that my mom is an attacker and the only way to beat her is to try to tire her out, then slip in some hits while she has her guard down.

Except she doesn't move, she stands there with her gloves raised and tears brimming in her eyes. I stand and drop my gloves to my sides. "Mom?" She shakes her head and tries to blink away the tears. I look over at my dad to see he looks just as devastated as she does, he nods once and then out of nowhere I'm sent stumbling to the side when Mom clocks me across the jaw. She may have pulled the punch slightly but it still hurts. I immediately throw up my guard and brace myself for her.

"I'm so sorry," she cries out before she comes at me. I'm stunned and fucking confused by what is going on that I don't even fight back for a minute. "Do it!" she screams at me. I suck in a deep breath, then duck and land a blow to her stomach and swivel out of reach when she tries to hit me again. I bounce on the balls of my feet, trying to get a read on her next move like Dad has taught me.

"Tell them!" is screamed from the other side of the ring. I spin around, forgetting all about the fight as I stare at Taylan standing at the edge of the ring behind my dad. Mom tackles me to the ground from behind. Instinct takes over and I buck my hips. Rolling, I get her off me and jump to my feet, she doesn't fuck around when she comes at me this time. Something inside her has snapped, her punches aren't pulled anymore, she's mad. "She's not going to stop until you break those fucking walls down and let them in!" Taylan's words hit me in the chest. I bite down on the inside of my cheek refusing to allow his words to distract me. I strike back, hitting Mom twice but she manages to get a good jab into my ribs that has me groaning.

"Let me help you!" she pleads as she continues to fight.

"You can't!" I scream, then trade rolls, forcing her to go on the defense as I attack. I pin her in the corner of the ring forcing her to put her guard up as I go for a quick jab.

"Please, let me in," she begs but I can't, if I do they'll know I'm a fraud and I'm weak. I can't let her see me like that, she raised me better than that. I know better. I lose all control and unleash every ounce of pent up rage inside me as I attack my mother. I know in my mind that she is my mom but all my eyes see is Koda standing before me.

"Destiny, stop!" Dad screams.

"I hate you! I want you to die!" I yell as I continue to hit him. "You fucking hurt me, you took everything from me." I hear him grunt and relish in the sound. "You destroyed the good in me, I'll show you I'm not weak!" I scream.

"You aren't weak, baby." The voice penetrates through the haze of my anger and I stop fighting. "You are so fucking brave. You are my little fighter and our champion." I blink my eyes a couple of times and the sight before me has me stumbling backward.

"Mom," I cry, her face is bruised and bloody—I did that. Horror cripples me as I stumble backward only to fall to my ass. She rushes forward and drops to her knees in front of me.

"You aren't broken, baby," she chokes out through her tears. She uses her teeth to help get the gloves off, then she's cupping my cheeks.

"Mom," I sob. "I'm so sorry," I cry out as tears trail down my cheeks. Dad appears out of thin air and is kneeling beside us looking distraught at the sight of us.

"No, you have nothing to be sorry about. We failed you—"

"No, Mom, you both did everything for me. I fucked up and he... he... I fought him. I didn't stop fighting, I swear, but he... arrgghhh," I cry out when the pain rips me apart. Both of them wrap their arms around me, holding me tight as I let all the emotions I have suppressed for years break free. My chest grows tight and burns from the pain. I force the words out past the lump in my throat, if I am to heal then I need to say out loud. "Koda Novikov raped me."

Chapter Twenty-Eight

Taylan

"Koda Novikov raped me." I slam my eyes closed and breathe through my nose. Pride swells inside me that she was strong enough to admit it out loud to them, but anger, bloodlust and pain also war for control. That son of a bitch hurt her and no amount of torture will ever change what he did.

"Fuuuucccckkkk!" Gage roars, the pain and heartache in that one word has me fighting back tears of my own. Gage's hold on both of them tightens. He buries his face in the crook of Destiny's neck. The three of them stay like that for over an hour. When Gage finally pulls back, his eyes are red and puffy. Not wanting him to think I was standing here judging them, I look away when he stands and helps both girls to their feet. "We're going to go home, sit down and talk this through. We're here for you whatever you need, baby girl. I swear to Christ almighty we will never think any less of you."

Destiny sobs and launches herself at Gage, wrapping her

trembling arms around his waist and burying her face in his chest. He cups the back of her head with one hand and grabs Anya with the other, pulling her in close enough he can rest his head against hers.

"You both are the most important people in my life," he mutters as he releases them and then turns to me. I still as his gaze bores into mine. A moment passes before he gives me a slight nod of thanks, then climbs out of the ring. I remain silent and wait as Destiny and her mom embrace in the ring. I feel like I should give them a moment, so I head outside. I lean against the side of my rental and look up at the night sky feeling utterly useless. I preyed on her like a lion, I made a fucking bet that I could bag her without realizing how disgusting that was until I got to know her.

"You ride alone, we need this time with her." I lull my head to the side and stare at Gage.

"Yeah, okay," I say as I push forward and turn to get in the car but his words have me pausing.

"How long have you known?" His tone is hard but I know his anger isn't directed at me, I do him the courtesy of meeting his gaze.

"A while. Consent is a huge thing for me, Gage. I swear on my honor that I never took advantage of your daughter. No matter what those pictures showed you, I never forced her, not a single fucking time." He eyes me warily for a moment before nodding and stepping back.

"You get to be there but you stay silent, you are only here because my wife agreed to your terms."

"I understand," I say firmly before climbing into my car,

it fucking kills me that I can't be the one to hold her right now but I know she needs this. I know I have no right to feel the way I do after I just let her walk out of that hotel room and did nothing to stop her, but never again.

The fucking cock sucking bitches manning the gate of the Murdoch compound wouldn't let me enter, so I've had no choice but to wait out on the fucking road for Gage to get here. The second I see his headlights, I pull up behind and follow him through the gates, but I roll my window down and shoot that cock sucker the bird as I drive past.

When he pulls into the driveway of his house, I park mine at the curb and kill the engine, suddenly feeling nervous. I climb out of my car, pull my hoodie on, then stuff my hands in the pocket and make my way up the drive. Gage glares at me before opening the back door. Anya steps out, followed by Destiny who won't even look at me.

I deserve the cold shoulder but fuck that shit hurts.

Gage leads her inside and I follow behind slowly, before I can make it through the door, Anya stops me. She looks shattered and torn apart. Without overthinking it, I pull her to me and hug her, she instantly melts into me and returns my embrace.

"Thank you for helping us," she says low enough for only me to hear, then she pulls back.

I shoot her a kind smile as I stuff my hands back in the pocket. "There is no thanks needed, Anya, truly." She nods, then gestures for me to head inside before her. Their home is spacious and has this real homey feeling to it. I smile at the sight of all the photos of Destiny and her cousins that adorn the walls. She looks really happy in a lot of them but that smile slowly fades when you reach the ones of her in college and now her parents know why. Anya leads me into the living room where Gage and Destiny are sitting on one of the sofa's.

I claim the single seat while Anya takes the vacant space next to her daughter. You could cut the tension in the air with a knife. I feel out of place and awkward but I'm trying to show her without words that I'm here and I want this!

"How are you feeling?" Anya asks her quietly.

Destiny twiddles her fingers in her lap and keeps her eyes downcast. "Like a fraud."

"Why the hell would you feel like that?" Gage snaps. Anya shoots him a look telling him to rein it the fuck in.

When she still doesn't answer he sighs and slouches back looking defeated. I know I'm supposed to remain silent but fuck him and his rules. I stand ignoring his look of warning and drop to my knees in front of Destiny. Anya stands and moves to sit beside Gage, giving us some space. She still won't meet my gaze so I reach out and grip her chin, forcing her to look at me. Those gray-blues eyes look haunted, I'd do anything to never see that look in them ever again.

"You aren't a fraud. You coped the only way you knew how, they don't see you as anything less." A soft whimper escapes her, I see Gage trying to stand out of the corner of my eye but Anya stops him with a hand to his chest.

"I let them down," she says quietly but they hear. Gage growls and Anya sniffs.

"No. You could never do anything for them to be disappointed in you. Nothing that happened to you is your fault, baby, you didn't ask for him to..." I take a deep breath and rein in my own anger before continuing. "You didn't ask for that cunt to do what he did. He took what didn't belong to him and for that, he will fucking suffer. I swear it." I reach up and swipe away her tears with my thumbs.

"I want my mom," she chokes out. Within a split second, Anya is at her side and pulls her into her embrace where she breaks down. "I'm so sorry, Mom."

"No, I'm sorry I never saw the pain in your eyes until now." Both of them are bawling and it pains me to see it.

"I never wanted you to be disappointed in me." Anya pushes her back and cups her face between her hands.

"Destiny Laurel Murdoch, there is nothing and I mean *nothing* in this fucking world that could make me see you differently. You are my miracle, my greatest gift. Never ever forget that, baby girl." Sobs wrack my girl's body and I clench my fists, forcing myself not to haul her away from her mother.

"Move," Gage snaps a second before shoving me out of the way and pulling both girls into his arms. I stand here and stare at them in awe. What I wouldn't have given to have parents like hers growing up, maybe I would have turned out differently if I didn't have a junkie for a mother and a rapist for a stepfather.

I reclaim the chair I had just vacated and sit silently as

Destiny tells them everything. I may have already heard the story before but it doesn't make it any easier to stomach. Gage looks murderous, like he is hanging onto his sanity by a thread. I can already tell he won't be able to transport that cunt without killing him. Anya looks like she wants to maim someone but I see the blame in her eyes as well, she thinks what happened to her baby is her fault.

"I never should have kept that fucking formula," she forces out through clenched teeth.

"No, Mom. None of this is on you, I had... stars in my eyes where Koda was concerned. He said and did all the right things. I fell into his trap," Destiny says bitterly.

"The blame isn't on either of you. I should have left this life behind the second I married your mother. I thought we were invincible and untouchable," Gage admits.

Fuck this!

"None of this is any of your faults." All three of them snap their gazes toward me. "You cannot control the actions of others. The trauma she suffered through doesn't make her a victim, it makes her a fucking warrior who came out the other side stronger. Both of you raised her to be the fighter she is and it's because of your teachings why she was able to survive such a traumatic event on her own."

"Shut up," Gage snaps. I roll my eyes and slouch back in my seat but Destiny keeps her eyes glued to mine.

"I'm kind of tired." Gage and Anya both climb to their feet, muttering about how they will both sleep on her floor or offer her to sleep between them but she shakes her head ignoring them as she asks me. "You planning on running again?"

"No," I answer without hesitation, she looks skeptical and I don't blame her.

"Somehow I don't believe you."

"And I don't blame you for doubting me, Slayer, but I'm here, aren't I?" She narrows her eyes and studies me for a moment before turning to her parents and hugging them both again and telling them how she loves them before making her way toward the stairs. I deflate.

"You coming?" I perk up at her invitation and immediately jump to my feet, ready to follow her but Gage blocks my path, glaring down his nose at me.

"I kept my end of the deal, honor yours."

I return his glare with a hardened look of my own. "I'm no bitch. I'll be there and ready to take care of business." He nods once before I step around him and follow his daughter up the stairs. I feel like a naughty teenager sneaking into his girlfriend's room instead of a thirty-three-year-old man who owns his own fucking home and doesn't need to sneak in anywhere. Her room is the last one at the end of the hall. I follow her in and close the door quietly behind us. My eyes widen at the color scheme of her room.

Pink.

Clearly her parents didn't change a single thing in here when she moved out, it's like time was frozen in this place and she's still a sixteen-year-old kid.

"I'm gonna take a shower," she mutters as she pushes a door open on the left hand side of her room. She doesn't close it all the way and a part of me is wondering if that's an invitation to join. I push that thought away and scold myself, seeing me fucking his daughter in photos is one thing but hearing her scream my name in *his* house is asking for him to murder me.

Instead of following after her like I want to, I distract myself by looking around her room. She has photos on her desk. I know I shouldn't breach her privacy but fuck me, it's hard not to when I spot a picture of her in her swimsuit on the top. She looks stunning in that all white two-piece bathing suit. I flip to the next one and feel a twinge of sadness for my friend, Chaos and Havoc stand there with a beer in each hand and an arm around each other as they smile at the camera. I feel for him, losing a piece of your soul must be fucking heartbreaking. When we thought we lost Waverly it nearly destroyed our family.

When I hear the shower shut off, I drop the pictures and claim a seat at the end of her bed. I am man enough to admit that my palms are sweating and my heart is racing as nerves spur to life inside me. My breathing grows choppy the longer she takes to come out. When that bathroom door finally opens, I stop breathing for a second. I slowly turn to face her and have to bite back the groan that wants to rip free at the sight of her in nothing but a towel. Her long blonde hair is wet and dripping, she is a wet fucking dream.

"I'm all talked out, Taylan."

I swallow and nod. "Okay," I say dejectedly and slowly stand.

She frowns. "Are you leaving?" I hear the pain in her

voice but I can also hear the undertones of anger there as well.

"I don't want to," I answer honestly. "But, I also don't want you to feel pressured—"

"I don't feel pressured."

"Then tell me what you want, Slayer. I'm right here."

She takes a deep breath and peers up at me through her lashes. "Stay." One word, that's all it takes before I'm pulling my hoodie and shirt off in one swift motion, then pushing my pants down my legs, leaving me in my boxers. Her eyes drink in the sight of my near nakedness. She nibbles on her bottom lip and fuck me, the sight has my cock growing hard at the thought of sinking into her tight wet pussy but tonight isn't about that. I snatch my shirt off the floor and toss it to her. She catches it, only to shoot me a frown.

"Keep making fuck me eyes while you're standing in a towel and I'll say fuck it to respecting your father's house and fuck you." A wicked gleam enters her eyes and I groan. "Slayer!" I scold her, earning an eye roll and huff from her. The dirty rotten little shit makes a show of dropping the towel, exposing all of her naked glory before slowly pulling my shirt on. "I swear to God you are going to pay for that move."

"Making more promises you can't keep?"

"Oh, baby, you and I both know I can have your fingertips gripping those sheets like it's a lifeline." Before the conversation can continue a knock sounds at her door, I groan internally. This is going to look real fucking good, me standing in my boxers and her in my shirt. Before I can even move to grab my pants the door opens to reveal her mother. I snatch the cover off her bed and wrap it around my waist, doing my best to hide my raging hard on! I sigh in relief at the sight of her and not Gage.

Fuck!

The second Anya takes a step to the side, Gage is right there with a dark look on his face, my hackles raise immediately.

"We have a problem," he grits out, his tone leaves no room for argument. I snatch my pants off the floor and turn my back to them as I drop the comforter and pull them on. Before leaving to follow Gage, I step in front of Destiny and cup her face between my hands. She looks apprehensive and I can't blame her.

"I'm not running, I promise."

"Don't make promises you can't keep, Taylan," she whispers.

I place a quick chaste kiss to her lips, ignoring her father's growl. "This is one I'm going to keep, I swear it." I release her, step past Anya and follow Gage downstairs. When we make it to the living room I cringe at the sight of all his brothers and Vincent.

Definitely should have stolen my shirt back.

They all take in the sight of me shirtless with my jeans still unbuttoned and they don't look impressed by the sight at all, but there isn't much I can fucking do about that now. I try to gauge why they would all be here at this hour but their faces give nothing away except for the disdain at the sight of me half-dressed and coming from their nieces room.

"What's going on?" I ask.

"Koda isn't going to Ireland." I inhale sharply at Vincent's reply.

"Why?" I press.

"It appears the mother of his child has had a change of heart regarding his punishment and we can't risk her setting him free." I stare at Bishop in shock, thinking I must have heard him wrong.

"I won't chance that cock sucker getting free after what he did to my..." Gage clamps his mouth closed, unable to finish his sentence. Fuck this. I rip my phone out of my pocket and hit dial on Kimber's number not caring about the time difference, she answers on the fourth ring.

"Taylan?" she says when she answers.

"Don't you fucking Taylan me!" I roar.

"Let me explain," she pleads.

"Explain what?" I snap, not caring that everyone in here is listening to my one sided conversation, with how loud I am yelling I have no doubt Anya and Destiny would be able to hear me. "He is going to fucking suffer and I don't give a shit if he is Lila's father. That cunt is on borrowed time for what he did!"

"I'm not doing this for me!" she defends.

"Your kid is better off without him!" I snarl. "Do you really want a rapist to be part of your kid's life, Kimber?"

"No, but—"

"No, buts! I swear on my brotherhood with Knox and Xander, if you try to rise against the Murdochs to free him it won't be the Re Della Strada coming for you, it will be *me!*"

"Lila loves him!" she screams into the phone.

I drop my voice low so she can hear every word clearly as I speak. "I helped you get your kid back," I say my tone dripping with malice. "You try anything, Kimber, and I will take her from you, she won't just be fatherless, she will be motherless as well."

"You don't mean that." Her tone is watery.

"My love for Wave won't keep you safe from me. Xander loves Waverly but make no fucking mistake, he won't help you hide and will lead me straight to you. Fuck around and find out, Kimber, I dare you!"

"Fuck you. I never wanted him to live but my daughter does. I'm sorry he hurt Destiny but he hurt me too and I am prepared to let that shit go for the sake of my child. I don't want him to be free, all I am asking is for him to rot in a cell so when she wants to see him he isn't beaten and bloody which will scare her."

"I thought you were different, Kimmy, I really did, but you are just the same as my mother. You keep making excuses for the cunt that hurt you and I promise you that you will lose the respect of everyone you love, even your daughter won't forgive you. Tell the kid the fucking truth, that her father is a rapist and see how much she misses him then!" I snarl before ending the call. I take a minute to try to calm myself before slowly lifting my gaze back to the guys who all stand there staring at me. I run my gaze over each of them before settling on Gage. "You have my word that I will put a bullet between her eyes before she can even think about freeing that cunt."

"She tries to come anywhere near my family again and I will slit her fucking throat in front of her daughter, mark my words on that," he answers. I nod in agreement.

"How did you find out what she was planning?" I ask the group.

"Knox Bronson got a tip from his sister's man," Bishop says.

"Xander," I mutter.

"Your boys are loyal to you and I respect that, but he betrayed his Don, Waverly could have him killed," King adds.

I shake my head. "Wave would have been the one to tell Xan to give Knox the heads up, knowing he would tell you," I admit.

"Why wouldn't he just call you?" Knight pushes.

I smile. "He knew something like this would happen and what my reaction would have been. He was giving me a chance to prove myself loyal to Destiny in front of all of you." I'm going to beat the shit out of Knox for this but I am also grateful for him for doing this. The looks on all their faces show a tiny amount of respect for what I just did. "He may not be going to Ireland but I want him to suffer just the same, but not here."

"You don't make the call, we do!" Gage snaps.

I shake my head at the idiot. "And how is your daughter supposed to feel fucking safe here when the guy who fucking hurt her is right fucking there?" I roar.

Chapter Twenty-Nine

Destiny

I take a shuddering breath, expecting to feel shame at Taylan's declaration but it doesn't come. Mom and I are standing at the top of the stairs eavesdropping. She clutches my hand in hers and gives it a reassuring squeeze. I can already tell Taylan is winning her over but my dad clearly hates him.

"She isn't your concern! She is my daughter and I decide what is right for her." I flinch, Dad is being an overprotective asshole and I hate that he is talking about me like I am a child.

"She may be your child but she isn't a *child*! She is a grown fucking woman and can make her own choices, stop treating her like she is made of fucking glass!" My heart swells hearing Taylan defend me. I know this is a hard position for him to be in since Kimber was one of his close friends and I hate to admit it, but I can understand why she wants him alive. I hate that I can empathize with her, but her child is innocent and only knows the good side of her father, not the monster he truly is.

"Get the fuck out of my house!" Dad roars. I snap my gaze to my mother with wide eyes, pleading for her to stop him.

"He needs to fight for you, baby, let him," she whispers. I frown but remain silent, needing to hear Taylan's answer. If he walks out, I won't let him back in again, he promised me he would stay and I need him to prove to me that he meant it.

"Not without *her*." I close my eyes and smile, he's fighting for me.

"You are alone here, boy, my brother has told you to leave and unless you want to be thrown out, do as he says," Uncle B adds. Before they can push him out, I tear away from my mom and race down the stairs, all their heads turning toward me when I rush into the living room. I don't stop until I'm standing in front of Taylan. He tries to grab my waist and shift me out of the way, but I elbow him in the ribs earning a grunt and a growl from him.

"No one is going to touch him." I force strength into my tone as I look at each of my uncles and then settle on my father. "If he's leaving, then so am I."

Dad's face falls, Mom comes to stand beside him and places a hand on his back in silent support. His mouth opens but no words come out, a frown slowly mars his face when my mom begins to speak.

"No one is making anyone leave." My uncles all drop

their gazes to the floor. "Here is how this is going to work. Destiny is going to take a few days to decide what *she* would like to happen with that cunt." I bite back my smile, my mom is a badass who can bring a room of men to their knees with just her words. "If any of you try to sway her or go against her wishes, I will call each of your wives." All five of my uncles snap their gazes to my mom in a panic.

"That's not fair!"

"Snitch!"

"They have nothing to do with this."

"I'm the Don!"

"You're a traitor!" All five of them shout. Mom walks to the center of the room with her back to me and Taylan while staring the others down.

"You all seem to think it's okay for you all to butt your noses into my family's business, so it seems only fair that I get the rest of the family involved. Want to try me and find out how far I am willing to go?" No one utters a single word. Mom slowly turns to my dad, who looks green and sheepish knowing he's about to get his ass handed to him. "If that boy leaves and takes my daughter with him, I will fucking destroy you, Gage Murdoch. Am I crystal fucking clear?" Dad cringes but nods. "Use your fucking words!"

Dad snaps his head up and shoots Taylan a glare before looking at my mom. "Yes, you are clear. Now, can we be excused so I can plan that *boy's* murder well enough that no one suspects it was me?" Taylan snorts out a laugh behind me and quickly coughs to cover it, while my father and uncles all shoot him death glares.

"No. It's late and you need to get to bed, and the rest of you need to get the fuck out of my house and home to your wives." My uncles all grumble their agreement and shoot my dad a glare.

"Oh, like any of you spineless fucks would stand up to your own wives!" Dad defends himself as my uncles file out of the room, muttering about how much of a bitch he is. Once the front door clicks shut, Mom turns to me and Tay, then smiles.

"You both must be exhausted—"

"No, not really, we don't mind staying," Taylan says with humor clear in his tone. Mom shoots him a disapproving look.

"Go to bed, Taylan, before I change my mind and let my husband and brother-in-laws at you." Before his mouth can get us into more trouble, I grab his hand and lead him from the room so my dad can get yelled at in private. I kind of feel bad for him, I've been on the receiving end of Mom's verbal lashings a couple of times and they never end well.

Once we get inside my room, I lock the door and head straight for the bed, I am mentally and emotionally spent and need to sleep for a week. Taylan rids himself of his jeans, then switches the light off and climbs in beside me. The instant he wraps his arms around me and pulls me into his chest, I sigh in contentment. His warmth seeps into my tired bones and I relish the feeling of having him here with me, it still kind of feels surreal that he is really here.

"Never leave your family for me," he says breaking the quiet moment. I remain silent, not sure how to answer that.

"Your parents and extended family love you so much, don't ever think you are alone, Slayer, because they all have your back. They proved it tonight."

I smile against his chest, I know they love me and I am so grateful for how close my family is but they also need to learn boundaries. No one cared when the boys started dating but the minute Chanel started dating Kacey, Uncle Vin lost it. Royal and Uncle B both wanted to wipe out the Greeks when London started dating Artemis. Even Uncle Rook tried to kill Unique's boyfriend and staged it so it looked like a car accident.

"Then they better not make me choose because it would break my heart to say goodbye to them," I mutter sleepily.

"Slayer?"

"Hmmm?"

"Don't break my heart."

"You have to give it to me first before I can break it," I say before sleep begins to pull me under.

"I already did." I swear I hear him say before I sink into deep oblivion.

Waking up the next morning, being cocooned in Taylan's arms feels fucking amazing, I missed this! Last night was the first night I actually slept peacefully in weeks, no nightmares to wake me and my parents didn't barge into my room. With him beside me I feel safe. I slowly untangle myself from him and slip out of bed so I don't wake him. I creep into the bathroom and pee, then brush my teeth before I quietly creep into my bedroom but stop at the sight of him laying there, fuck he looks so sexy. If my parents weren't home, I would wake him by sucking his cock.

I force those thoughts out of my mind as I exit and make my way downstairs to get some much needed caffeine. The moment I hit the landing, my mouth waters when the smell of bacon hits my senses. I practically run into the kitchen and grin at the sight of my dad cooking breakfast.

"I'm starving!" I say as I make my way to the coffee maker to get my fix.

"That's nice." I spin around and balk at my dad.

"What?" He looks back at me over his shoulder and smirks.

"Get that useless weasel to cook your food." My jaw unhinges.

"You always cook me breakfast!" I snap.

"Nope, not today. This is for me and your mother." I stare at him in utter disbelief. "You're a dirty little traitor and left me alone with her and her wrath last night, so I'm punishing you. Cereal's in the cupboard, help yourself." I stand here utterly stunned as I watch him plate the food, then carry them out back where Mom sits at the table with her laptop in front of her.

"Oh, it's on!" I growl into the empty kitchen as I take a sip of my liquid gold.

"What's on?" I nearly jump out of my skin at the sound of Taylan's voice. I spin around and glare at him but it drops off my face the moment I take in the sight of him shirtless and sporting the cutest bed hair I have ever seen. "Stop looking at me like that!" he chastises but it lacks heat. I place my cup on the counter and close the space between us, laying my hands flat against his bare chest. His eyes darken in warning but he doesn't push me away. "Slayer," he warns.

I bat my lashes up at him as I slowly snake my arms around his neck. His hands drop to my hips, pulling me flush against him. "No good morning kiss?" I taunt. He growls low in his chest, then bends down and captures my lips in a kiss that robs me of air and has my toes curling. I brush my tongue against his and moan, then lift up onto my tiptoes, trying to deepen it but the sound of a smashing glass has us jumping apart and turning toward the back door. Dad stands there with his fists clenched at his sides and eyes spitting hate at Tay.

"One hour, be ready to leave." A whoosh of air escapes Taylan as he nods.

"I'll be there," Tay answers.

"Be where?" I ask, both of them keep glaring at each other as Taylan answers me.

"I have to do something with your dad, I'll be back after." Something is off, I can hear it in his voice.

"Will you?" Dad taunts.

Taylan throws his arm over my shoulders, pulls me into his side and places a kiss to the top of my head before answering. "Oh, definitely." Dad looks like he wants to murder Tay, something is brewing between them and I hate not knowing what it is. If they think for a fucking second I'm staying behind in an hour's time, they are dead fucking wrong!

After Taylan kissed me goodbye and followed my dad out of the house, I waited ten minutes before I hijacked my mom's car and brought up the tracker on my dad's car. I frown at the sight. He's at the gym? I start the engine but before I can pull out of the garage, the passenger door opens followed by both the back doors. Mom, Aunt Kiara, Aunt Ally and Aunt Koby all slip inside. I stare at each of them with wide eyes.

"What are you doing?" I ask them, each of them wear disapproving looks but it's Aunt Kiara who answers.

"Bishop pissed Royal off this morning, so my son called me to give us the heads up that those six idiots plan to beat the shit out of your boyfriend." I gape at my aunt.

"Koby and Clare are parked out front in Rook's car, they'll follow us," Aunt Carlina says.

"Come on! We don't have all day, I need to beat my husband's ass, then get back to work," Aunt Ally shouts. I shake my head so I can focus as I put the car in drive. I am so fucking angry at my dad and uncles that I'm white knuckling the steering wheel.

"Is it wrong that I'm excited to fight Bishop?" Aunt Kiara asks, sounding giddy.

Aunt Carlina snorts. "All my brothers are pussies when it comes to their wives, ten bucks says they all turn white as a ghost the moment they see your faces."

"Twenty says Vincent blames the others for making him join in," Mom says, getting in on the action.

"I got fifty on Knight dropping to his knees in front of Koby so she won't hold out on him," Aunt Kiara says, waving a fifty dollar bill in the air.

"Fuck no, I got a hundred on Gage shitting himself at the sight of Anya *and* Destiny catching him out lying," Aunt Carlina shouts above the others.

"I got five hundred on all of them pissing their pants when they realize I will never speak to any of them again for doing this," I say. The car falls silent at my declaration, the mood shifts from joking to tense. I can't believe my dad and uncles would do something like this and Taylan isn't exempt either, he should have told me! All at once my aunts and mom begin shouting about how much each of them are betting on me making my dad cry and how long it will take for Taylan to grovel his way back into my good graces. I roll my eyes and ignore them, even when mom calls Aunt Koby through the Bluetooth system in her car and my other two aunts get in on the bets.

They are children, all of them!

I've barely put the car in park outside the gym before I'm jumping out and rushing inside, those assholes even closed the gym for the day so they wouldn't be interrupted. I take the staff entrance and run past the offices, my mom and aunts hot on my heels. The instant we break into the gym area my heart drops. Taylan stands in the middle of the ring panting, bleeding and covered in sweat. My uncles and dad all surround him, each of them are shirtless and none of them are wearing gloves, except for Taylan. They wanted to make sure that they hurt him. My breath lodges in my throat when Uncle King and Uncle Knight move in tandem toward Taylan, he turns sideways to keep them both in his sights but it's no use, it's two on one and all of my family are skilled fighters.

The instant my uncles descend on him landing punishing blow after blow, I snap. I race forward toward the ring and at the last second I jump and slide under the bottom rope, the momentum propelling me forward until I am in the middle. I leap to my feet and shove Taylan from behind, my eyes widen when I see Uncle King's fist coming at me, the other guys begin yelling but it's too late. I brace myself for impact but at the last second I'm tackled to the mat and land with a grunt.

"What the fuck were you thinking?" Taylan yells right in my face. I blink up at him in surprise.

"Me?" I yell. "What the fuck were you thinking agreeing to this bullshit?" I scream. Taylan is shoved off me, then my dad is pulling me to my feet. I shove him away from me, scowl at him, then turn to the rest of them, pinning each of them with a scathing look. "You all fucking disappoint me." I look to Taylan next who looks pissed off at seeing me here. "You don't need to prove anything to any of them, my opinion is the only one that should fucking matter." Taylan at least has the decency to look sheepish and drops his gaze to the floor.

"What are you doing here?" Gage barks. I slowly turn to face him and scoff.

"You're fired as my stand-in trainer and I'm moving out."

Chapter Thirty

Taylan

I stand here feeling like a real piece of shit as she climbs out of the ring and stalks out of here, ignoring her aunts and mom as she brushes past them. The second she disappears out the door her aunts and mom all focus their eyes on me.

"You gonna go after her or are you more worried about what those idiots think of you?" Koby snarls. I spy Knight out of the corner of my eye, cringing. I nod once before tearing the gloves off and dropping them to the ground. I flinch in pain when I bend and slip out between the ropes. I jog toward the exit but Anya stops me in my tracks when she cuts in front of me. The angry look in her eyes has me feeling like a scolded child.

"The next time you think about doing something as fucking stupid as this, remember there is only one person you are going to hurt. Make this fucking right with her fast, she's been through enough."

"You have my word." She scoffs and waves me off. I run out of the gym, praying I'm not too late to catch her. When I spot her leaning against her mother's car, I sigh in relief. At the sound of my approach she stiffens and crosses her arms over her chest, then hardens her features. I stand in front of her, keeping a foot of space between us.

"I don't want to talk to you," she grits out.

"Good, because I have a few things I need to say and you need to hear them." Her eyes shoot me an icy glare but I won't be swayed. "What you saw in there was me taking the punishment for my mistake."

Her jaw locks. "*I'm* a mistake?"

"No. The mistake was me giving my word to your father and agreeing to keep my good for nothing hands off his little girl and then breaking my word. I knew what I would face when I came back here. He made it clear that the only way he would let me back into your life without facing the wrath of your family was to take a beating for breaking my word. Getting my ass handed to me means nothing if it means I get *you* at the end of it."

She searches my eyes trying to find any sign of deceit. "You did all of that for *me*?"

I close the space between us, resting my hands on the roof of the car, caging her in. "Yes. You may be pissed off about that but I couldn't be a bitch about it. Your father needs to know the lengths I am willing to go to for you. I will take that beating every fucking week if it means I still get to come home to you at the end of every day." Her eyes soften.

"You don't have to do that, you have me, Taylan! I am right here, you just need to choose me too and I promise I will fight for us. I won't let you lose who you are for me." She reaches up and cups my face between her hands imploring me to believe her and I do.

"I never thought I would find an undercover angel who would make me change everything in my life, you mended my heart, restored my faith and made me want to change your last name." Her eyes widen at the last part and her mouth parts in a gasp. "You will be Destiny Carter it's not an if, it's a *when*."

"Do you really mean that?" she whispers as tears gather in her eyes.

"I do," I say with a grin. "I have a lot of making up to do and I know that, but just don't ever give up on me, baby. This is all new to me. I've never wanted to try before but I want to do this for *us*. I won't ever walk away from you again, I promise."

She smirks. "Don't make promises you can't keep, Tay Tay." I smile down at her and rest my forehead against hers.

"I would punish you for that comment, but making you scream in your father's house doesn't seem like a good way to get into his good books."

She presses in and ghosts her lips over mine. "Well, aren't you lucky I got the keys to my new place yesterday." My eyes burn with need and my cock presses painfully against my shorts.

"Don't tease me, Slayer," I growl.

"Take me home and fuck me on every available surface, I need to feel you and taste *us*."

The second we burst through the front door, I grab her and lift. She wraps her arms and legs around me. I slam into the wall, loving how she moans into my mouth, she likes it when I get rough. I grind my erection against her, she throws her head back and whimpers.

"Tease me later, I need you inside me now!" Not wanting to release her, I use my hips to keep her in place and reach between us. I rip a hole in the center of her tights, she gasps but I know she fucking loves me being a caveman. I free my cock and push her panties to the side as I line up with her entrance.

"Want me to make love to you?" I tease, her eyes narrow.

"Stop fucking playing around—Fuck!" she screams out when I slam inside her, cutting off her reply. Jesus Christ, this is what home feels like. Her pussy fits my dick perfectly. She scrapes her nails down my bare back when I start to thrust inside her. "Fuck, harder," she begs.

I draw almost all of the way out before slamming inside her again. "Show me my tits, baby." She rushes to yank her top off but I'm too impatient to wait for her to remove her bra. I yank the cup down with my teeth and suck her nipple into my mouth.

"Ah, fuck, yes!" She starts bouncing up and down, meeting me thrust for thrust. I release her nipple with a wet pop and pull out of her, ignoring the glare she shoots me. I lay on my back on the hardwood floor.

"Ride me." She rids herself of her torn pants then peels her panties down her legs and holds them in her closed fist as she climbs on top of me. She leans forward and places a kiss on my lips before sitting back.

"Open your mouth," I obey her order and groan when she shoves her wet panties into my mouth. "Now you get to taste me while I fuck you." My eyes blaze, my cock is aching to be back inside her. She shifts and grips my shaft, lining it up with her entrance, then slowly sinks down, pulling a moan from the both of us. "I need to come so fucking bad."

"Hmmm," I say in agreement. She adjusts herself and squats on top of me, resting her hands flat on my chest. Our eyes lock and then she begins bouncing up and down on my dick like a pro bull rider. Fuck, she feels so fucking good, the sound of skin on skin sounds out around the room, adding fuel to the burning desire between us. Her moans turn from controlled to strangled as she tries to silence herself. I grip her waist in my hands and hold her still as I thrust up inside her.

"Fuck, yes!" she screams. "Don't fucking stop, please, don't stop," she begs, her wish is mine to come true so I keep going. My balls begin to tighten, I'm so fucking close but I'm not coming without her. I need to taste her come mixed with my own as I suck it out of that perfect cunt. "Taylan!" she screams as she clamps down on my cock, forcing my orgasm to rip through me. I bite down on her panties and growl as jets of my cum shoot inside her. Tremors wrack her body but she knows what I need now. She plucks the panties from my mouth, then moves so she is kneeling above my face. I grip her ass and pull her down onto my waiting tongue. "Oh fuck, yes. Suck that cum out of my pussy then spit in my mouth."

I do as she says but I'm greedy and swallow some of it, loving the taste of our releases mixed together. She shuffles back enough so I can sit up. Gripping the back of her neck, I pull her forward. She opens her mouth greedily, I spit into her mouth and love the way her eyes turn hazy as she tastes us.

"Hmmm. We taste so fucking good together," she praises after she swallows. I press a kiss to her lips, then pull back so I can stare into her eyes as I utter the three words I have never said to any woman before in my life.

"I love you, Slayer."

She gasps, her eyes fills with tears but she quickly blinks them back. "I love you, too," she whispers before kissing me. I groan when she grinds down on my sensitive cock. "Now, fuck me again and tell me you love me as you come."

Jesus Christ, God really did make her just for me!

We spend the rest of the day fucking on every single surface of this new apartment and still we can't seem to keep our hands off each other. I have this insatiable hunger for her that never seems to lessen. I think I finally understand how Knox and Xan feel now. She is my sole focus and all I can think about, all I need. We sit here in the large tub in her ensuite with her between my legs and resting back against me with her eyes closed.

She is so fucking beautiful.

"I can feel you staring at me," she grumbles sleepily. I smile and kiss her forehead.

"Well, it's my right as your boyfriend to stare at you whenever I want." She pops her eyes open and grins at me.

"Boyfriend, huh?"

I playfully glare at her. "Damn fucking right, you're my woman and that means I get to shoot any fucker who looks at you." She snorts out a laugh.

"Okay, caveman."

"That's right, *me Tarzan, you Jane.*" She bursts out laughing and I can't help but join her.

"Don't ever do that again!" she says between fits of laughter. The sound of her phone ringing has our laughter dying off, it's been ringing nonstop for hours. She sighs in my hold and closes her eyes, we both know who keeps calling and she can't avoid him forever.

"Slayer—"

"If I answer that call it will shatter the bubble we are in and I'll have to face reality. I don't want to face it." I can read between the lines. She isn't just referring to the fight today, she means if she speaks to her dad she will have to worry about what to do with Koda.

"What if we hopped on a flight tonight and went back to Canada? My house is secluded and only my brothers and the girls know where it is?" She sits forward and turns around, straddling my lap. Water sloshes over the sides but she doesn't seem to care or notice.

"I never considered what would happen next."

I frown up at her. "What?"

"Your life is in Canada, mine is tied here for another three months until after the fight but I want to go back to school and then there are my parents and—"

"Stop!" She clamps her mouth closed and inhales a deep breath through her nose. "Nothing has to be decided right now, we can take it slowly and work out what is best for us." I say that shit aloud but the truth is, my life is back in Canada and I can't keep blowing off my job as Knox's underboss. But, the longer I stare into those gray-blue eyes I know without a doubt, I would give it all up for her and make a life here in the States if that meant keeping her happy.

"D-do you even want to move in with me?" Her cheeks redden and I find the sight so fucking cute I can't help but smile.

"I told you, I'm not running. I'm in this for the long run, baby."

"What... what if I wanted to try living in Canada?" My eyes widen in surprise.

"Are you serious?"

She shrugs. "I mean, I can do school online and my mom and dad can visit whenever they want, right?"

I nod eagerly. "Of course they can."

"Can you wait three months?"

"I can wait a lifetime." She beams down at me. "If you need me to, I will train you for three months and work from here until your fight."

"Really?"

I nod. "Yeah, Knox won't mind and Xan will help him if

he needs it." She opens her mouth but snaps it closed when her phone rings again.

All traces of excitement vanish from her face. "Will you come with me?" I inhale sharply, knowing what she is asking and hating that she even wants to do this but I won't let her go alone, I'll stand by her side the entire time.

"Of course I will."

Chapter Thirty-One

Destiny

Taylan pulls his car to a stop in front my mom and dad's house. When he kills the engine, I make no move to get out, feeling suddenly unsure about my decision. He reaches across and grabs my hand, giving it a squeeze to draw my attention to him. His eyes shine with love and seeing that look on him has butterflies taking flight inside my belly.

"I got you, baby." His words have me exhaling and nodding.

"I need you beside me the entire time, I need to know he can't get to me. With you there, I know it won't happen." I can see the guilt churning inside him. Twice now he has had no choice but watch me be hurt at the hands of the prisoner currently sitting in my family's bunker. I know it pains him to think back to those times but none of it was his fault, without him there with me I don't know if I would have made it out with my mind still intact,

"I promise, I won't let you go," he says, then leans over and presses a kiss to my lips that has me relaxing slightly until knuckles rap on the window behind me. We break apart, sighing. "Come on, he's already glaring at me," he mutters as he climbs out of the car. I fight back my laughter as I open my own door but before I climb out, I grab Taylan's gun from the console and stash it inside the pocket of the hoodie I wear, then climb out, only to be met by my dad standing there with his hands stuffed in his pockets. He runs his gaze over me and frowns. I'm in one of Taylan's shirts with his hoodie on and a pair of his sweats. I don't have any clothes at my place so this was the best option since he had a bag in his car.

"If he makes you happy then... I won't hurt him." Taylan scoffs but dad doesn't take his focus off me. "I just want you to be happy and safe. I guess after learning what I did yesterday, I took that anger out on him. I never want to be the cause of your pain but I can see now that I was and I'm sorry, Champ, I mean it." I wrap my arms around his waist and press my cheek against his chest, Dad sighs and returns my embrace.

"I love you, Dad."

"Love you too, baby girl. Whatever you need, we are here. I know it's gonna be hard to hear but with your mother it was different helping her heal." I pull back and stare up at him.

"How?"

"I could hold her while she had bad days. Sometimes she would go months without thinking about it but when she did, I was there to hold her and tell her how perfect she is and remind her that she is the strongest woman I know." My heart melts inside my chest hearing how my dad helped my mom overcome the horror she lived through. I have always envied their love, they are the perfect pair.

"You can still do that for me, you know." He smiles sadly and shakes his head, then shoots a look at Taylan over the roof of the car before looking back at me.

"I would love to be that rock for you, baby girl, but unfortunately I think you went and found someone of your own to remind you of all those things. It pains me to admit it but I think he is the one you need to remind you of how truly fucking amazing you are, hearing that stuff from your old man wouldn't be the same." Love and warmth spread through me at my dad's acceptance of my relationship with Taylan. I know it's going to be hard for him to get used to the fact that I have a boyfriend—it feels so weird saying that— and he isn't going anywhere. Dad pulls me in for another hug and presses a kiss to the top of my head, no matter how old I get I will always be my daddy's little girl.

"Are you sure about this?" Dad and I break apart at the sound of his voice.

"I am," I answer honestly. He looks reluctant to accept my answer but nods. "I also have something else I want to tell the both of you." Dad steps back and stands beside my mom and Taylan comes to stand behind me, he doesn't touch me but his presence alone offers me the support I need. "After my fight against Tiana, win or lose, I am hanging up my gloves and going to law school." Dad looks devastated but proud while my mom just looks... stumped.

"You don't want to fight anymore?" Mom asks quietly.

"I love fighting and I will never give it up fully but I also don't need to use fighting as a way to escape my past. I already proved that bastard wrong." At my declaration Taylan wraps his arm around my waist and pulls me back flush against his chest, I melt into him.

"You proved he didn't break you years ago by surviving." The conviction in Taylan's voice makes me love him even more.

"I'm just grateful you don't want to be a housewife like Nytress and Unique." I snort at my dad's answer. Uncle Rook had plans for his girls to study and become librarians or some shit but instead, he got two girls who want to be kept women and he fucking hates it.

The four of us walk to Uncle B's house and the closer we get the more my nerves grow. Before we can make it inside, Taylan uses his grip on my hand to pull me to a stop. I stare up at him in question.

"We walk through that door, you put your game face on, you don't let him see any cracks in your armor. You are the feistiest, most aggravating woman I know." I narrow my eyes. "But, you are strong, loyal and have me and your family here to protect you. He is your past, leave him there and don't allow him into our future." I roll my lips over my teeth and nod. He turns and leads us inside after my parents. My mom shoots me a smile over her shoulder, clearly liking what she heard from Taylan.

We walk through the living room and head straight out the back where my aunts and uncles all stand waiting, each of them shooting me smiles as we walk past. They fall into step behind us, their support in this moment means more than they will ever know. A surge of strength races through me knowing I have my man and family with me as I face the nightmare of my past. Uncle Luka is manning the door of the bunker and at our approach, he opens it and winks at me.

"You got this, Dest," he murmurs as I walk past. I shoot Uncle Luka a smile and follow my parents through the door. When we approach the second door, Billy opens it for us. Taylan squeezes my hand, offering me his strength and reminding me he is right here with me. My parents step aside as we enter and my breath hitches.

Koda is strapped to a chair, naked except for his boxers, purple and black bruises covering his entire body. His left eye is crusted with blood and sealed shut from the swelling. His lips are chapped and split. They have sliced him with a knife. The wounds are clear on the tops of his thighs but it's the sight of the pin marks seared into his ribs that have me raising my brows.

"Cattle prongs," Taylan whispers in my ear. Well, that's very resourceful. Koda lifts his head and I can see it takes every ounce of strength he has to do it, but at the sight of me his right eye widens slightly, clearly surprised to see me here but when he looks to the man standing at my side that eye narrows.

"Suka," (*Bitch.*) he snarls at Taylan, who tries to step forward but I use my grip on him to hold him back.

"You told me I was special." Taylan tenses beside me at my words. "You told me I had the power to bring the most powerful man to his knees and I did." A smug smile crests his face. I snort. "I wasn't talking about you." The smile vanishes from his face as he looks at Taylan, catching exactly what I'm putting down. "Unlike you, he didn't have to hurt me to get the answers he needed."

"Ty byl vsego lish' peshkoy v igre mesti svoye materi." (*You were nothing but a pawn in a game of revenge against your mother.*) My mom and dad both shift closer to me, wanting to pulverize Koda but a look from Taylan has them both stopping.

"Yi vy ostanetes lish dalekim vospominaniem. nicto yi nikogda nay vspomnite, kto the, krome tvoyei doceri." (*And you will be nothing but a distant memory. No one will ever remember who you are except for your daughter.*)

At the mention of his daughter he begins thrashing in his seat. Uncle B and Dad step forward and each clamp a hand down on his shoulders, holding him in place. Fear spurs to life inside me. Taylan drops his hold on my hand and pulls me in front of him, wrapping his arms around my waist and burying his face in the crook of my neck.

"Breathe, baby, I'm right here," he whispers low enough for only me to hear. I suck in a large intake of air at his request.

"Derzhis' podal'she ot moyey docheri, malen'kaya gryaz-naya shlyukha!" (*You stay the fuck away from my daughter, you dirty little slut!*) Before I can form a reply, my dad is there reigning down blow after blow.

"Ya, chert vozmi, dolgen otplatite tvoyei doceri saa to, chto the sdelal s moei, tvoyei nikchemnoy pizdoy!" (*I should fucking repay the favor to your daughter for what you did to mine you worthless cunt!*) Dad roars. Uncle B and Uncle King haul him back until he is across the room. When I hear my mom grunting, I turn and see her being held back by Uncle Vin and Uncle Rook. Uncle Knight is trying to calm her down but it isn't working, I need to finish this.

"You have my word that Lila will come to no harm by the hands of my family, we aren't dogs like you." Koda looks dazed and barely hanging onto consciousness. "You will never get to say goodbye to her or ever see her again." For the first time ever I actually see pain in his soulless eyes. "Koda Novikov, I sentence you to death." I pull out of Taylan's hold, reach into the pocket of his hoodie and retrieve the gun. My hold and aim is steady when I point it at his head, loving the sight of fear in his eyes as I pull the trigger. The bullet has just left the gun when Tay darts forward and rips the gun out of my hands, but he's too late.

Relief.

Freedom.

That's what I feel when I look at the bastard who defiled my body and tried to break me. Taylan spins around and faces me as everyone around us remains silent. He shoves his gun into the back of pants, then cups my face, searching my eyes.

"You didn't have to be the one to pull the trigger," he whispers, I can see the worry lines etched into his features and I hate the sight of them on his beautiful face.

"*I* had to do it for myself. I never wanted him to go to Ireland, he didn't deserve to live and now I won't have to live with the fear of him ever getting free and coming after me," I admit honestly. His shoulders deflate, then he pulls me against him, crushing me against his chest.

"You will never be alone, baby. I'll be there for you to watch your back always, I promise."

Epilogue

Taylan

3 months later...

Nerves thrum through me as I stand on the outside of the cage and watch her bounce around the ring with her hands in the air. The crowd goes wild at the sight of Destiny *'Havoc Slayer'* Murdoch—she is the underdog in this fight but when you look at her you wouldn't think so. The ref checks them both over and lists the rules. Gage stands beside me, feeling exactly as I do. With the both of us training her every day — even her mom helped us and so did Kiara—Gage and I have actually started getting along.

Destiny isn't pleased when we both gang up on her, but I can see it makes her happy to see me and her dad getting along. Her whole family is here for support. Royal and the others flew in and so did London and Artemis to watch her fight. It made me fucking ecstatic to walk out with her and see my brothers here as well. Knox and Lake, who is six months pregnant, sit with the Murdochs. Xan, Trey and Wave being here means a fucking a lot as well—I know Wave doesn't like crowded places but the fact she came to support me and my girl is a testament to the love we share.

"Fuck, I feel like I'm going to throw up," Gage says.

"I think I'm more nervous standing out here instead of being the one actually fighting," I admit.

"Tiana looks hungry," he says somberly.

"Yeah she does but our girl has the upper hand here."

"How?"

"She can draw on her past anger and use that to her advantage, I got faith," I say just as Destiny turns to us and winks. "Get it, baby!" I yell when the bell sounds, my stomach in my fucking throat when Tiana *'Prime time'* Lawson rushes my girl. She does everything we taught her and keeps her guard up as she's shoved against the cage.

"Get the fuck out of there!" Gage roars.

"Fuck her up, Dest!" I hear London call out from behind me. The rest of her family begins roaring and shouting out, their shouts seem to give her a boost, she manages to get her leg up and kicks Tiana in the stomach, sending her stumbling backward.

"Now, Slayer!" I roar, she knows in order to win this fight it has to be by knock out or tap, there is no other way for her to win. Tiana is the crowd favorite. Destiny runs forward and leaps into the air landing on her back. With one arm wrapped around her neck, she uses the other to land punches to the side of her head. In an unexpected move, Tiana pushes backward and uses all her weight to slam Destiny into the ground.

"Get up!" Gage screams as he smacks his hands against the cage. Destiny manages to roll away from Tiana when she tries to stomp on her face and my stomach bottoms out.

"Fucking destroy her, baby!" I roar as my anger surges to the surface when that fucking bitch tries to stomp on her again. Fuck, if she was a dude I would beat her ass for trying to hurt my girl. Destiny swipes her leg out and manages to take Tiana to the ground but before she can do more the bell sounds, signaling the end of the first round. Gage and I grab our supplies and rush into the ring. He begins patting her down with a towel as she spits her mouth guard into my hand. She snatches the water bottle out of my grasp and guzzles it down.

"You need to take her down this round, don't go to the third. That's when she tends to do the eye gouging and fights dirty," Gage barks at her. She nods and hands me back the bottle. I place her mouthguard in her hand and shoot her a wink.

"Go for the knockout, she's favoring her left side so attack that side. I want to see you using your fists more. She knows you like to use your legs so switch it up and keep her guessing." Gage and I are pushed out of the ring. We resume our positions and both grip the side of the cage as we wait for the bell to ring. The second it does, Tiana takes off like a raging bull and tackles Destiny to the ground, the girl is a shark. She climbs on top of my baby and hails down blow after blow.

"Knock her the fuck out!" I roar. Destiny is doing her best to shield her face but if she doesn't do something soon this fight is over.

"Right jab, left uppercut!" Gage screams over the roar of the crowd. Destiny swings out with a right hook to Tiana's jaw dazing her slightly but she still takes a hit to the rib. Adrenaline is riding her so the pain hasn't registered. Just as Tiana cocks her arm back for the final knockout, Destiny swings out with her left hook, sending Tiana flying off her and falling to the side of her in a heap. Gage and I jump up and down cheering, grabbing each other and hugging but then realize what we have done and shove a part. The ref is there counting down. I wait with bated breath. When he waves his hand in the air signaling the end of the fight, I rush for the gate, shove it open and run to my girl. She jumps into my arms, locking her legs around my waist as she raises her arms.

The crowd is going nuts!

She leans down and presses her lips to mine, then draws back so our noses touch. "I love you so fucking much, Tay Tay."

My heart swells inside my chest. "I love you too, so fucking much I can't even put it into words, baby." Gage tears her out of my arms and I stand smiling at the sight of them, he looks so proud.

This is the definition of what your heart beating outside your chest looks like, how I ever thought I could walk away and live without her is a mystery to me and one I never hope to discover the answer to. Destiny Murdoch is mine and it feels fucking amazing to say that.

I got the girl!

THE END

Thank You

The final in Re Della Strada is finished!

Fuck I miss each of these characters already and I don't want to let them go. This world is so close and near and dear to my heart, I love these books so much.

At least this one didn't end in a cliffhanger so you're welcome! I hope you all enjoyed getting to see the Murdochs again. I loved writing each of them and having them play a part in Tay and Dest's journey.

Thank you so much for reading Tay Tay and Destiny's book,

I cannot thank you enough for reading *Tainted Essence*, it means the world to me that you have taken a chance on reading one of my books!

If you would leave a review that would be amazing!

ACKNOWLEDGMENTS

Marky-motherfucking-Beez, my bestie, my homie, my Tay Tay inspo. I love ya dick and love how you make me scream your name. Get it, daddy!

My darling demons, I love you both as much as a fat kid loves cake! You two are my greatest blessing and the best gift I have ever received. Hand on the Bible, I would do anything to keep a smile on your faces and never think for a second I would ever be disappointed in anything you do in life.

Leah, you slayed the covers on this entire series and I'm not even surprised because you are an evil genius my Wednesday Addams, I love you!

My alpha's, Debbie, Clare and Sarah, thank you for coming on this wild as fuck ride with me and helping me shape these books into what they are. I wouldn't be able to write any of these books without your help and guidance.

My beta girls, Erin, Rizzo, Morgan and Patti, you ladies are absolute magic weavers and I am so grateful for each of you ladies. Truly, from the bottom of my heart, thank you!

Lizz, there are no words to describe how important you are to me. NONE of these books would be out or even as good as they are without you my friend. I appreciate you so fucking much!

My darling dark delicious readers, thank you again for following me and reading each of these books. I know I break your hearts and leave you mad when I end a book on a cliffy but I love that you trust me enough to heal those hearts and come back for more, I love you.

Sam xxx

<u>Fairytales With A Twist</u>

<u>Condemned Beast</u>

Sports Romance

<u>Playing For Keeps</u>

<u>Offside</u>

<u>Touchdown</u>

<u>End Game</u>

<u>Hail Mary</u>

<u>Blindside</u>

RH Sports

<u>Hate Us Like You Mean It</u>

MM

<u>Love Me Like You Mean It</u>

Paranormal Romance

<u>The Dream Series</u>

<u>A Beautiful Dream</u>

<u>A Twisted Fate</u>

<u>A Beautiful Nightmare</u>

<u>Redemption</u>

<u>Anarchy</u>

<u>Brutal Savages</u>

<u>Savage Lies</u>

<u>Brutal Truth</u>

<u>Savage Beast</u>

<u>Brutal Beauty</u>

ABOUT THE AUTHOR

Samantha Barrett is originally from Auckland New Zealand but living in Brisbane Australia

Sam writes all things dirty dark and delicious with a side of twisted mind fuck

She is the love of all things red flags and an anti-hero is a must.

www.ingramcontent.com/pod-product-compliance
Lightning Source LLC
Chambersburg PA
CBHW030606170726
48283CB00002B/485